The Audacious Ghost Adventures of Phineas A. Pennypacker

(Book #4 of "Lily and the Ghost of…" book series)

-NP Haley-

Copyright © 2017

1st edition

ISBN: 978-0-578-19786-9

Formatting by: Ron Haley

Cover by: Pink Ink Designs

Editing by: Ron Haley, Ron Vincent, David Shorten

Library of Congress Cataloging-in-Publication Data

Also by NP Haley

Lily and the Ghost of Michael Thorne
Lily and the Ghost of Tillie Brown
Lily and the Ghost of Peg-Leg Paddy McGee

Chari,
I hope you
enjoy Lily's new
adventure!

JP li

-"Ron, if I had this life to live over again I would find you sooner so I could love you longer."-

The verbiage and grammar used in this book is normal for the time frame. After reading you will notice that some of the slang still exists in today's conversations.

The Mighty Mississippi

The Mississippi is a North American wonder and the fascination with its massive power has existed since the first Native American stood on its shores awestruck with its fascinating, immense power and spellbound with the unbelievable supremacy it possessed when compared to other rivers.

The Missouri River, after rising from the majestic Rocky Mountains, is the Mississippi's main water contributor as it joins with this mighty river north of St. Louis, Missouri. The Mississippi is approximately four thousand three-hundred-miles long. Interesting enough is the fact that as the crow flies it is six hundred and seventy-five miles long. It receives water from fifty-four large subordinate rivers in which boats can navigate on and over one hundred smaller rivers.

Remarkably, the mud which dumps into the Mississippi from the Missouri gradually moves into the Gulf and extends the land mass. Over the past three hundred years' mud from the mighty river has extended the land mass a mile or so into the Gulf. At one time, it is believed, the mouth of the Mississippi ended at Baton Rouge, Louisiana but over the course of the rivers life-span it has extended its mouth two hundred miles south where it now empties its belly into the Gulf.

Prophet's Island (which is written about in *Lily and the Ghost of Tillie Brown*) at one time contained only one thousand five hundred acres of land but now the river has deposited soil and mud from the northern states and added over seven hundred more acres to the island.

Along with all her history and movements; as she winds through the United States on her way to the Gulf of Mexico, the Mighty Miss is full of hauntings and untold secret deeds done by mankind, ghost sightings and paranormal activities she keeps well hidden within her dark underbelly.

One such secret she did give up is the discovery of a heavily damaged ship found near the confluence of the Wolf and Mississippi rivers during a drought. It is a Viking ship constructed in the design of a "Knarr" ship which was built during the Viking Age between 793 to 1066 AD. It was capable of sailing 75 miles in one day and held a crew of approximately 30 men.

Many myths from local native tribes tell of the Chickasaw and Choctaw fighting against "red-haired devils" and winning many generations past.

But the mighty Mississippi rarely gives up evidence of her countless hidden secrets.

Davey Jones Locker

"By the Lord, Jack! You may say what you will but I'll be damned if it was not Davey Jones himself. I know him by his saucer eyes, his three rows of teeth, his horns and tail, and the blue smoke that came out of his nostrils. What does the blackguard devil want with me? I'm sure I never committed murder, except in the way of my profession, nor wronged any man whatsoever who din't deserve it since I first walked."

-T'was whispered to one pirate from another while both were clinging to a ship's beam adrift on the glassy sea during the calm after a violent battle with mother nature and another pirate ship, *The Black Raven* in 1755 -

1

The Grizzly

(As told by Mr. Phineas himself to Olivia Gisel)

The forest held the silence of a tomb as Phineas A. Pennypacker laid his head on the short, stiff mane of his mule, Big Bess. Three gaping claw marks stretching from the top of his shoulder to the center of his chest oozed blood into the fibers of his shirt. It seeped through his dirty undershirt, down along his upper arm and slowly dripped onto the sleeping flower heads growing along the trail. He had managed to struggle out of his outer shirt and twist it tightly around the deep wounds.

Phineas carefully urged the mule through the shadowy tunnel of dense, thick trees. The moon had slipped behind the dark, low-hanging clouds as if it was trying to hide its face from the lingering feeling of terror. Night creatures were holding their chirps and croaks, all staying still as if waiting for something else to happen. Four raccoons sat half-hidden behind a fallen tree trunk with their eyes opened wide, silently looking from side to side in anticipation. They seemed too frightened to scurry away as they normally do when a person on a mule passes by. Not a peep was heard from nary a bullfrog or even a tiny cricket. The air was tense with fear; the metallic smell of his blood mixing with the grizzly's blood and the odor of putrid rotting flesh permeated the woods around them. The path was narrow and branches brushed against the mule's sides trying to block their escape from the dark woods of Missouri. Every so often Phin would have to stop his mule, reach out with his uninjured hand and push aside the intruding branches so they could pass through.

***

When Phin first spotted the enormous grizzly, he knew right off it was the old silver–tipped grizzly known to the locals as the Banshee. Phin had stood frozen to the ground in fear with his hair standing straight up in terror as the massive beast lumbered closer. The rapid beats of his heart echoed in his ears as sweat began pouring down the back of his neck like a waterfall. His rifle remained in the saddle on his mule and the dang mule had taken off like a firefly flash the very instant Phin slid off the saddle to retrieve his fallen harmonica. The dang mule must have smelled the beast way before Phin had a chance to get a whiff of the odor. The only weapon on his body was a long sword hanging from his belt, and it was covered by leather which would hinder him from being able to jerk it out quickly.

Knowing he dare not move a muscle, Phin stood quiet as a church mouse, watching and praying as the partially blind bear ambled slowly through the brush crushing and breaking small branches as it pushed through the dense forest undergrowth. He hoped the monster would veer away, but the big brute ambled closer, grunting with each laborious stride as if each step was an extreme effort. Thank the good Lord on high, it was still unaware of Phin's presence, but the monstrous giant was only twenty feet away. Phin knew if he dared to twitch one muscle in an effort to escape, the nightmarish madness of hell would be upon him in seconds.

As the grizzly drew closer and closer, Phin could tell it still had not caught his scent, probably because the wind was blowing in Phin's direction. It continued ambling through the brush, swaying back and forth with his mammoth head slowly shifting from side to side.

But then — as was the luck of an ill-fated mountain man—the wind shifted when the brute was about ten feet away. The beast stopped, flared its nostrils and lifted its ugly muzzle into the air. Violently it shook its powerful head from side to side, alerting Phin the giant had caught his scent. The creature inhaled deeply then exhaled with a powerful bellow. Phin was so close

2

he could smell the rotten stench of its breath. Then it drew in another breath, curling its lips outward as it exhaled once again and immediately Phin was certain the bear knew his whereabouts because it took two massive steps, stood straight up, and looked down at Phin with white milky eyes, lips drawn back and its enormous teeth flashing in the night. Its size was absolutely astounding. It must have stood twelve feet tall.

The thought flashed through Phin's mind that maybe the local rumors were true: the bear's eyes were the white eyes of a haint and that meant it was almost totally blind. Maybe that would work to Phin's advantage - or so he hoped. On its underbelly was a wide, gaping gash which had festered and was now oozing rancid, putrid pus trickling down its hind legs.

In a speed like none other, the giant beast dashed toward Phin, reached out and quicker than Phin could react, swung its colossal paw; shredding the front of Phin's shirt with razor sharp claws. Phin frantically whipped out his sword as best he could, and slashed upward at the enormous bellowing head, catching its left jaw and opening a long gouge between its ear and mouth causing blood to spurt out of the wound with every beat of its heart, but it did not stop the beast's advance. In fact, it angered the fiend into a frenzied madness; it began lashing at Phin with rapid, violent blows.

Phin began doing the duck-and-dodge dance of survival, but the grizzly quickly got the upper hand. Again and again the ogre stepped toward Phin and swung its powerful paws. After each swipe of its claws, Phin would lash out with his sword, hoping to injure the monster enough to make it retreat. For a bit, Phin was able to outmaneuver the grizzly but then he found himself backed against a huge fallen tree with nowhere to run. The hideous creature raised its head to the sky and proceeded to let out another terrifying, earth-shaking roar.

Trying to take advantage of the quick few seconds the grizzly roared, Phin took a quick step to the side in an effort to escape. With an agility Phin had never seen in a beast before, the behemoth once again swung out at him, its mouth slinging drool, and caught Phin on the side, flinging him into the air like a rag doll. The bear grabbed him mid-air and slammed him onto the marshy earth with the force of a locomotive, leaving Phin on the ground gasping for air and seeing lights.

The Banshee bellowed again, standing over him, its drool dripping profusely onto Phin's face and chest. The grotesque stench was so horrendous that if Phin had not been fighting for his life he would have vomited. Its mouth was open wide with lips pulled back, exposing enormous yellow teeth and a long tongue curled upward. Bits and pieces of its last meal were stuck in its teeth and flowing out of its mouth with its slobber. Immediately the bear stepped onto Phin's chest and began bouncing up and down. Thankfully the ground was marshy-soft from the recent rains, so Phin's torso was able to sink deeper and deeper into the damp earth leaving only his head, shoulders and legs sticking out of the marsh. The grizzly stuck his muzzle into the wet earth and began biting Phin on the arm and shoulder, then locked its jaws around Phin's head. Phin could feel the grizzlies tongue, an animal of its own, lapping at his face and scalp but miraculously the bears massive jaws did not close. As it pulled its teeth from around Phin's head it bit off part of Phin's ear, causing blood to drip into his ear canal and down the side of his neck.

Playing dead, Phin lay petrified with fear as sweat continued to run off his head like a faucet; waiting for the bite that would put an end to his pain and agony. But it didn't come. Instead, the giant again lifted its head to the sky, let out one more thunderous roar and gave Phin a half-hearted stomp on the chest. Then it ambled off, grunting and rumbling deep within its colossal chest, leaving behind the reeking stench of rancid breath and rotting flesh. Phin stayed as he was for a good five minutes, catching his breath quietly before gaining the courage to lift his head and take a look around the area. His mule was missing, but thankfully so was the grizzly.

Slowly he eased himself up out of the hole he had been stomped into, whistled for his mule and waited for what seemed like an eternity before he spotted the cantankerous mule peeking around a large elm tree as if making sure it was safe to show himself. Seeing no grizzly and only Phin sitting in the mud, the ornery mule presented himself in a skittish side-stepping prance as if at any time he might take off in a mad dash. Phin's head and shoulder were throbbing; blood was dripping from his ear down onto his body to mingle with the blood oozing from the claw cuts. Carefully Phin eased his shirt over his head and wrapped it around his shoulder to make a sling for his arm. Then he took the scarf off his neck and bound it around his ear in hopes of stopping that flow of blood. Slowly and carefully he dragged himself up into the saddle and coaxed the mule into a slow walk.

"Take us to Elijah's, Bess", Phin muttered.

Now all he had to do was get out of the strange tunnel of trees and hang onto Bess so he wouldn't slide off the ornery animal. Gradually the path opened up a bit, enabling Big Bess to walk with ease along the trail. Not one sound could be heard in the shadowy forest tunnel. There was something still amiss in the air, as if the world around Phin was waiting and watching for something else to happen. Gradually the grove of elm trees thinned and became a pine forest. The tree branches began growing high above the earth, permitting Phin to see distant objects resting on the ground amongst the blanket of dry pine needles that had dropped off the trees.

With the hands of fear still gripping his chest, Phin spotted four dark shapes gliding silently from tree to tree. They looked strange and seemed to be stalking him. Blinking quickly, he wiped the blood dripping into his eyes from a claw-cut on his forehead and squinted to get a better look-see at the dark shadows. They were like nothing he had seen before. Whatever they were had four legs but scrambled from tree to tree like a man running bent over using his knuckled hands as feet. Except for their white glowing eyes, they were solid black against the pine needles on the forest floor.

Bess began twitching nervously and side-stepping as if he wanted to run, but Phin sensed if the mule started running the creatures would begin their chase. Even though his mule was a Tennessee walker mule, a breed known for its speed, Phin had no idea what the creatures were or how fast they could run.

Unfortunately, one thing was certain: they could most assuredly smell the blood dripping down his body.

Relaxing the grip on the reins, Phin let the mule ease into a trot. He knew his shoulder would begin to bleed more but it was the chance he would have to take. Sitting upright, he tightened the scarf around his ear hoping to stop that flow of blood. Keeping a close eye on the creatures, he let go of the mule's reins to tighten the scarf; that was when Bess shot off in a run which made Phin grab frantically for the reins and hold on for dear life. Glancing to his left he saw the creatures dashing through the pine trees in hot pursuit.

Within seconds the trail led the two of them into an open field bare of trees with only low-growing grass and brush covering the meadow, sweeping for miles on either side of the path. And just like that, the creatures were nowhere in sight. The usual sounds of the night were again echoing across the fields; the sweet fragrance of night Jazmine floated in with the gentle wind, carried along and mixing with the smell of smoke from campfires along the river bank a mile or so away. The moon had emerged from its hiding place and clouds had been pushed further east as if they knew the danger had vanished from the land.

Slowing the big mule down, Phin leaned forward and groaned. The pain in his shoulder was getting worse and now his head was throbbing like a hammer. He knew he had to make it to Elijah's cabin soon or he would probably fall off his mule and the dang old cuss would walk off and leave him to rot in the wilderness. That idea did not set well with Phin.

"Ahhh, Big Bess," he mumbled to his mule, "Would ya leave me alone to die in these strange woods?"

"Hee-aww," the big mule answered, followed by a grunt and a head nod.

"Yeah, that's just what I thought. You're an ornery ol' cuss, Bess. Ya ain't got no sense of loyalty a'tall. I reckon I should take ya to the glue factory in Memphis and be done with ya."

"Hee-aww," Bess bawled loudly and nodded.

"Well hee-haw, yourself, Bess. Yep, I'm gonna sell ya to the glue factory just as soon as I get into Memphis then I'm gonna buy myself a real horse. So how ya like them apples?"

"Hee-aww," the mule gave another nod and a snort, as if he was understanding what Phin was saying but knew he was lying.

"Okay, Bess, take us on home to Elijah," Phin said, slumping back down onto the big mule's back.

Phin and Big Bess continued on down the path with Phin dozing off and on, letting Big Bess go whatever speed he wanted. Phin knew he wouldn't start running unless something menacing came along.

Long about early dawn, Phin felt Bess come to a stop and realized they had finally arrived at Elijah Bonheur's cabin, located not too far from Memphis, Tennessee. Elijah Bonheur was an old farmer nigh onto 100 years old and he lived alone with his dog and his old horse, Samson. He had been like a father to Phin from the day Phin was left alone by the passing of his Aunt Abby, and he loved the old man as if he was his own pa. Barely sitting up in his saddle, Phin slid himself off Bess and stumbled into Elijah's small cabin.

As he opened the door, a chilly breeze welcomed him instead of the usual smell of early morning coffee. Instantly Phin forgot all about his injuries and went in search of Elijah.

"Paw?" Phin's worried voice echoed through the house. "Paw? Where are ya?"

"Back here taking me a bit of a rest!" Elijah's feeble voice called out from his small bedroom. "I'll be right out in a jiffy and fix up a pot a coffee fur ya."

Not waiting for the old man to come into the main room, Phin walked to the small bedroom door and there, sitting on the edge of the bed, was Elijah. His hair was in tangles and his body was as thin and gaunt as a scarecrow.

"What happened to ya, Paw?" Phin asked in a gentle, concerned voice, walking to the bed. He smoothed Elijah's hair down and put another blanket around his gaunt body.

"I'm thinkin' I'm just getting a mite old, son. A little long in the tooth, ya might say."

"Why, that's not true a'tall, you're only nigh onto a hun'ert years old. What makes ya think you're a mite old? You're pretty much a spring chicken!" Phin laughed softly, lifting the old man's legs and easing him back onto the bed.

Phin had not seen Elijah for almost six months and he was surprised at how fast the old fella had taken a downhill slide.

"Well," Elijah laughed easily, "I ain't no spring chicken - that's fur sure. I reckon I ain't even an old stewin' hen. My old bones are creakin' and crackin' every step I take and my food ain't feelin' too good when it goes down. I'm getting tar'd, Phin, I'm jest gettin' tar'd. I been dreamin' 'bout my sweet Esther and Molly and them young'uns running 'round laughin' and a'gigglin'. What'cha think, Phin? Ya think it's 'bout my time ta go? Cuz iff'en it is, I'm durn tootin' ready ta take off inta that wild blue yonder. I'm 'tar'd and my giddy-ups done got up and gone."

"Well," Phin answered in a slow, soft voice, "I'm hoping it ain't your time to go, but iff'en you're wantin' to go, then I guess I'll honor that and hope ya go too. Ya been here a mighty long time, Paw, a mighty long time. Ya seen many a thing I ain't never seen and I ain't never gonna see. If you do pass on, would ya tell Aunt Abby that I'm missin' her all these years and say a big 'how-do' to my Maw. I ain't never remembered her but I'm sure she will remember me." He paused. "Let me warm up your blanket a bit for ya then I'll fix us up some stew. How's that sound?"

"Mighty fine Son, mighty fine. And I will, for sure, have a right-nice talk with Abby and your Maw."

With that said Phin didn't even mention his fight with the grizzly. Instead he pulled another thin blanket up over the old man and carried the thicker blanket, along with Elijah's socks, into the small living area where he started a fire in the pot-bellied stove. Then he threw the thin, worn socks into the belly of the hot stove, pulled out a thick pair of his own socks and held them close to the flames until they were warm as toast. Walking back into the bedroom he slipped the big socks onto the old man's feet, pulling them up to cover his boney legs and knees before returning to the stove to get the warmed blanket. He would fix up a pot of stew and some hot coffee just as soon as he got Elijah warmed up, he thought to himself.

"Ya better tend ta them grizzly wounds, Phin. They kin fester-up really quick-like. Ya had ya'self ah run-in with ol' Banshee, din't ya?"

Looking back through the bedroom door, Phin saw the smile on the old man's face. It was tough getting anything past him. He still had the eyes of a hawk and he himself had experienced battles with that same gruesome grizzly.

"I'll be doin' that, Paw. Just as soon as I get your blanket warmed up and some stew going. You rest easy now."

2

Elijah and the Soldier

Silently they sat, the old man Elijah and the young soldier, staring solemnly into each other's eyes. The soldier was obviously an apparition. Elijah sat hunched over on the edge of the narrow, rumpled cot, grasping the thin blanket tightly about his bony shoulders. His trembling hands nervously fumbled with the ends of the blanket, trying to tug it closer to his gaunt, shivering body. The old man's skin hung loosely from his feeble frame and his face was worn from years of struggling with the life he had been dealt. In days long past, the old man had been a dignified, stately gentleman - not rich by any means, but full of integrity and honor.

He had started out as a strong, young farmer in the fertile Missouri delta farmland, and after his grandson left to fight in the War Between the States, he moved his family to Memphis where he became a preacher as well as a farmer. He spread the love of God by helping out folks as far as his horse could carry him during the cold winter months. During the long, hot summers of western Tennessee, he tilled the soil and fought the elements to provide food for his daughter and her children, and also for anyone passing through who might be in need.

His young grandson perished during the war so after the long, dreary conflict finally ended, Elijah moved back to Missouri with his daughter Molly and her little gals, just a few miles north of Memphis but on the other side of the Mississippi river. The previous years of working and saving enabled him to help others without struggling to support his own family after the move. Every year, he and Molly put in a large vegetable garden for themselves and strangers

10

traveling along the river road to St. Louis who might need food for a day or two. Every traveling man and woman knew they could get a hearty meal at what folks called Elijah's Farmhouse. Elijah never set a monetary price on the food he fed strangers, he let them decide what they thought they owed him. More times than not, travelers would stay a few days and help Elijah and Molly with chores in exchange for their shelter and food.

But now, sadly, the last chapter of Elijah's life was coming to an end. So it seemed to Phin, anyway. The kind old gentleman had lost Esther, his lovely wife, many, many years ago to Cholera. He lost his grandson Isaac to the War and then a few years later, his daughter Molly and her two sweet little girls passed on due to the Yellow Fever epidemic. Finally, and much to Elijah's relief, it was time for Elijah himself to leave this earth. It was the last paragraph in the book of Elijah Bonheur's adventure, and thus he lay in the small narrow cot waiting for his maker to release him from his earthly body.

No longer was his hair thick and black as midnight. It had become thin and hoary-white with age and hung loose about his head in wild disarray. Every bone seemed to press against his skin as if trying to escape. Small brown time-spots covered his face, arms and hands. Years of labor in the cotton fields of Missouri and Tennessee had left his bony knuckles swollen with arthritis. Only his eyes stayed strong, holding a sense of knowing. They were still the bright, soft blue-grey of his youth, but now they seeped water somewhat constantly - as if tears from losing loved ones had built up over the years and were overflowing from a broken heart.

Elijah's blue-grey eyes locked with the eyes of the apparition sitting in front of him, dressed in the blue uniform of the Northern army. The soldier's hat was pulled low on his head and on the epaulettes of his uniform hung two gold bars, telling Phin that at the time of his death he had been a captain in the Union Army. The uniform was torn and scruffy with dirt clinging to its sleeves; he must have been buried in the very spot where he lay dead, as soldiers often were.

Phin stood quietly beside the open door, suppressing the urge to walk in and wrap the old man with the warm blanket, for he feared he would chase the apparition away. He knew the old man was cold, but he also knew Elijah wanted to see this soldier. Something unseen and powerful held him beside the door. Whatever it was, it wanted this meeting between the living and the dead to continue.

Phin knew who this apparition was. It was the spirit of the Elijah's grandson Isaac, the one who had joined the war effort when he was but twelve years of age. Elijah had repeatedly told Phin of how he had pleaded with his grandson to stay home and help the family survive until he reached the age of manhood, but the young boy had been restless and tired of farm life; he was lured by the romantic image of fighting for what one believed in. Even though the old man told and retold the story, Phin always knew by the emotion in his telling that he was proud of his grandson and how he had fought for the freedom of mankind. But, two days after his fifteenth birthday, Isaac died in the Battle of Chickamauga.

With Phin watching from the hallway, Elijah continued to tug gently at the blanket, keeping his eyes locked onto the apparition, fearing it might vanish.

"How are ya, son?" Elijah's voice cracked with emotion as tears ran down his wrinkled cheeks slowly; his lips quivered slightly, trying to keep from sobbing.

"Fair-ta-meddlin', Paw," Phin heard the young soldier whisper back in a thick southern accent. "How ya doin' ya'self? I been wantin' ta see ya. I sure do miss talkin' to ya ever' day."

Phin could not see the apparition's lips moving but he could hear the whispers of the loving words as if they were blowing in with the gentle breeze drifting through the cracked window. The young soldier appeared a bit misty, constantly coming in and out of focus. At times, his facial features were clear and Phin could see the soft grey–blue eyes so similar to his grandfather's.

"Doin' far-ta-meddlin' too, Son. Jest fair-ta-meddlin'."

"I've been wanderin' 'bout tryin' ta find my way back ta see ya, Paw. I know Ma and the little'uns passed on. Ya doin' okay?"

"Well, I'm jest puttin' in my time here on this earth and it's coming nigh onta the last chapter fur me. I'm ready ta go see the rest ah y'all. I'm powerful glad ya found me, son, I been missin' ya somethin' awful. Since the very day ya left there ain't been one day gone by that I din't think 'bout ya. I love ya like ya was my own young'un. We coun't find your body ta give ya a proper burial and all. The War Office said they din't know where ya was."

"It's a'right, Paw. It don't make no difference a'tall. I should'ah stayed here with ya like ya said. Might be Ma and the little'uns might not'ah passed on. I'm mighty sorry for that, Paw. I love ya more than ya'll ever know."

"I love ya too, Son. Don't ya be frettin' none, now." The old man reached out to touch Isaac's hand. "Thur ain't nary ah thin' a body kin do against the Yeller Fever and thur ain't no fightin' it. It's stronger than any man can be. Your ma and sisters suffered some but the fever don't waste no time a'tall takin' whoever it wants. That's a good thing, iff'en thur ever was ah good thing about the fever. I thought it might leave me lil' Pansy but it took her too." Elijah shook his head in sorrow. "I had 'er with me the longest and she was a delight fur my old soul. She held on till her ninth birthday, but then it came again one more time an took 'er. She was the lest'un to go and I sure did try ta save 'er, I surely did. Iff'en you'd ah been here I fear you'd been sufferin' right along with 'em. I ain't never figgered out why the good Lord din't take an old codger like me a'fore he took our lil' Pansy." Elijah shook his head. "But don't ya be frettin' none a'tall, son. It all turned out right nice. I raised up ah young'un named Phineas who lost his Aunt ta some sickness, and he turned out ta be ah right nice fella, so's I guess that's why the good Lord left me here."

The old man slowly laid back on the cot with a deep sigh as if he was just too exhausted to sit up any longer. Carefully he eased his legs up and slipped them under the thin blanket as the young soldier smiled broadly at him and bent over as if to kiss him on the forehead. Elijah reached out to shake the soldier's hand as best he could, then Isaac's apparition began slowly floating away in the warm morning breeze. The sense of his presence hovered over the small cot and filled the little cabin for a few more minutes.

Attempting to not let the floorboards creak, Phin tiptoed into the room, covered the old man with the warmed blanket and tucked it around and under his thin body gently so as not to wake him. The old man did not open his eyes when he spoke.

"Thank ya kindly son. Did ya see 'em? He came to see me. He sat right here and we had us a nice talk. I knew he would come. Yep, I knew he would come jest as soon as he could. He's a good boy."

"Yep, Paw, I saw him. I knew right off who it was, too. He's a mighty handsome soldier-boy, ain't he."

"That he is. I'm mighty proud of that boy. And this blanket is warm as buttered toast in the mornin'." Elijah smiled happily and sighed with contentment. "Yep, I'm feeling much better, Son. I've had me a good day. First off you shows up and then my Isaac comes to see me. It's been a fine day indeed. Ya been ah blessin'. My life is purt-near finished being writ' and I can say I've had me a good run." Chuckling, he continued. "I married-up with a good woman, had me a couple good farms, made a good livin' fur my family, had me ah good daughter who gave me a good passel of young'uns and 'long the way I had many a good laugh with good friends. Life don't get no better'n that, Phin. Yep, I had me a grand adventure here on earth." Elijah's voice grew softer and Phin had to lean over the bed to hear what he had to say.

"It's been a grand adventure." Elijah's face brightened with a big smile, and the two sat in silence for a moment.

"I'll fetch you some stew, Paw".

"Nope, don't bother, Son. I ain't hungry a'tall. I'll jest take me a quick nap."

Phin sat down on the rocking chair and watched the old man with wonder. This was the first time in his life that he hoped a person would die. He knew the old man wanted to leave; to Phin, whatever the old man wanted was fine with him. Elijah Bonheur was the kindest man he had ever met and he deserved to have peace from his pain.

Elijah's eyes fluttered open and he stared into Phineas' face a moment before speaking softly.

"Did ya see 'em, son? Did ya see my Isaac?" he asked again, not remembering that he had just asked Phineas that very question. "He's a fine-looking soldier, ain't he?"

"He is, Paw," Phin said with a warm smile.

Elijah laid quietly for another minute. With his eyes closed, he said, "I'll be goin' now, Phin. This cabin and all I have in it is your'n. Come back whenever ya want cuz its yours now along with my cabin over in Memphis." Elijah's raspy voice was getting weaker. "I'll be seeing ya my boy, make sure ya live good 'nuf ta meet me over yonder along with yor Aunt Abby. Remember, Son, as ya write your book of life thur ain't no goin' back and changin' the words."

Phin silently nodded his head because he had no idea how to answer without sobbing. Elijah raised up on one elbow, looked towards the window and lifted his feeble hand as if waving to someone outside.

"I see them young'uns laughin' and gigglin' and peekin' in the winder over there. That lil' Pansy gave me a wave with both of 'er hands!" Elijah said with a smile and a soft chuckle, motioning for Phin to look out the window.

15

"Do ya see my Esther? Iff'en ya look real close-like you can see 'er over there next to the well talkin' with my Molly." Elijah gave a feeble wave at the window, "My Esther is a lovely woman, ain't she?"

Phin turned his head, looked out the window. He raised his hand and gave a wave even though he didn't see a thing. "Yes, indeed she is, Paw."

"Well," Elijah whispered as he eased back down, "they're leavin' so I'm gonna lay back down here for a spell, Phin. Once I'm gone, get ya'self ah shovel and bury me alongside my Esther and Molly and the young'uns. Ain't no need ta be goin' inta town fur the preacher-man. I been to so many burying's I could prolly say the exact words he would say with my own dead brain. Ain't no need fur it. I'll be gone and I won't even know 'bout it. You go right on ahead and say ah good word or two over me a'fore ya put me inta the dirt. I'll be needin' all the good words I kin get when I'm standin' thur in front of my maker.

"Then ya go and pull up the boards ah my front stoop and you'll find ya'self ah box your Aunt Abby left fur ya. I ain't knowin' what's in it, but she told me ta give it to ya when I'm on my last leg and that your ta be doin' some good thin's with it. I'm guessin' I'm on my last leg so's that's the only reason I'm tellin' ya. When she passed on, an I'm sure-ah-shootin' it was somethin' other than the dropsy that killed 'er, I promised 'er I'd teach ya the right way ta live and now I done did my job. You're a grown-up man full of respect and honor."

Elijah stopped for a minute to draw in a shallow breath before continuing. "It ain't gonna be long and I'll be seein' ya, Son," Elijah said quietly as if speaking to Isaac's apparition again. "I done finished my work here and I'll be on my way. I'll be seeing ya soon, Isaac, I'll be seeing ya soon."

Elijah continued mumbling to himself. For the rest of the day Phin sat beside the old man, rocking slowly in the rickety rocking chair and wishing he could do something to ease Elijah's discomfort. Every so often he would heat up another blanket for Elijah and tuck it in around his thin body. Phin's arm and ear was throbbing like a son-of-a-gun but he ignored the pain.

Just before the sun slipped its last rays of light beneath the western horizon and the sky turned itself into an amazing array of reddish pinks and purples, the night creatures hushed their singing and Elijah's big hound sat up on his haunches and began a soft, sorrowful bay, sending shivers up and down Phin's spine.

As the gentle hoot of a night owl's call echoed from across the mountain's hollow into the bedroom window, Elijah opened his sparkling blue-grey eyes, grinned, and gave Phineas a wink as he breathed his last.

***

After sewing up his arm and ear the best he could, Phin buried Elijah behind the little cabin in the shade of the giant oak trees next to his wife Esther. Phin bowed his head and said all the good words he could muster up about the old fella. He felt Elijah didn't need any words to help him enter the pearly gates, but he did it because Elijah had asked him to. Then he sat there thinking about the old man until the soft greys of pre-night were totally gone and darkness surrounded him like a cloak. There wasn't a soul walking on this earth who was a better man than Elijah Bonheur had been.

Phin walked slowly back into the little cabin, cleaned it up and packed a bag of the perishables to take along with him. He realized he now had a home to call his own whenever he tired of wandering.

After putting Big Bess into the lean-to with Elijah's horse Samson, he fed Elijah's hound dog, fixed himself some supper and eased down onto his bedroll where he fell sound asleep with the hound pushed up close to his back.

Well before the first fingers of sunlight slipped through the forest and reached into the cabin window, Phin got up and made himself coffee. He then hitched up Big Bess, tied Samson to the back of his buckboard, lifted Elijah's old hound dog onto the top of his pile of pelts then went back inside and grabbed the shovel, walking out the door into the dusky dawn of a promising warm day. Bending down, he pulled up the flimsy boards to the front stoop and peered into an empty hole.

"Well, son-of –a-gun, Elijah, I guess some other fella beat me to it."

<u>Twenty years later</u>

3

Olivia

Silently she sat on the long front row pew with her head lowered, fiddling with one of her dress buttons. Her vivid green eyes flowed with tears as she focused her attention on the button she had twisted from the sleeve of her dress, tumbling it from thumb to thumb while slowly swinging her legs back and forth under the hard, wooden pew.

Her large green eyes were beautiful and strikingly captivating. They overpowered her delicate facial features and seemed to look past a person's eyes and gaze straight into their very soul. These eyes unknowingly made people uneasy occasionally, giving one the feeling she could look into their soul and see all the sins which they had buried deep within the hidden depths of their hearts. Those people tended to not look her in the eye.

Looking down at her feet, she noticed how shiny her black shoes were and knew Mrs. Turner had polished them especially just for this occasion. Her glossy black hair hung forward, hiding the tears slipping down the delicate, freckled, twelve-year-old face. Her skin was pale but her high cheekbone and refined features confirmed the unmistakable presence of Cherokee blood running within her veins.

She sniffed loudly. Mrs. Turner, sitting directly behind her, slipped a lovely embroidered handkerchief over her shoulder. Taking the handkerchief, Olivia thanked her with a nod, wiped her eyes and nervously began twisting the handkerchief around the button she still held in her hand. She didn't know if her heart would actually break in half and stop beating, but it surely did feel as if it was starting to. She truly hoped it would! Then the church folks would carry her right up to the coffin and put her in with her mama and she would be out of her misery. She wanted so badly to leave this cruel world and go with her mama where she could see Pa, Opal and Oliver. She suppressed the urge to walk up to the coffin, climb inside, snuggle up next to her mama, take her hand and walk into the next life where she would once again be with her family. Grief swelled up within her as she thought of her family all being together without her. She was supposed to be there with them. Something had not worked out the way it should have, she thought. "This is not right," she whispered softly, laying her head back against the pew and letting out a deep sigh.

She gave a loud sniff, not caring if it sounded rude or obnoxious to anyone in the church-house. She didn't want to be sitting on this pew, she didn't want to listen to the preacher-man say the same words he said every time someone passed on, and she sure didn't care what anyone thought. Well, maybe she did care a smidgen about what Mrs. Turner thought.

Once again, she wore the same black dress, black shoes, stockings and black hair bow Mrs. Turner had given her one year ago on this very day for her Papa's funeral. She had also worn the same outfit for her baby sister Opal's funeral, then again for her twin brother Oliver's funeral, and now here she was wearing it for the funeral of the last member of her family, her Mama. The dress was a bit shorter and the shoes were a bit snugger, but they still fit her small slender frame.

Alone she sat on the pew designated 'Reserved for Immediate Family Members only'. She had wanted Mrs. Turner to sit beside her, but she was gently told that it would not be proper for anyone else to take the seat. She felt so alone in the world, sitting on the loathsome pew made to accommodate large families. She squeezed her eyes shut and tried thinking of Mrs. Turner's new litter of kittens to get her mind off the droning words coming from the preacher-man but instead her mind went back to Oliver's funeral when she and her Mama were the only two sitting there. Mama had sat tall, stately and beautiful with her head held high and proud tightly holding onto Olivia's hand

21

throughout the entire service. Her mama was a Cherokee Indian. She had been tall, slender, and what most people called a delicately framed woman. She had jet-black hair, tanned creamy skin and eyes the color of midnight.

Because her mama had been a Cherokee, a few folks in Malden shunned all of them, but Olivia had never given a rip about what other people thought. Her mama was the most beautiful, most kind mama there was and anyone who thought less could stay away. Mrs. Turner, the retired schoolmarm, was the closest friend Olivia's mama had and after Olivia's Papa died, Mrs. Turner would be often found at the house helping them with planting, canning or harvesting. After the death of Opal and Oliver, Mrs. Turner tried talking Mama into moving in with her, but Mama said no because she needed to keep a home for Olivia and herself. Then when Mama died, Mrs. Turner came right over and moved Olivia into the pretty little spare bedroom at her house on Main Street, and that's where Olivia had slept for the past few days. Other than her own mama, Mrs. Turner was the kindest woman Olivia had ever met. She often thanked God for placing Mrs. Turner in Malden, Missouri.

Olivia had tried her best to make her mama stay with her. Even Mrs. Turner had been there the entire time Mama was sick, trying to help heal her body, but the Yellow Fever was stronger than she or anyone else. It was a mean, nasty disease. Only two weeks passed from when Mama started feeling poorly to when she was gone. The day before her ma's funeral, in an effort to follow her family into the next world, Olivia had visited five people who had the fever with the hope of catching it. It didn't work.

"Maybe I'll get sick tomorrow," she thought to herself as she looked up at the roof of the church house and counted the wooden beams, still twisting her button in Mrs. Turner's handkerchief.

The preacher-man was still droning on and on; Mrs. Turner reached from the pew behind and patted her on the shoulder with a warm, comforting hand that brought Olivia's attention back to the present. Glancing up at the pulpit, Olivia watched the preacher's mouth moving but had no idea what he was saying.

Looking to her left, she saw three of the Pruiett brothers sitting in the second pew on the other side of the room; all three of their heads were nodding and jerking as they struggled to stay awake. Tom, the younger of the three, gave up and leaned his head against the back of the pew with his mouth wide open and began giving out little snorts of air. She watched him with a slight smile on her face. When he gave out a loud, nasal snort, his Pa reached up and smacked him upside the head. The smack surprised Tom so much he jumped to his feet and stood there blinking, thinking it was finally time to stand up and leave the church building. Immediately his brothers Paul and Ott grabbed his shirttail and jerked him back down between them. Paul and Ott shook with laughter as they tried to compose themselves. They put their heads down between their knees, shaking with laughter, so their Pa wouldn't give each of them a smack on the head or a whooping when they got home for being disrespectful at a burying. Olivia let out a tiny laugh.

After a bit, the preacher's blah-blah-blahing finally came to a halt and Mrs. Bullock began playing the organ as the congregation stood to their feet.

"Stand to your feet, dear," Mrs. Turner whispered gently, leaning forward.

Olivia stood to her feet as folks slowly began filing by and, as was the custom, either shook her hand or gave her a hug. After what seemed like a mile of adults passing by, it was the Pruiett boys' turn. They were all barefooted but dressed in their Sunday best. Ott Pruiett, who was close to Olivia's age, reached her first and stuck out his hand to shake her hand and slipped a shiny new penny into her palm, then his brother Paul shook her hand and gave her a fairly new whistle and whispered that he had carved it out of gypsum wood. He was followed by Tom, who slipped a small piece of cow bone into her hand and said he had carved it into a cross just for her and that he was sorry he had fallen asleep during the preaching. He gave her a cockeyed little smile and pushed Paul further ahead.

Then along came Robbie and Frankie Pruiett, the two youngest Pruiett boys and Robbie, who's hair was standing on end, gave her a fist full of wilted flowers and a shiny green stone. He whispered that he had polished it with hog fat to make it sparkle. Then Frankie gave Robbie a push so he could stand right close to Olivia and slipped a big, white mule's tooth hanging from a piece of twine into her palm. In his loud, squeaky little boy's voice, he told her he had pulled it out of the mule's mouth himself, wiped it clean of all the blood and then polished it with lard; it was his most treasured treasure in the whole wide world.

He looked her in the eyes and whispered, "My cousin Charlie told me it is more valuable than a chunk of gold!"

Then Frankie gave her a tight hug and a big front-tooth-missing smile. He stood and stared at her for a bit before reaching up and pulling her down so he could whisper in her ear that she looked just as pretty as a daisy in her Sunday dress.

"Move along, Frankie," said Lily Quinn, standing right behind him, giving him a sharp nudge. Paul reached back, grabbed Frankie by the shirt-tail and pulled him along so the next person could give her their sorry's.

"I was trying to talk to my gonna-be wife, Paul," Frankie said in a shrill little voice. "I'm gonna marry-up with Miss Olivia when I get grow'd up!" Paul rolled his eyes and drug Frankie out the side door.

Lily Quinn and Ophelia Knudson came up next in line. They hugged her and whispered that they would be seeing her in Memphis. Each of them gave her a pretty piece of fabric, which she stuffed into her pocket with the treasures she had gotten from the Pruiett boys.

After what seemed like an eternity, Mrs. Turner, the last in line, finally stood beside her and held her hand as the pall-bearers picked up her mama's coffin and carried it out the door to the graveyard. Once again the preacher spoke. Once again Olivia did not listen. The congregation sang "Shall we Gather at the River" as the pall-bearers lowered her mama into the ground next to her papa and covered the coffin with dirt. To most of the congregation her Mama would not be remembered.

The congregation walked quietly and solemnly to the shade trees at the backside of the church property where the women-folk had set up a picnic with tons of food. The entire congregation began eating, talking and laughing as they enjoyed each other's company. Olivia sat alone in misery. She knew they were not jovial in disrespect, it was just the way things went at a burying and she knew life had to go on, but the pain in her heart was like a sharp knife being thrust into her very soul.

She sat at a table silently waiting for Mrs. Turner with her head once again hanging down staring at her hands and wondering - which she would probably do for the rest of her life - if she had missed something that would have saved her mama.

"Olivia, dear," Mrs. Turner said softly as she sat a plate of food in front of her, "Here. Eat a bit of food, dear. I also want to introduce you to Mr. Phineas Pennypacker. Mr. Pennypacker will be taking you into Memphis to live with your Aunt Katy. Just as we talked yesterday, your Aunt Katy is a good woman. She'll make a good mother for you. You're the onliest blood kin she has left and also her for you." Mrs. Turner scooted her ample body onto the bench seat beside her.

Olivia looked up into the smiling face of Mr. Phineas Pennypacker. He was a friendly looking fella, standing there with his pipe in his mouth, both his hands holding a heaping full plate of food.

"How-do, Miss Olivia," Mr. Phineas said, bowing his head slightly.

25

He sat his plate down and whipped off his leather skull cap. His white hair shot up about a foot in length straight up on his head, making Olivia's attitude lighten and smile.

"Tis a mighty beautiful day to bury your mama, that is iff'en ya have to do such ah dreadful thing. It best be done on a sunny day to put a wee bit of happiness inta your soul. The folks on Piel Island, where I was birthed, say iff'en the sun shines on the day of a buryin' it means the soul of the lovely person passin' over shoots straight through those Pearly Gates and skids right into Heaven with a graceful-light landing. And your mama was a mighty-fine lovely lady. My deep, sincere sorrow I give ta ya and my soul feels your grief, my dear young lady."

He paused for a moment; Olivia could see the genuine concern in his eyes.

"In fact, another piece of important information to remember is, 'tis said that whenever ya see a red bird close by it means your loved ones are comin' ta see ya from the great beyond. So, ever'time ya see a red bird or a cardinal, you remember there's your mama and papa come to visit with ya."

Mr. Pennypacker was a strange looking fella. He was skinny and probably close to six and a half feet tall, with wild hair looking as if he had been frightened out of his skin. His face was long, gaunt, furrowed with deep wrinkles, and tanned as dark as a deerskin hide being dried in the hot summer sun. His white eyebrows were so long he had to give them a trim every so often to keep them out of his eyes. His snowy-white beard ran along the sides of his face, joining up with his mustache at the bottom of his chin before braiding into one long braid hanging to the middle of his belly. He had a thin, narrow nose. His eyes were as blue as a robin's egg and looked as if God had dotted each eyeball with tiny black specks among the blue. He had deep laugh lines reaching from the corners of his eyes to the back to his ears. He had all his own teeth— quite unusual for a mountain man—and he claimed that he kept them white as snow by scrubbing them with a wet rag dipped into wood ash from his fire pit every night before he took his sleep.

He was seldom seen without his unlit Brandy pipe hanging from his mouth; when he spoke he would grip his pipe with his teeth and speak around it. It was a pretty comical thing to watch since he laughed often. When he would laugh, only one side of his mouth would go into a smile. He was full of stories and tales, as most mountain men were, and he loved to grab someone's ear and tell his tales whether they sat willingly or not.

Mr. Pennypacker wore a deer-skin skull cap with goggles attached to the top; he very seldom took his hat off. He wore a long, tan capote coat which hung down to the top of his moccasins. His moc's were the usual mountain-man style of knee-high leather loaded with colorful beads. His shirt was loose, red, long-sleeved, and durable. His pants were made of heavy fabrics and were held up by bright red suspenders. He smelled of pipe smoke, horse sweat and the earthy aroma that came from living off the land and sleeping on the pine needles which lay abundantly in the Ozark mountains. His very being seemed to radiate the fragrance of peace and harmony with nature.

Olivia automatically smiled when she looked at him. It was as if she felt a kindred spirit with the strange looking mountain man. Mr. Pennypacker bowed deeply as if standing before royalty.

"How-do, Mr. Pennypacker," Olivia said as she stood and stuck out her hand. "Thank you kindly for sharing my grief and I thank you for taking me to Aunt Katy 's house. I will try my best to be a great help along the way."

"No thanks to me," Mr. Pennypacker said with a broad smile. "Thank you kindly for keeping me company on my travels. And ya can call me Mr. Phin or Mr. Phiney iff'en ya want ta. And how 'bout I call you Livy? Would that be a'right?"

"That would be fine, Mr. Phiney," Olivia said with a smile. "Livy would be just fine and dandy. That's what my Pa always called me. In fact, he called me Livy-Bean most times and my brother always called me Liver-Beans." She gave a slight giggle.

"Well now, I reckon I kindly like the name Olivia or Livy, but I'm not too fond of the name Liver-Beans, that's kindly strange fur a pretty young gal. But then again brothers do some strange thin's, don't they? I'll jest call ya Livy or Olivia iff'en ya don't mind."

Olivia gave him a broad smile and nodded her head.

Mr. Phiney slipped his hat back on and turned to Mrs. Turner. "Milly, my lovely lass, mind if I have me a sit-down next to you and Miss Olivia here while I eat me some tasty vittles?"

"Well," Mrs. Turner said with a stern huffy sniff, "Be polite and take your hat off in the presence of ladies. And I'm not your lovely lass, in fact I'm way too old to be anyone's lass - and stop calling me Milly. My name is Mildred. But if ya must sit down, do what you gotta do." She laughed and cleared a spot for Mr. Phiney to sit across from her.

"Now, Olivia, dear, Mr. Pennypacker can be a fair-ta-meddling nuisance when he takes a mind to it, but all-in-all he's a right nice fella."

Mr. Phiney took off his hat again and bowed deeply to Mrs. Turner before taking a seat.

"Why, thank'ye fur the compliment, madam." He laughed.

Both Mrs. Turner and Mr. Phiney had a laugh at what had been said between the two of them, and then he gave out a loud, gurgling burp. Olivia could not help but grin and let out a soft laugh even though she knew Mrs. Turner would not approve of Mr. Pennypacker's vulgar burping.

"Well, heaven's ta Betsy's britches! Pard' me all ta pieces ladies. That thur burp jest jumped right up and popped outta my mouth like a dog fartin' in the wind a'fore I could citch it. That peach pie I ate earlier din't settle in yet."

28

"Well, Mr. Pennypacker," Mrs. Turner said with a sniff and a loud gasp, "Watch your language. And, I saw you, with my own eyes, gobble down that entire peach pie without taking nary a breath. If ya hadn't been such a hog and shared some of that pie maybe your stomach wouldn't be protesting so powerful much."

"Oh, my dear Milly," Mr. Phineas rolled his eyes towards the sky, put his hand over his heart and signed deeply as if reciting in a play, "Ye pierceth me soul with ye sharp arrows of scorn; truly ye do me, lass." He stopped reciting and looked mournfully at Mrs. Turner. "I ain't no selfish hog. I'm jest ah poor hungry mountain man desirin' some good home-cookin'."

Then he sat straight up again and put his hand over his heart one more time and spoke as if he were performing. "Thou do tear me heart in twine."

"Oh poot and horse feathers, Mr. Pennypacker," Mrs. Turner huffed as she put her hands on her hips. "That's a bunch of poppycock and you know it. And, I am not your lass, I am an honorable widow woman so show me some respect."

"Ah, but 'tis true, me lass! You are my favorite honorable widder woman. Of all the widder women in town, you are the best!" He lifted his fork into the air and continued talking while eyeing his heaping plate of food. Another loud burp surged up and popped right out of his mouth.

"Whoa! I do beg your pardon again, ladies, that'un snuck right up on me and made my ears pop. But, I surely cain't stop 'em cuz I heard some medical advice straight from old Doc Gibbons himself, a'fore he passed on, God rest his soul. While sittin' on the porch of the jailhouse he tol' us fellers that iff'en a man was ta try and hold them burps in or stop ya'self from breakin' wind for a long time, your whole insides will most likely start swellin' up and burst right outta your belly button and shoot smack dab onto whoever you're talkin' to cuz them burps and smelly winds don't never leave your body, they just keep buildin' up and buildin' up over the years 'til they have no other place to go 'cept through your belly button. Doc Gibbons said that's why we have belly buttons. He said we see so many men with big ol' belly's and skinny bodies and it's 'cuz thur wives ain't lettin' 'em burp or break wind so sure 'nuf they're gonna just pop and it'll be done and over for 'em!" Mr. Phiney looked at Olivia and Mrs. Turner with his eyes bugged out and a slight smile.

"You are full of hot air yourself, Mr. Pennypacker." Mrs. Turner shook her head and frowned at Mr. Phiney over the top of her spectacles, "I personally knew old Doc Gibbons and he was an old wind-bag. That was just his made-up excuse for having that big pot-belly of his that was caused by him nipping from that jug he kept hid in the barn. But, unknown to him, Mamie knew all along about his hidden jars so every month or two she would go out, dump his jug of brew and replace the entire contents with some horse pee. So, don't you be telling my Olivia any of that rubbish, you hear?"

"Rubbish? That ain't no rubbish, my dear Milly. It came straight from the mouth of a genuine certified doctor."

"Horse-feathers," Mrs. Turner waved her hand in the air as if dismissing his statement as pure nonsense. "The only training Doc Gibbons had was from an old horse doctor who spent his time pulling rotten teeth out of mule's mouths. And please stop calling me Milly. I told you I'm a respectable widow woman and you should address me as such."

"Well now, Milly, that you are. Yes sir, you are a respectable lady. But Doc Gibbons was a durn good doc, iff'en ya know what I mean."

Olivia decided right then and there she liked this Mr. Phineas Pennypacker. He looked a bit like her Papa's older brother might look, and he emitted a feeling of laughter which made her heart feel light for the first time in many months.

"Well," Mr. Phiney said with his mouth full of food, "Livy, how 'bout we get goin' first thin' in the mornin' afore the sun comes up. How's that sound to ya? Milly, did ya send Katy a telegram that we're comin' this week?"

"Of course, I did!" Mrs. Turner said with another huff, insulted that he would think she hadn't. "You are trying my patience today, Mr. Pennypacker. Trying my patience indeed."

"Sorry, Milly. Ya think ya can be ready ta go early in the mornin', lass?"

"Yes. I already packed up what I wanted and the rest Mrs. Turner said she would see to finding someone who wants the rest of our things," Olivia said with a shaky voice.

Mrs. Turner reached over and gave Olivia a tight hug.

"Olivia, dear, I'm going to go through all the things you had to leave behind in your home and I promise I will put away everything I think you may want to keep. Whenever you come back it will all be stored safe and sound in my spare room. In fact, I already spoke to the banker and since your Papa had your house all paid for, he said he would sell it for you and put the money in the bank just for you."

"Thank you, Mrs. Turner."

"It will be a pleasure, my dear. Now, you go on to your Aunt Katy's house and have yourself a good time. Katy told me she wants you to live with her and that's the way it should be. I just want you to know that if you ever decide you want to come back, I will be as happy as a new born pup to have you as my very own daughter."

Olivia gave Mrs. Turner a big hug and with misty eyes told her how much she loved her.

"Okay," Mr. Phiney said as he stood up with his mouth full of the last bit of food from his plate, "I'll be by bright and early ta pick ya up. Maybe Milly will pack up some vittles ta take 'long. Would ya do that iff'en I ask ya real nice-like, Milly?"

"Mr. Pennypacker," Mrs. Turner said with a stern frown, "I already have a basket ready for Olivia but I guess I can throw in the scraps I was saving for my old hound dog. Just don't you be eating Olivia's food, mind you?" Then she laughed loudly. "And don't you be hogging the peach pie I've already put in the basket."

Mr. Phiney's eyes got wide as a big smile spread across his face.

"Ya don't say! You are an angel from the pearly gates, my dear Milly." He held his hand over his heart.

"Now shoo! Go away and leave us be, you troublemaker." Mrs. Turner said loudly as she shooed him away like a fly after a bit of food.

"Shoo!"

"Okay, I'm shooin'." He bowed deeply to Mrs. Turner, walked a fair distance from the table then turned and waved as he called out, "See y'all later, Milly dear!"

"He's a fuss and bother most times, but all and all he's an upstanding man," Mrs. Turner told Olivia with a sigh. "Mr. Pennypacker is a right nice fella. A bit rough around the edges but his heart is good. He is what I call the perfect example of a kind-hearted, gentle mountain man. You just have to prepare to have him talk your leg off as he tells you a heap of haint tales."

"Haint tales?"

"Oh, yes indeed. He is full of haint tales and adventures that will scare the skin right off your bones, iff'en ya know what I mean. He's been here and there and everywhere. He came from overseas somewhere and he knows folks in every country on this earth, I do believe. Now, some of his tales may be him making up stories to scare folks but a few I have heard may be close to the truth."

"Wow. I hope he tells me some of his haint stories."

32

"Well you won't have to bother hoping. When it comes to him talking about haints and such, it's as sure as the sun coming up in the morning. You'll have a jolly good time riding along with him. You might have to tell him to stop his telling a time or two if you get scared or tired of listening to his voice droning on and on, but it won't hurt his feelings none; he's used to folks telling him they've heard enough."

Mrs. Turner continued talking without stopping to take a breath. "I hear-tell Lily Quinn and Ophelia Knudson are also going into Memphis for a spell. Maybe you'll meet up with them and share some fun. I also hear-tell Mr. Alexander Bushman is the one taking them down to visit Granny Cora. And, word is, those rowdy Pruiett boys are going down to help pick cotton for their Uncle George Thomas. Maybe you'll meet up with them too. You should have a quite a good time on your travels."

"That's what Lily Quinn whispered to me at the end of Mama's service."

"Is that right? Well now that's a great thing and a not so good of a thing. Those two are some mighty nice gals but you be careful now. Word is Lily and Ophelia like to do some adventuring."

"Adventuring?"

"Yes. They like to solve other people's problems and the sheriff over in Caruthersville, who by the way is Lily's brother-in-law, has to keep a close eye on those two."

"Oh, I'll behave. Aunt Katy is too nice for me to cause her troubles."

"Humph," Mrs. Turner snorted. "Your Aunt Katy might just cause *you* some troubles. She is an adventurer herself and by the time you get to Memphis she'll probably be all healed up from her fall off that tractor and she'll be itching for some adventures. But she too has a kindly heart so I'm not the least bit worried about you living with her. You just remember, if anything ever happens to your Aunt Katy you have the sheriff telegram me immediately and I'll drop everything and catch the next train. As soon as your Aunt Katy gets over her broke leg I'm sure ah shootin' she'll be up and having a jolly good time right along with you."

Mrs. Turner gave her a tight hug. "I hate ta see you leave, Olivia dear. Other than your Aunt Katy, I am your closest relative. Even if we don't share a drop of blood - it makes no difference to me." Olivia returned Mrs. Turner's hug and gave a sigh of relief because now she knew she was no longer alone in the world.

"Well now, speak of the devil. Here come those two rowdy gals right now."

Olivia looked up from the table and sure enough Lily Quinn and Ophelia Knudson were running their way.

"Yoo-hoo! Hello gals!" Mrs. Turner called out, waving her handkerchief at Lily and Ophelia well before they got close to the table.

"Hello, Mrs. Turner," Lily called out. "Olivia, ya wanna come sit under the trees with us for a bit?"

Olivia looked at Mrs. Turner.

"Go right ahead, dear. Go on with the gals, I'm going over to sit with Maude Ann and Beulah Mae for a bit and find out the latest gossip. I'll clean up our dishes." Mrs. Turner shooed Olivia away from the table.

Olivia timidly followed Lily and Ophelia off to sit on the packed ground beside a large cluster of oak trees growing between the picnic tables and the forest.

"Like I said at your mama's service, we're going to Memphis too, Olivia," Lily said with a smile. "We're gonna visit with Granny Cora for a while and she lives on the farm right next to your Aunt Katy, doesn't she?"

"I think so."

"Yep, she does," Ophelia replied quickly. "During the funeral service, my mama whispered that Olivia's Aunt Katy lives on the farm next to Granny Cora's."

"Well," Lily whispered quickly, "you'll never guess what I heard last week when Mr. Phiney came out to the farm to visit with Uncle Pud - he knows Uncle Pud from way back when they were young'uns picking cotton on all the farms." Lily leaned in close to the other two girls to continue telling them how Mr. Phiney knew Uncle Pud.

"I don't care how Uncle Pud and Mr. Phiney know each other, I just want to know what you heard," Ophelia said anxiously. "What did you hear?"

"Well, okay," Lily whispered softly. "I heard Mr. Phiney telling Uncle Pud that right before Elijah Bonheur, the man who raised him, died, he had told Mr. Phiney to dig under the front porch stoop and he would find some family valuables, but after Elijah passed on and Mr. Phiney buried him, the next morning he went to dig up the valuables and they were gone! Someone had gotten to it before he did, and the thing is, Mr. Phiney said the dirt was freshly dug up - so it must have happened the very day Elijah passed over. And he said it must have happened while he was back behind Elijah's cabin burying his body or during the night while he was asleep. But he said he wakes up at the drop of a pin, seeing that he's a mountain man and sleeps outside most nights and all. And Elijah's hound dog was sleeping right up close to him and that hound never let out a peep all night long. Mr. Phiney told Uncle Pud he has not one clue as to who or what took it, but it was gone. Then after talking to Uncle Pud for a while I heard him say that maybe Elijah was mistaken and that the family valuables box was at his cabin in Memphis and the thief might be on his way to Memphis to snatch it up."

"Wow," Ophelia sucked in a deep breath. "Wow. That's exciting. Maybe it was one of them red-haired haints who are always looking for treasure and souls to take up north to the salt mines. But if it had been one of them red-haired haints, they would have tried to take Mr. Phiney, wouldn't they?"

"I think it's a real person," Lily replied. "There ain't no haint around that could carry a box of valuables. But it must have been treasure of some kind or they wouldn't have taken it. If it was just family valuable stuff, no one would want it, right?"

"Right, I agree," Ophelia whispered. "They must have dug that hole hoping to find the treasure, and when they couldn't find it maybe they figured out Mr. Elijah had another cabin in Tennessee. What do you think, Olivia?"

"I don't know anything about red-haired haints or buried treasure," Olivia said quietly, looking at Lily and Ophelia with wide eyes. "I just met Mr. Phiney for the first time a few minutes ago. Mrs. Turner introduced us because Mr. Phiney is taking me to Memphis to live with Aunt Katy."

"Oops," Lily said softly. "We're sorry. Sometimes we forget most folks outside of Caruthersville don't know about those red-haired haints. Let me tell ya about them scary ghosts. One time a few months back, Ophelia found a dead person down in the river bottom not too far from our farm. It was dark as pitch when she knocked on my bedroom window all shaky-like and climbed through the window and told me 'bout the dead body. Well, we snuck on out of the house, went down to the river bottom and sure 'nuf, we found the dead body. It was the body of Tillie Brown! Do you know who Tillie Brown is?"

"Yes, I know Tillie Brown, she's some kind of distant relative to my Pa," Olivia replied. "But I thought she was alive and living back east with her Pa and a new husband."

"Well," Lily said, "She is. it's a long, strange story but the first time we found her she was dead. Just as dead as can be. Then she came back to life!"

Olivia stared at Lily and Ophelia with open-mouthed disbelief.

"Well, it's true, but anyway," Lily continued, "One thing led to another and low-and-behold, some other fellas were hunting for her dead body, so in the dark of the night, we lugged her dead body up onto the side of the levee and stuffed it into a hollowed-out dead tree that was barely standing. We climbed inside with her dead body and then Ophelia fainted cuz she faints every time she gets scared, but I kept right on watching through a hole in the old tree for the fellas to come out of the river bottom woods. Well, two of them came running out of the pathway and began searching around for the body. When they couldn't find her, they built themselves a fire and waited for the third fella to show up. When finally the third fella showed up they started in talking 'bout haints and things cuz they thought they might have heard a haint, when actually it was Ophelia snoring," Lily laughed before continuing. "But, anyway, they started in telling about some red-haired haints that, I guess, swoop down from up north in Michigan trying to find souls they can take back with them to work in the salt mines.

"Well, I ain't ever heard of salt mines up north, but that's what the three fellas were saying. They said these red-haired haints have great big teeth and big, bushy heads of red hair and can put a smile on their faces stretching from the top of one ear to the top of the other ear and it makes their giant teeth shine like lanterns. Sounds kindly strange to me, but that's what they said, didn't they Ophelia?"

"Yep," Ophelia whispered quietly. "It was pretty dang scary. But I don't think those red-haired haints could carry off a heavy box of treasure, do you?"

"Nope," Lily whispered back, "but let's think on it some more. Maybe we can help Mr. Phiney find his missing family treasure."

"Wow," Olivia whispered quietly. "I'll ask Mr. Phiney tomorrow on the way to Memphis and maybe he can help us think on it."

"Yeah, that sounds like a fine idea!" Lily said.

"Duck!" A boy's voice rang out.

Immediately the three girls ducked down and covered their heads as the Pruiett boys sailed over them. Ott, Paul and Tom, with their legs churning the air with someone's hound dog following them, whooped and hollered as they flew over their heads. All three of them landed about a foot from Olivia, creating a big cloud of dust which engulfed the girls as the boys fell to the ground in a tangled heap and rolled a bit before jumping to their feet.

"I beat ya, Ott, I beat ya!" Tom yelled, jumping up and down with his arms in the air.

"No, you didn't!" Paul yelled back at Tom, "My feet touched the ground right before Ott's and you didn't touch the ground 'til after me."

Tom turned to the girls. "Who won, Lily?" he asked.

"I don't know, you morons," Lily replied with a frown, standing to her feet and putting her hands on her hips as she brushed off her dress. "Go away and leave us be. We don't want to be bothered by y'all today. Olivia's still mourning her Mama's passing."

"Sorry Olivia. We didn't mean no disrespect. We were just having us a race," Ott said kindly.

All three boys plopped down beside the girls, causing more dust to float into the air like flour. They had changed out of their Sunday clothes and were dressed in pants held up with ropes going from the front loops of their britches, crossed across their chests and attached to the back loops of the britches. None of the three wore a shirt and on their heads were frayed straw hats.

"Guess who we saw over by the side of the church-house," Ott whispered as the three of them scooted in close with the girls.

"I don't know, who?" Lily asked as she rolled her eyes.

Ott leaned in close and whispered, "We saw Tater James and Hawg-Jaws Jackman squatting on the ground over by that big tree on the side of the church-house and they were talking real low 'bout some kind of gold they're gonna dig up from Tater's Granny Josie's tomato patch down in Memphis. Tater said she's just a old crippled-up old woman who can't hear worth a pip and they could get at it really easy-like. He said she's so deaf she couldn't hear thunder if it was in her kitchen, much less the two of them digging of a night in her tomato patch. Me and Paul were hiding around the corner and when we heard what they were talking about, we snuck off quick, grabbed up Tom and started in hunting for you gals. Ain't that right, Paul?"

"Yep, it is," Paul said quietly. "Cuz we know y'all love a mystery and since y'all are going to Memphis like we are, we can all hunt up Tater and Hawg-Jaws and figure out what they're up to. Ain't that right, Ott?"

"Yep," Ott said a bit louder. "We already know where Tater's Granny Josie lives 'cause me and Paul picked 'maters for her last summer. We have to help Uncle George bring in his cotton during the day, but after that we can help ya. Ain't that right Paul?"

"Yep, we know where she lives," Paul said. He looked at Olivia. "Sorry 'bout the dust we caused when you're in mourning for your ma and all. We'll leave ya be for now. But we'll be seeing y'all on the way down to Memphis. Pappy Smith might not be able to take us down, so we might have to ride with Mr. Bushy."

"Yep," Ott said with a big grin as he looked at Lily. "Ain't that gonna be fun."

"What??" Lily and Ophelia said at the same time, looking at each other. "But me and Ophelia are riding with Mr. Bushy!"

"Yeah," Ott and Paul grinned as they laughed, "we know!"

"What'd you boys hear us sayin'?" a deep voice came from behind the clump of trees where they were sitting. "Ya better be tellin' us the truth or you'll be sorry, cuz I got me a big ol' snake here."

"And ya best not be jumpin' up yellin' and screamin'," Another deep voice said quietly with a snicker.

"Iff'en ya do, I'm gonna throw this snake on y'all," Hawg-Jaws laughed as he lifted the snake so they could see how long it was. "I've trained him so iff'en I give 'em a throw he bites whoever he lands on." He gave out another evil snicker.

All six of them got wide-eyed and slowly turned to look at the clump of trees. There stood Tater James with his head stuck through a V in a big oak tree; Hawg-Jaws Jackman was peeking through a clump of wild ferns at the bottom of the same tree with a big water moccasin being held by the back of its head. The snake was twisting and writhing, trying to get loose.

Immediately the girls and Pruiett boys jumped to their feet and slowly began backing away from the clump of trees.

Tater James was a tall, skinny fella with britches well above his ankles held up with a string going from a loop on the front of his britches, circled around his neck and back down to the other loop on the front of his pants, leaving the back of his pants hanging down with a gap at the waist. He wore no shoes and his white shirt was so dirty it looked to be brown. He was a known thief and a rascal who would swipe anything not nailed down. His face was always filthy and his hands grimy as if he had been digging in a mud hole. He had his frayed straw hat pulled down low over his ears causing him to bend his head back so he could see whoever was standing right in front of him. His long, brown hair hung in greasy strands over his face as usual. Each strand of hair was full of lint and debris picked up from sleeping on the ground in the forest.

Hawg-Jaws, whose real name was Hawley George Jackman, was a short, skinny fella with a big pot-belly and a ruddy red complexion. He kept his head shaved of any hair that might happen to grow and gossip said it was because he was covered with lice. His jaws looked just like a big old hog's droopy jowls, thus his nickname. He said he was from Sikeston, Missouri, but he wandered through the Missouri boot-heel with Tater James stealing and committing all sorts of unlawful deeds. The two of them didn't bother doing odd jobs for a bit of money or asking for a hand-out; they just took whatever they wanted with no regards to respectability at all. Most of the local hobos who rode the rails and wandered through the small towns refused to associate with Tater James and Hawg-Jaws, because they claimed the two of them were the bottom-dwellers of the hobo country and couldn't be trusted enough to save their own granny's lives.

"We didn't hear nothing," Paul stuttered as they all kept backing away. "Did we Ott?"

"Nope, we didn't!" Ott said.

"Nothing a'tall," Tom spoke up boldly, pointing his finger at the two men. "Get on out of here and stop bothering us or I'm gonna yell for the preacher-man and he'll come running with the sheriff and take both of y'all to jail!"

The two backed off from the trees and slowly eased into the woods, still holding their snake. Hawg-Jaws turned, glared at Tom, pointed a dirty crooked finger at him then pointed at the big snake. He gave Tom the evil eye and in a chilling, whispery voice said, "We'll be gettin' ya, boy, we'll be getting' ya good. And I've always got my snake with me." He gave the snake a shake and acted like he was going to jump at them with it, but then the two of them quickly disappeared into the woods. They didn't know the kids could still hear them.

"Let go of that evil thing and let's get outta here, Hawg," Tater said.

Tom's face turned white as a sheet as he stood staring into the woods. "Whatcha' think, Ott? Ya think they'll be gettin' me with another snake? Maybe I ought not go to Uncle George Tomas's farm with y'all."

"Nope, you're going," Paul and Ott said at the same time.

"They're full of hot air, Tom. They're just a couple tramps," Paul said calmingly. "We'll take care of ya, ain't that right, Ott?"

"Yep, ain't nobody gonna be getting' ya, Tom."

Tom stood there quietly not saying another word, just looking into the woods.

"Well," Ott said slowly as he and Paul took a few more steps towards the church-house, "We best be going. We'll leave you gals alone so's Olivia can grieve for her ma without us scuffing up dust."

With that said, all three boys turned and took off running toward the eating tables.

"Come on," Lily said still glancing at the woods. "Let's go see what the rest of the folks are up to."

4

The Wraiths and Napoleon Bonaparte

(As told to Olivia by Mr. Phiney who swore it was the gospel truth)

"The sky was black as pitch that stormy night so long ago," Mr. Phiney began telling and reliving another tale to Olivia as the day began to wane on their journey to Memphis. They could not yet see the shadows of the night coming from the east, but it could be felt.

"Not a sliver of light peeped through the angry black clouds and it was entirely up to my horse Atticus ta keep us upright on that slippery, muddy road 'cuz the blindin' rain was pouring down upon us in buckets, blockin' out everthin' round about us. I could hear them haints comin' up fast as poop goin' through a goose and I could tell my Atticus knew it as well. His thunderin' steps bore a sense of urgency. My ears were keen to the sound of those haint horses' hooves hammering the earth like spikes being driven into railroad ties, and I knew the hounds of Hades were upon us!

"Shivers and chills raced up and down my spine like water on a hot stove," Mr. Phiney said with a shudder. "and it wasn't just the rain. I knew good-and-well that if we were caught it would be me against the five of them wraiths cuz thur weren't nary another livin' soul on that road. I was afraid to take a peek behind me cuz ever once'st in a while Atticus would slip a bit in the mud. But he kept right on moving fast and that muddy road was getting as slick as goose grease; if by chance he lost his balance, I was a goner. The pounding of those haints' hooves was almost as loud as the ear-splittin' claps of thunder as the storm whipped and roared above us as we raced along the

French coast. I could feel their presence behind us tryin' ta tug at my very soul like they wanted to snatch my soul from my body and leave me soulless. They chased us with a vengeance I ain't never seen a'fore. It was like ole Lucifer himself had set 'em upon me.

"Now, Livy," Mr. Phiney turned and looked at her with a furrowed frown as he spoke in a low, whispery voice as if maybe old Lucifer himself might jump right up beside him if he spoke louder. "I've had me some serious run-ins with that evil feller from the pits of fire afore and I had no DE-sire ta have any more run-ins with 'em, iff'en ya know what I mean. No DE-sire a'tall.

"Rain was coming down like bedsheets flappin' in the wind on a clothesline," Mr. Phiney continued in a quiet whisper. He let go of the reins and began demonstrating with his hands and shoulders. He started waving and jerking them around to emphasize how the clouds and rain had rolled, tumbled and twisted with anger. His voice grew louder and more forceful until he was basically shouting.

"Those clouds roared and rumbled furiously," Mr. Phiney said in a gravelly voice. "They were twistin' and churnin' in the skies above me then started in shootin' down to the ground lookin' like little cyclones, then back up into the skies, plundering and ravishin' the heavens into shreds as they churned and tumbled. All the while shootin' jagged bolts of lightnin' ever which way. I took a peek up to the sky and watched as the clouds pulled away from each other fur a quick second and there, for jest a flash, was the blue sky. But then, with a mighty, earth-shakin' roar," Mr. Phiney raised his hands in the air, gave out a mighty roar and slammed one fist into the palm of his other hand making Olivia jump, "they collided like two locomotives plowing full throttle head first inta each other. Lightning bolts burst forth from the clouds like far-works, then cracked sharp between the rumblin' clouds as the wicked battle continued. It was like the old tales of the war gods Honos and Ares and they were battlin' like savage beasts in the skies above me. I could feel the tingling of the lightning in my bones as if it would strike me dead at any time. The good and

44

the evil were mixin' up in that ferocious battle of power. Massive bolts of lightning shot down, one right after the other - Boom! Boom! BOOM!" Olivia shrank back a little from Mr. Phiney's thundering voice as he continued. "Where lightning had hit the ground, it would sizzle as pillars of steam shot up like hot coals. The smell of burning sulfur filled the air, making it hard to take in a good gulp of air.

"Then an ear-piercin' scream of a horse being struck down by lightnin' shot through the wind and rain; at the same time, the sound of my horse gasping for air reached my ears and my poor heart purt-near came to a stop. I forced myself to turn and take a look-see under my armpit and when I did, I saw one of them haints' horses vanish inta a million pieces of sparkling light, then, POOF! It was gone. That's when I saw my horse's tail catch a'fire and start burnin' straight up in a big 'ole streak ah fire like a torch. But, just in a snap, it was put out by the deluge of water. I felt the back ah my britches and low and behold thur was ah hole burnt straight through to me under drawers! Good gosh a'mighty I was scare't."

Mr. Phiney laughed loudly. "Now, Livy, don't you be spreadin' 'round that I told ya 'bout being scare't. It ain't manly for a man my size to be scare't, now is it?"

Olivia laughed and said she wouldn't tell a soul his secret, and Mr. Phiney continued.

"Now, frothy foam started in flying from Atticus' mouth, causing great gobs of foamy slobber mixed with rainwater to splat and slap me about the face and shoulders 'cuz I was leanin' as far forward as I could so the wind would whoosh over me and help old Atticus run. We continued on down that nightmarish road and I listened to Atticus gaspin' for air, and I suddenly feared he was gonna slow down—or maybe fall over dead in his tracks—and that put the clinch of death inta my bones.

"But that horse kept right on fighting to escape them wraiths and I knew if we could jest make it into the little village of Roscoff-by-the-Sea, we would be safe. I couldn't yet see the lighted winders of the cottages, but a hint of salty seawater smell came upon us really quick-like mixed with the smell of smoke from chimneys as lamb's legs and such were being roasted and right then I knew we were drawin' closer to shelter and safety.

"I turned my head again, jest a wee bit, and peeked under my armpit and low and behold they was still coming on strong like nothing even happened to the fifth feller. The remaining four haints were sitting tall in the saddle an every last one of 'em was holding a shiny glistenin' white scythe straight up in the air. Atticus was still foamin' at the mouth and I was still holdin' my breath in fear. I knew we had to get to shelter fast or my Atticus was gonna fall over lifeless and I would be another victim of the Five Horsemen.

"Now, I ain't knowin' where them fellers came from and I ain't knowin' why they decided ta give us a chase, but, let me back up in my tellin' and tell ya the whole tale from the very beginning so you can understand it all. How's that sound to ya?"

Olivia gave Mr. Phiney a grin and told him it was fine with her.

***

Mr. Phiney sat up straighter on the wagon bench, clicked his tongue to signal to the horse to pick up the pace a bit, then cleared his throat. He shook his head and shivered as he blew out an uneasy breath.

"Whew. It's fearful jest memberin' it." He leaned closer to Olivia and in a low, whispery voice, resumed the telling. Olivia edged closer to his shoulder so as to not miss a single word of his tale along with easing the feelings of fear. A bit of a shiver began dancing up and down her backbone in anticipation of the tale she was about to hear. She gave a slight shudder, lifted the blanket she was sitting on and pulled it tightly about her shoulders. The pre-dark shadows of the night began collecting behind the leaves of the trees and a faint hint of the misty fingers of fog began slipping up from the mighty Mississippi River into the trees where it would eventually wind its tendrils through the bushes, searching for something or someone to envelop.

Peering into the forest in front of them, Olivia saw the giant elm trees leaning further and further across the narrow path creating a tunnel of dark shadowy green leaves. The coming shadows and fog was already changing the shapes of the trees, making them seem to shift and sway, transforming them into frightening silhouettes of unknown creatures lurking about, ready to pounce upon whomever ventured close. Hues of gray pushed the crystal blue sky of summer away and cast a sinister spell upon the earth.

Shaking her head to clear her mind, Olivia knew most of her thoughts were her own imagination working overtime, but she couldn't shake the shadowy images out of her head. Gone was the bright sunlight which had filtered through the passage of trees with blue jays and cardinals flitting and dashing from tree to tree. In its place came the gray gloom of the pre-evening sky. Branches and leaves began rustling in the warm night breeze making a body wonder if the rustling was the breeze or actually the movements of unknown spirits slipping through the air. High-pitched cicada screams dwindled to a low murmur then swelled into another high-pitched chorus. The calls of the Mocking Jay faded into the west as the Missouri farmland settled in for the beginning of another warm summer night. In the distance, the melancholy howls of wolves reverberated softly across the mountains. Up from the Mississippi River rose the hauntingly repetitive notes of a river loon's song; its wavering treble floated gently off into the dusky pre-night air until it softly faded away. Slowly, there came the forlorn song of its mate as it answered. The lonely songs of the river loon always made a soul feel alone and isolated as if the loon was the sole survivor on a lonely, deserted planet.

The sudden screech of a large barred owl, swooping down from the trees, jerked the minds of Oliva and Mr. Phiney back to the present. Mr. Phiney began his tale again; the old mule was plodded along the narrow path, pushing fluffy clouds of misty fog up with each hoof beat. Mr. Phiney looked over at

Olivia with a grin and once again leaned down so he could continue his story in a whispery voice.

"You see, Olivia lass, back when I was a young man I decided to take me a trip across the ocean and have me a visit to Piel Island in England where I was born, where I know'd some of the folks I grew up with was still livin'. Well, I stayed there visitin' and havin' me a fine time until it came on into September and the sea started gettin' rough with waves sometimes reachin' ten feet high and slammin' inta the rocky cliffs, the air was bitter cold and nippin' at my skin every night with its cold icy fingers.

"Well, one early afternoon when the cold winds started whippin' around I decided I was gonna take my leave of that pretty little isle and come back home to Memphis where the air is warm and the nights are balmy. Well, I was staying up at the King's castle, so I determined to take a short stroll down to the Ship's Inn and pop in for a spot of tea and a few biscuits ta go 'long with it while doin' a wee bit ah jawin' with the bar-keep and anyone else who popped in for a spot. Well, I was sitting on a stool enjoyin' my tea and talkin' to the bar-keep 'bout whether I should leave the island on that very day or iff'en I should wait 'til morning. Well, after a bit, in came some more fellas and when the bar-keep walked away ta wait on the fellas, into the pub shuffled ah strange lil' fella with a bushy head of white hair and a long, white bushy beard. Real sly-like he slipped up beside me and slid onto the stool next to mine. He pulled his stool real close-like, all the time dartin' his head back and forth as if lookin' for someone in particular. Then he bent his head over purt near onto the tabletop, all the while jerkin' his head back and forth, still checkin' the room ta see who might be watchin' or listenin'. Then he says in a whispery, raspy voice, 'They be coming for ya, lad; they be coming for ya quick on the next ferry. I'd shinny on outta here if I was ye. They're comin' ta get the treasure box and drag ya inta the London Tower dungeon ta rot with the rats even iff'en ya give 'em the box.'"

Mr. Phiney stopped talking for a minute and laughed softly. "Ya see, some fellas 'round there thought I had some stolen treasure, which was just a bunch ah poppycock.

"That feller smelled so bad I wanted to pinch my nose shut and let out with a "phew" a'fore I keeled over in a faint like ah woman onta the floor. But I din't want ta hurt the ole fella's feelings and I surely did want ta hear what he was talkin' bout so I acted like he smelled like a rose, then asked 'em to tell me his tale. He went on to tellin' me the London Bobbies knew I was there on Piel Island and he himself knew they were on their way. Well, without hearing anymore, I figured it warranted some action so I din't say anythin' a'tall ta insult the lil' feller and instead of sittin' there questionin' him I remembered how fast Aunt Abby whisked me off that island so many years ago and right then and there made up my mind to do the same. I could actually hear Aunt Abby whisperin' in my ear to get a move on and leave as quick as possible afore it was too late. So, I pulled out some coin ta pay for my spot of tea and quietly slipped the old fella a farthing for his warning. He grinned broadly and whispered 'thank'ye lad'. Well, right away I stood up, kept my eyes down to the floor and started walking out ah there, and the lil' old fella scurries out the door after me. When I got outside onta the stoop, he grabs aholt ah my coat, still hunkered over, and again dartin' his eyes from side to side while whispering that his name was Timmy Rimini and he knew my Aunt Abby way back in the days a'fore I came 'long. He whispered to me that she had the missin' royal treasure trove hidden som'ers and when I got back to America it would be right nice if I was to remember 'em doing me this favor and send 'em a wee bit of the treasure. He said he ain't never told ah soul 'bout that treasure and he wasn't gonna snitch on 'er now, cuz Abby Ann was a beautiful woman with a heart of gold. Now that's his words, not mine, cuz the Aunt Abby I knew sure wasn't no good lookin' woman. She had a big heart ah gold, but she wasn't so comely ta gaze upon. Well, I looked at 'em sorta curious-like, shook my head and told 'em I didn't have no treasure but if I ever acquired one I would most definitely send 'em a wee bit cuz I sure didn't like the idea of spendin' time in a watery dungeon with them rats. And I knew how them

Bobbies threw many a bloke inta the dungeons for less'en havin' the Royal treasure trove. Well, that old fella gave me a gnarly bad-toothed smile and jest as he turned to leave I heard him say in a whispery voice so low I couldn't hear him so well, 'they killed 'er, lad. They killed 'er.' Then quick as a wink he turned, broke a bit of wind and whisked off around the back ah the Ship's Inn and vanished.

"After that little fella vanished, I remembered he was the very one who had given Aunt Abby the warning to leave the island so long ago when I was just a young lad. Only then he was a tall, ominous fella dressed in black.

"So that very afternoon, me and Atticus, the horse I bought from the King of Piel Island, left on the last ferry goin' to Liverpool where we would straightaway go for the next ship going to America. But just when I was no more than twenty feet from the gangway leading inta the ship for America from Liverpool, I spied six Bobbies walking real slow-like to the gangway lookin' 'round for me, or so I figgered. So calmly I put my head down and changed my course for the ship sailin' for Roscoff-by-the-Sea on the Brittany Peninsula along the coast ah France. Luckily I was wearin' the same kind a disguise I wore as a lad when me and Aunt Abby fled to the Americas. I was dressed as a stevedore leadin' my horse close beside me so's I could hide my face behind his head 'til I got inta the stock hold of the ship where I stayed with the farm animals 'til we was way out inta the English Channel. All the time I was wonderin' where that ole fella got the idee that Aunt Abby had the lost Royal treasure. If she did have it she sure did hide it from me cuz after she passed on, God rest her soul, I went through every last thing ah hers and I didn't find no treasure, that's for sure.

"But that's another story I'll be tellin' ya later on. Let me finish my tale of them wraith-like haints and my friend Thomas Pierre Charron, a Frenchman I know'd from way back in my childhood days on Piel Island. Now, Livy-gal, I know your Pa's ma had the same last name as my friend Pierre but I ain't thinkin' he's any blood relation to ya."

Mr. Phiney turned his head to look at Olivia for a moment.

"Well, now that I'm lookin' at ya real close-like, it jest might be. Hmm...". He scratched his bearded chin in deep thought. "Ya know, Livy-gal, I best be thinkin' on that a spell."

Olivia glanced over at Mr. Phiney as he sat relaxed on the hard buckboard seat. His legs were longer than most men's legs were so he sat on the wagon bench with his feet hanging over the front board of the wagon box. Just as Mrs. Turner had said, Mr. Phiney talked so much a body could sit right next to him for hours never saying a single word and he would keep right on talking just as happy as a clam while telling his tales, not caring one bit if you replied or laughed. Local gossip did say, Mrs. Turner had told her, he was born on a small island near the coast of England and came to America when he and his Aunt were forced to flee. So, after hearing what he just told her, Olivia knew the gossip was true.

"Well, let me continue telling my tale about the wraiths where I left off and 'bout what happened when we reached the coast of the peninsula and was making our way to Roscoff. We were mindin' our own busy-ness when out from that dark forest burst those five wraiths on horses and that was when the whole thing started," Mr. Phiney said with a smile as he shifted in the hard buckboard seat.

"So anyway, Atticus was still laborin' for his breath and my heart was still bangin' like a drum in my ears with mud and foam still flying ever'where and I was tryin' ta slap it away the best I could."

Mr. Phiney was using his arms to demonstrate how the mud and foam was flying all around him.

"And all that time I was shootin' up flare-prayers." he laughed. "But when I smelled that salty sea and the smoke from the fireplaces, my heart slowed down a beat or two. The smell of those roastin' lamb legs floated inta my nostrils like sweet honeysuckle blooms on a hot summer night and Atticus sensed safety cuz I could feel 'em give a burst of energy, as if it was his last chance ta get ta shelter, and then, there we were flying along the path inta town. I saw the lighted winders of my friend Tomas Pierre's cottage glowin' like a beacon on a dark stormy night. Immediately I pulled Atticus to a skiddin' stop, vaulted out of my saddle, flung open Pierre's door and surged inside pullin' the heavin' horse right along with me and slammed the door shut boltin' it as I went. Pierre jumped up from his table where he was sittin' and with a cuss word grabbed his gun and pointed it directly at me poor heart but just as he was 'bout to pull the trigger he recognized me, and with another cuss word, lowered his gun to the table and started in cussin' at me for being such a mugger as to burst inta his house without callin' out. Then I yelled back that the Five Horsemen were in hot pursuit of us. Well, that made him stand bug-eyed for a few seconds before he muttered something under his breath and motioned for me ta have ah seat. Taking Atticus' reins, Pierre led the poor heavin' fella out through the back door and into his lean-to, while I was tryin' ta get aholt ah my breath while Pierre gave Atticus a quick rub-down and set a feed-bag filled with oats about the poor fella's neck.

"Then he stomped back inta the big room, bolted the door to the lean-to and poured me a mug of steamin' bitter English tea, and there we sat for purt-near five minutes afore I could get 'nuf air inta my lungs ta tell the tale.

"Jest as I was 'bout ta start in my tellin', the candles flickered out and the fire in his fireplace got real low-like and started ta sputter. So t'was lucky for us we were sittin' real close ta the sputterin' fireplace so's we could kindly see each other's faces.

"'It's them', Pierre mouthed ta me so low I could barely hear 'em.

"'Yep,' I whispered back, 'I tol' ya. They follered us in.'

"Turning to his fireplace, Pierre tossed some water onto the embers, making it hiss and sizzle for a bit. Then the room was pitch black and we could barely see our hands in front of our faces, ya know, just like it is here in

Missourah on them pitch-black moonless nights down in the Ozark mountains? Well, it's like that in Roscoff."

Mr. Phiney hesitated a few seconds before continuing. Olivia sneezed quietly.

"God bless ya," Phiney whispered. "Now, the story goes that those wraiths can't see through glass but they have ears like the good Lord himself."

Mr. Phiney stopped speaking and cocked his head to one side as if listening for something before continuing his tale. Then he continued in a lower whisper prompting Olivia to lean in closer so she could hear.

"The two of us sat there waitin' in the dark fur something ta happen, dartin' our eyes from one winder to the other cuz Pierre's cottage had two winders in the front and one winder on each side wall. They weren't big winders, but they were big enough that a body could see out fairly well."

Again Mr. Phiney stopped speaking and cocked his head as if listening for something. Then again he continued his tale.

"It was quiet as a cemetery for a few minutes then the hair on my arms and the back ah my neck started in tinglin' like a wasp bite and that was when I saw 'em." Mr. Phiney gave a quick shudder.

"First thing I saw was a black shadow movin' slowly from winder to winder. Those creatures were so black; they made the black sky look grey. Then, at ever winder stood one of them wraiths. And they were some bad-lookin' haints. It wasn't like no other haint I ever did see afore. As black as midnight they were, and I know it's hard to believe it, but they were blacker than midnight. They stood silently trying to see through the winders. All me and Pierre could see was an outline of a haint shrouded in a hood; then slowly and at the very same time, they raised their heads up and there they stood with glowing yeller eyes blazin' through the winders. I could tell they couldn't see us cuz they kept shiftin' their yeller eyes from side to side. Then a see-through, green fog floated in front of them and they left each winder and all of 'em gathered up at one front winder right next to the door; with each of 'em tryin' ta push to the front. Then, their black cloaks fell off and there they stood all white and ghostly-lookin', one of 'em reached its hand right through that winder-glass like it wasn't even there and slid it down all the way to the floor, then jerked it back out when a different haint gave a shove to the haint who stuck his hand through the winder; as if ta get 'em out of the way. Then the one who got shoved started in pushin' the one who shoved 'em, then all four ah 'em started in rippin' inta each other in a big ole brawl 'til one of 'em hit the middle haint-feller's head with a scythe and that made the haint with the hit head give the hittin' haint a big push and sent 'em slippin' and sliddin' right under the crack at the bottom ah Pierre's door with a loud 'oof'. And there he was all sprawled out like a hound dog on a hot Sunday afternoon. But the strange thing was, when he slipped under the door, his body was flat as a fritter and he came through that crack as one long tall flat haint. His feet were stuck outside the door but his body was stretched out neigh-onta ten feet long! And he was all green and glowing."

Mr. Phiney gave a loud chuckle as he looked at Olivia's wide-open eyes staring up at him.

"Don' look at me like that, it's the honest-Abe truth! Well, really quick-like, we scurried over ta where that haint lay sprawled out and stood starin' down at 'em with our mouths hangin' wide open. It was the strangest sight I ever did see. The glow from that haints body lit up the whole cabin and we could see 'em really good like it was broad daylight and it was the ugliest durn haint I ever did see. He was staring up at us jest like we was staring down at him. His eyeball holes were nothin' but empty black spots and right in the middle was this here itty-bitty white bit of an eyeball with a black dot right in the center and he had no nose a'tall. It looked like his nose had been cut clean off when he was still living. Now, I'm thinkin' he got tangled up with somebody who cut off his nose and that was what killed the poor feller maybe. And, its gappin' mouth was stock full of yeller teeth kindly-like two rows ah teeth on top and two rows ah teeth on the bottom! Then it's wide-open mouth turned inta a wicked smile, and I mean it was sure 'nuf really evil."

For the third time Mr. Phiney stopped talking and cocked his head as if he had heard something out of the ordinary.

"Now," Mr. Phiney kept turning around glancing behind the wagon and was barely speaking above a whisper. "Let me tell ya the worse thing 'bout that haint. His hair was all bushy and jest as red as a red bird and crawlin' all over it was millions and millions of little bitty white spiders. It looked like a big ole nest of them things and they started in crawlin' onta the floor. There were sacks a spider eggs hanging from his head and really quick-like them sacks started poppin' open and them baby spiders began scurryin' all over the floor. It was the awful'est durn sight I ever did see. I tell ya, Olivia lass, they were weavin' in and out an all about that haints eyeholes and crawlin' outta his nose and even its mouth! Well, Pierre calmly reached over, picked up his old beat up coffee tin off'en the eatin' table and gave it a dump right smack dab onta that haints belly. We stood and watched that haints ghostly body seep inta the wood leavin' nothin' behind 'cept little sparklin' bits ah light floatin' around on the floor and a bunch ah them spiders. It was like that floor jest sucked that haint right down inta the wood, and then - poof! - it was gone!

"But," Mr. Phiney continued, "I swear on my Granny's grave, all them little spiders stood up on their hind legs and I could hear them screaming at the top of their lungs and they were jest itty-bitty but I swear I could see 'em dancin' a jig! The strangest thing I ever did see.

"It was truly amazin'!" Mr. Phiney's eyes bugged out as he looked at Olivia, as if he still could not believe it. "Then Pierre turned ta me with a big grin and says, 'Phiney my man, now there are only three of them!'

"Well, me and Pierre looked back up at the front winder and the rest ah them haints was starin' bug-eyed at us like they could now see through that winder and slowly they all got a frown on thur ugly faces and started in glarin' at us. Well, I'm thinkin' they must be able ta see us cuz one of 'em was starin' right inta my eyes and it was givin' me the willies. I forced my eyes away from that haint and grabbed up Pierre's old straw broom and start in pushin' them bits ah flickering lights and the white spiders back outside through the crack under the door. Jest as soon as those spiders were back outside, the rest ah them haints startin' in runnin' like the hounds' ah hell was after 'em. Lickety-split and they were gone. So Pierre and me decide ta take us a sit-down and jest watch for a bit.

"Well, we eased quietly back to the table and Pierre poured us some lukewarm Buckeye tea then we sat jest starin' out the winder waitin' for the haints to return. And sure 'nuf they did. There they were again pushing up against that winder. They started in pushin' and shovin' each other again and soon we had to stand up close-like to the winder because they were all rolling around on the ground wrestlin' and gougin' at each other.

"Then all three of them rolled away into the forest and me and Pierre sat back down, lit the fire again and had us a fair ta meddlin' long talk before decidin' ta get some shut-eye. So, Pierre laid down on his cot on one side ah the room and I laid down on the cot on the other side ah the room and purt near right away we were snoring.

"Well, long 'bout midnight, or close to it, I woke up to the loud rumble ah thunder comin' in from across the sea and as I lay there real quiet, I could tell it was comin' inta Roscoff pretty quick-like. I glanced over at Pierre and he was sittin' straight up on his cot with his head cocked ta one side."

"'They're coming, Phiney,' he whispered to me in ah hushed voice. 'They're coming and we cannot stop them.'

"'Who's comin'?' I asked as I quickly sat up on the edge of my cot.

"'The *fantômes noir* are coming with vengeance and we don't want ta be here,' he whispered louder, already sitting on the side of his cot lacing up his boots as he told me that he had seen it happen before and the souls they were able to snatch never made it out of their cottage alive. The whole cottage fell in on all of them. They didn't ever have a chance at all."

"'Come quick, *mon amie*,' Pierre said as he stood up and swiftly walked to the back door of his cottage. 'The *fantômes noir* are on their way and we don't want to be here when they arrive. They are a bad lot and we must leave now!'

"Well, I jumped ta my feet, jerked on my mocs and grabbed my grub sack and started in follerin' 'em out the back door.

"'*Se dépêcher, mon amie, se dépêcher!*' Pierre called out over the roar of the thunder."

"'I am hurryin'!' I yelled back at 'em. "Do we take the horses?"

"'*Non*, they will not help us. These *fantômes noir* do not care about our horses, they are after us. Hurry now and let's go to Madeline's cottage. Maybe they won't look for us there.'

"What in the world is a *fantômes noir*?" I asked 'em.

"'A black ghost, *mon amie*. There is nothing more terrifying than those dark evil *compagnons*. Once they arrive, they will creep slowly; silently slipping from tree to tree and cottage to cottage until they find the cottage and persons they are seeking. They ride on the wings of the storm as it rumbles in from the open sea. If you listen carefully you can hear the heaviness in the thunder. And the lightning is sharper than usual with arrows of fire shooting down all about. They are the giants in the realm of ghosts; they stand neigh on to twelve feet tall with six fingers on each see-through hand and their faces are shrouded in black burial cloth. Neither man nor woman have looked into their eyes and lived to tell the tale. It is said if you happen to see their eyes, you are doomed forever from its wicked glare and you will walk the earth in dazed silence until the day you die. The old storytellers claim that the only thing more frightening than the glare of the fantômes noir will be the glare of God's anger if you ain't living right when you meet up with him.'

"Well, I got a bit edgy cuz I knew I hadn't lived the life of a monk, iff'en ya know what I mean. I ain't no bad guy, but I've done a little sinnin' here an' there every so often."

Once again Mr. Phiney paused his story to turn his head to listen to their surroundings.

"Do you hear something, Mr. Phiney?" Olivia asked quietly.

"No," he whispered hesitantly, "Well maybe. I ain't sure."

"Well," he continued, "the two of us scurried out Pierre's back door and then he whipped open the door leadin' into his lean-to, gave Atticus and his own horse a push and off they ran inta the surroundin' woods like maybe they knew what was gonna happen and wanted ta get far away as possible. Quickly and quietly we ran down towards the pond to Madeline's cottage, went 'round to the back and knocked softly. There was no answer. Not a soul was about her cottage, not even her hound dog. Pierre gave the door knob a rattle and a sharp nudge and slowly it opened. Easin' inside we stood looking 'round a bit, then Pierre called out to his friend a couple times but there was no answer, and we could tell jest by the feelin' in the air that the cottage was empty. Then we turned about and opened the backdoor to take a peep outside.

'She's gone, Phiney,' he said to me. 'Her buggy isn't in its usual place and her old horse isn't looking out the lean-to window. Even her old hound dog, Bijou, ain't out and about. That's strange Phiney, that's mighty strange.'

Mr. Phiney stopped talking and gave a shiver and once again clicked his tongue to get his mule moving a bit faster. He gave another quick glance over his shoulder.

"So as we stood there on Madeline's back stoop we could hear the thunder rumblin' over by the sea, but the sky over our heads was still crystal clear with all the stars shinin' and moon sendin' its light down upon us as it lit up the whole little village. Then it started. We watched as dark black fingers ah fog started creeping up the lane, round the cottages and slowly easin' round our feet. Within a second or two those slithering wet fingers turned into a giant black wall blockin' out the moon, stars and ever'thin round us. That fog was alive with somethin' 'er other an I didn't know what it was, but it wasn't normal. Straightaway me and Pierre jumped back inta Madeline's cottage, slammed and bolted the door and backed away like maybe the door was gonna catch a'far. Then, the walls started in shakin' and quakin' and ah mighty bangin' started in at the front door, then a few seconds later at the back door. Someone was bangin' on it like a war-drum. Then the person yelled out for Pierre ta open the door: 'Fichu, Pierre, ouvre la porte! I know it's you in my house!' It was Madeline.

"Pierre scrambled up from under the table where we had dived when the walls started shakin' and ran quick for the back door, whipped it open, and in tumbled Madeline and her dog Bijou. Madeline looked mad as a hornet and her dog looked kindly stunned. Maddy, as Pierre usually called her, was a skinny little woman with long, wild, black curly hair flying round her head like a bunch ah bats. Her blue eyes were snappin' with fire as she glared at Pierre. Her dog had dashed under the table with me and was all scooched up close-like and he was shakin' like a leaf in a whirlwind.

"'Get out!' Madeline screeched at Pierre. "I battled that wind and black fog all the way to your cottage and here you are shivering and shaking in mine like a coward!'

"'Nope,' Pierre calmly and quietly answered her back. "Shhh…"

"'Don't you shush me! Get out! Bijou, get 'em!'

"Well, I looked at Bijou and Bijou looked at me, and I swear he rolled his eyes, and he didn't move a muscle. He kept right on lookin' at me tryin' ta ignore Madeline. Well, Madeline was standing there with her hands on her hips when all of a sudden a howlin' came swoopin' through the village. It was like the howls of a million hounds. It started out real soft and low but then grew louder and louder and echoed 'cross the surroundin' green hills. It sent shivers through my soul; I hunkered down under that table lookin' out the winder. Bijou put his head between his paws and covered his eyes. It was so dark outside I couldn't see nary a thing."

Olivia shivered again and tried scooting closer to Mr. Phiney. "Mr. Phin, is this tale true or are you just pulling my leg?"

"Ah, lass, this tale be true! I ain't never been through something like that a'fore. But, iff'en ya want me ta stop with the tellin' I'll stop cuz I ain't wantin' ya ta get too scare't, iff'en ya know what I mean. Whatcha say?"

"No, keep on with the telling. I'll be okay."

Olivia pulled her blanket up around her head like a hood and waited for Mr. Phiney to continue with the telling.

"Okay, then. Well, when that howlin' started in, Madeline jumped all the way inside and slammed the bolt on the door then ran over and jumped inta Pierre's arms and plum forgot all 'bout her fussin'. Her eyes was as big as saucers and she started shakin'. Now, I knew ole Pierre was scare't himself, but with Madeline clingin' ta 'em he was tryin' his best ta be a man." Mr. Phiney snickered under his breath.

"Then," he said, still whispering, "It became quiet and as still and jest as calm as it is right afore a twister hits. Nothing moved, not even a single leaf on a tree and we waited with hushed anxiety. Then it came.

"It started with soft scratches on the door, then silence. A fingernail scratched across the side winder. Then we watched as the darkness became thicker and the moonlight once again hid its face. We couldn't see it, but we could hear the door latch start moving. I felt a soft tug on my sleeve and I turned to see Madeline motioning me and Bijou to follow 'em. We quietly hurried into her food pantry and slipped behind the jars ah pickle and 'maters and boxes filled with various thin's stacked along the back wall. There was no door on the pantry so we pushed ourselves up against the back wall pulling the boxes in front of us, hoping whoever it was would not be able to see us. I left myself ah tiny lil' openin' between two boxes so I could have a look-see, cuz I wanted to know if one of them haints started coming inta where we hid. Bijou was scrunched up against my legs shaking like a leaf in a storm.

"Then we heard it—the bolt on the door slid open with a sharp snap and the door creaked open with a squeak and a groan, and into the pantry rushed a blast of hot air; the smell of sulfur filled the whole place. I could see pretty good into the main room and fear grabbed aholt of my heart and purt-near stopped its beating when I realized what I was seeing. There standing in the main room of Madeline's little cottage was the haint of Napoleon Bonaparte himself! He had on them clothes they used ta wear and he was standin' thur all soldierly-like, puffed up like a banty rooster all full of his-self. It was the weirdest lookin' haint I ever did see. He had his hand inside his jacket and I knew for sure just who it was. Well, I looked straight inta his eyes, he looked straight inta mine, and then he took two steps closer to the pantry - but then I gave him the evil eye and he stopped. Out from his ghost belt he pulled a long sword and brandished it like he was gonna start fightin' us. Well, real quick-like I twisted open a jar of Madeline's dill pickles, reached in and got me a handful then threw 'em straight at that haint followed by the whole jar ah pickle juice. Well, Napoleon's mouth twisted inta this awful scream and - *poof* - he vanished with a scream of agony!

"Now, all my life I heard Aunt Abby say that haints will vanish iff'en a person throws vinegar at 'em cuz vinegar burns 'em bad and I guess it's been proven to be true! So, iff'en you're ever faced by a haint, grab ya'self a jar ah vinegar and give it a toss!"

Olivia started laughing so hard she almost fell off the seat. Mr. Phiney was doing the same.

"Okay," Olivia gasped, "I'll remember that!"

Mr. Phiney abruptly pulled up on the mule's reins and motioned for Olivia to be quiet.

"Listen," he whispered, as he reached out and grabbed ahold of the lantern he had hanging from the side of his wagon. "Can ya hear that?"

Olivia cocked her head to one side and listened.

"I can't hear anything at all, Mr. Phiney, except for the night critters."

"Listen real close now," he whispered, dousing the lantern. Again he looked over his shoulder. "I can hear the squeakin' of another wagon coming up the trail back behind us. Ain't nobody 'cept us crazy folks and thieves out this time ah night. Listen closer now."

They both listened for a moment in silence. "There it is," he whispered. "Ya hear 'em? They're coming closer. It's 'bout a half mile back but I can hear 'em."

Mr. Phiney clicked softly to the mule, easing the wagon into the head-high grass growing along the road.

"Come on, Livy-gal," he said uneasily as he soundlessly eased himself down from the squeaky wagon bench. "I'm not a'fear'd of ah fight, but iff'en I can avoid one that's what I do. Scoot over here and let me help ya down. We need ta move back inta the woods a bit. Ya gotta whisper real soft-like cuz a body's voice carries far during the dark of night."

Olivia nodded her head, scooted over and reached out so Mr. Phiney could swing her down from the wagon. Then, surprisingly, Mr. Phiney gave a soft rap on the side of the wagon bed and whispered, "Butler! You hear what's goin' on? Ya can either stay under them skins or scramble out and go further back inta the woods with us."

5

Uncle Puddle Dee and the panther

After a bit of rustling, out from beneath the huge pile of bear and beaver skins eased a big olive-skinned man. Olivia stood there staring at the man for a rude minute before clamping her mouth shut so as to not offend the fella. During the entire trip from Malden she had no idea they were carrying another person. Mr. Phiney must have picked him up at the last farm along the way when they stopped for water.

Mr. Phiney quickly introduced Olivia to Mr. Buford Beauregard Butler.

"How-do, miss," The big man whispered in a slow, deep rumbling southern drawl, bowing deeply. He was dripping sweat from being under all those skins and his shirt looked as if it had just come out of the river.

Turning to Mr. Phiney, Mr. Butler said with urgency in his voice, "Well come on Phin, let's get on outta here." Then the big fella took off running like a deer towards the dark shadowy forest with his shoes slung over his shoulder.

Mr. Phiney walked over to his mule, whispered something into one of the mule's big ears then turned to Olivia. "Come on Olivia, we best be catchin' up with Butler or he'll be runnin' all the way down ta the Gulf of Mexico."

With that said, Mr. Phiney and Olivia took off running after Butler. After taking a few lengthy strides, Mr. Phiney stopped, looked back at Olivia, squatted down and told her to climb onto his back then took off running faster.

Olivia turned her head and watched Mr. Phiney's mule amble into taller grass until all one could see of the mule and wagon was the tops of the mule's ears. Then the mule laid his ears back and both him and the wagon became invisible to folks passing on the trail.

Abruptly, Mr. Phiney burst into a small clearing and Butler, who had been sitting on the top of a fallen tree putting on his shoes, jumped up to meet them.

"It took ya long 'nuf Phin, what were y'all doing? Crawlin'?"

"No, we weren't crawlin'," Mr. Phiney gasped between breaths. "Olivia's legs are a bit shorter than mine so I had ta lift 'er up and carry 'er. Ya could'ah helped me some."

"I din't have time, Phin. When you said you heard a wagon coming I purt-near jumped right-on outta my skin! Sorry."

"Never no mind. It ain't no problem a'tall, Butler."

Mr. Phiney and Mr. Butler sat back down on the fallen tree as Olivia stood there watching and waiting for them to do something.

"Let's hunker down and slip on out ta the trail and have us a look-see. What'cha say?" Mr. Phiney whispered quietly, looking at his friend.

"Well," Mr. Butler whispered slowly, "I ain't wantin' ta get caught, Phin. I guess I'll go 'long with ya, but if it's somebody lookin' for me I'm outta there and I ain't gonna wait-up for you this time."

"I'm comin' too, Mr. Phiney," Olivia whispered.

Mr. Phiney and Butler turned and looked at Olivia for a bit.

"Okay, but iff'en I whisper fur ya ta run, you run as fast as your legs can carry ya, ya hear? You run for the old mule and wait in the tall grasses 'til that mule puts his ears straight up. He'll know when it's okay ta start movin' on down the road. He's hiding som'ers close and iff'en me or Butler don't show up, he'll take ya ta Memphis on his own. He knows the way back ta his barn."

Butler, Mr. Phiney, and Olivia took off walking through the tall grass towards the trail. Butler had to walk hunched over since he was so tall. Prickly thorn bushes grabbed onto Olivia's stockings and pricked her skin, and the tall grass kept slapping her in the face, but she kept up with the two men. Reaching the road, Mr. Phiney motioned for them to ease down into the grass and wait quietly.

They didn't have to wait long before they could hear the squeaking of another wagon approaching. Straining her eyes, Olivia made out a wagon and its driver moving haphazardly down the trail. The wagon was being pulled by two massive draft horses - Olivia's pa had raised a few horses, so she was quite familiar with these particular horses. They were fine-looking, and by the looks of the fella driving the wagon, he must have stolen the pair. He was a short, stubby looking fella with a little brown derby sitting on his head and a dirty, long-sleeved, greyish-white shirt under his overalls. He had a rifle lying across his lap and on the bench beside him sat a pistol and a bottle of moonshine.

Suddenly the driver burst forth with a verse of song.

"She'll be comin' round the corner when she comes. Yee-hah!

She'll be comin' round the corner when she comes,

She'll be comin' round the corner, she'll be comin' round the corner,

She'll be comin' round the corner when she comes! Yee-hah!

Then I'll grab 'er and I'll kiss 'er when she comes.

And I'll grab 'er and I'll kiss 'er when she comes.

Yes I'll grab 'er and I'll kiss 'er, I'll grab 'er and I'll kiss 'er,

I'll grab 'er and I'll kiss 'er when she comes! Yee-hah! Yee-hah!

I'll put 'er in my buggy and take 'er fur ah ride, Yee-hah! Yee-hah!

The fella drew out the next word before finishing the line.

"Buuuut,"

"If she's Widder Jones I'll kick 'er skinny bones! Yee-hah!"

He laughed loudly as he ended his song. "Well now, that thur's a purdy dang good song iff'en I have ta say so myself," He said to himself, laughing again. "Might be I ought'a take up song writin'."

Olivia was quite sure the fella was making up the words as he went along, but it didn't matter to her. Just as long as he left in a hurry was all she was hoping.

"Hey Pud!" Mr. Phin jumped up and yelled, causing Olivia and Butler to flinch. "Ya ornery old coot, What'cha doin' out here?" He started walking through the tall grass towards the trail.

Puddle Dee Patterson, who everyone in the county called Uncle Pud and was Lily Quinn's distance relative, jerked back on the reins, causing the two big draft horses to rear up on their hind legs and knock his bottle of moonshine onto the floor. He whipped up his pistol and pointed it to where he thought the yell had come from.

"Who's you?"

"It's me," Mr. Phiney called out again. "Phin the Brit."

"Well, I'll be ah hog's snoot! Is that really you Phin? I ain't seen ya in ah month ah Sundays! What'cha doin' with ya'self out 'ere in the wilderness?"

"I just saw ya last week out at the Quinn farm, 'member? What are you doin' out here in the dark hours, Pud?"

"Oh, yeah, that's right! I do 'member. That Caitlin can cook up a mighty fine mess ah food, cain't she? Well I got me a job deliverin' these two fancy boys to a feller down Memphis way. He's gonna give me twenty-five dollars iff'en I get 'em there all safe-like. He missed gettin' 'em on the train by ten minutes so he had ta get 'em there somehow. What'cha doin' hidin' out in them trees Phin? Seems like you're up ta no good? Ya fixin' ta rob me?"

"Rob ya? Rob ya of what, Pud?" Mr. Phiney snorted and laughed while walking closer to Pud's buckboard. "Ya ain't got nothing but the clothes on your back and I'll wager ya ain't even got two plug nickels in your pocket. Plus, it'd be a waste of energy ta take your clothes from ya, seeing that you've worn the same clothes nigh onta twenty years. And I'd wager ya ain't got no drawers on under them filthy britches. I'd rather poke myself in the eyeball with a fork than see ya naked." Mr. Phin looked up to the sky. "Whew! Good Lord on high, wipe that picture outta my brain!"

Mr. Phiney swiped his hands over the top of his head as if trying to erase the image of a naked Uncle Pud from his brain. "Good Lord a'mighty, Pud, don't even think a givin' 'em away. We heard ya coming and thought maybe ya was some fellas followin' us and wantin' ta rob us."

"Who's we? You and ah frog in ya pocket?" Pud laughed nervously looking behind Mr. Phiney.

"No, I got me some ride-alongs I'm taking down ta Memphis."

"Ya up to somethin' shady, Phin? Who ya carryin' and how ya carryin' em? I ain't seein' no buckboard 'round here and you're too skinny to be carryin' ah scrawny dog much less ah ride-along. Where's your buckboard, Phin?" Pud spoke a bit louder and raised his pistol a bit as he looked around the trail.

"Good grief, Pud! Ya known me most of twenty-five years. I ain't no robber, so stop puttin' on the stupid."

"Come on outta thar and show ya'self," Pud yelled, "iff'en ya be some honest folks get out here with your hands up high. Or should I be shootin' Phin here fur hangin' with some no-gooders?"

Olivia and Butler jumped to their feet with their hands in the air and walked onto the trail.

"Well, what'cha know?" Pud jerked up straight on his seat and bent over close to Olivia and Butler. He lowered his voice and looked around as if maybe there was someone else lurking in these deserted woods who would hear what he had to say. "Put your hands down! You're lookin' the fool! I know you, lil' gal, you're that pretty lil' gal who buried 'er mama over Malden way, ain't ya? I know'd your pa and ma and they was good folks. Sorry for the loss, Miss. Hope you're doing okay with these two ruffians. Iff'en not, jump right on up here with me and I'll rescue ya." Pud stood up and bowed deeply to Olivia.

"And I know you," Pud said as he bent over to get a better look at Butler. "You're Buford B. Butler. They be lookin' fur ya, son. Ya best be high-tailin' it outta' here really quick-like. I know'd ya din't hurt nobody, and I know'd ya din't steal that gold from the Widder Jones, and I be knowin' who did! T'ain't you, that's fur sure." Uncle Pud shook his head, "Hit was that phony ol' sawbones Doc Wally. He ain't no more a doc than I am the Queen ah England. I see'd 'em do it too. In fact, I was hidin' outside Widder Jones' house waitin' ta snatch a peck ah apples off'en her porch, and I saw Doc Wally slip quiet-like through her door. Then I hear'd a scream and a loud thud, 'parently when she hit the floor. Then ol' Wally came running out with a box, and that box was heavy, cuz he kindly staggered when he lifted hit up onta his horse. I guess that Widder woman fainted dead away and din't get a good look at 'em, cuz when she came-to and cried out, her handyman Leroy went chargin' inta the house from the woods. I din't even hang 'round cuz I din't want that sheriff ta think I was the thief. I high-tailed it out of there without getting' any apples. But later on I heard she tol' the sheriff she was sure-ah-shootin' it was you, cuz you was the first'un that popped inta her head when she came-to and she was quite sure it was a sign from heaven. That woman is crazy as a bat and is a pickle short of a full barrel. She's always making up crazy thin's and blamin' folks fur stuff jest cuz she don't like 'em. I'm thinkin' she's mad at ya cuz ya turned 'er down when she asked ya ta marry-up with 'er."

Butler signed a breath of relief that Pud believed he was innocent. "Nope, it wasn't me. I stay as far away from that widder woman as I can."

Uncle Pud laughed and shook his head as he continued talking. "Lord have mercy on the poor soul who marries up with 'er, she's a homely woman. Now, I ain't got no good-looks myself, and I ain't against havin' me an ugly woman, but that widder Jones would scare the skin off'en a cat with that tongue ah hers. Ya know, she's done asked 'bout ever' feller around this county ta marry-up with 'er. She asked you yet, Phin?"

Mr. Phiney nodded his head to say no while he laughed.

"No? Well," Uncle Pud laughed loudly, "she ain't asked me either, cuz she says I smell like a horse's patoot. That's fine with me. I won't take a bath fur the rest ah my life iff'en it keeps 'er away."

"Have ya ever taken a bath, Pud?" Mr. Phiney asked, still laughing.

"Not as fur back as I can 'member. I take me a dip or two in the river ever' once'st in a while and that's good nuf for me."

"Well," Mr. Butler said with a frown on his face, "I din't take any of her money, and even if she is a mean old woman, I wouldn't scare her half to death. On the other hand, I wouldn't marry-up with such as that woman either. Are the Sheriff and his men far behind?"

"Well," Uncle Pud said real slow-like, as he scratched his chin. "I'm thinkin' they prolly won't start out 'til tomorree, iff'en they do a'tall. The sheriff knows the widder is kindly crazy, iff'en ya know what I mean. She even asked him ta marry-up with 'er, an' he's already got himself a purdy lil' wife an' seven young'uns."

Olivia was staring at Uncle Pud with fascination. He looked like a jolly fella with a ruddy complexion and a short, white beard, but no mustache. His hat was a small, brown derby hat which sat on the very top of his head making her wonder how it stayed put. His ears stuck out like barn doors on either side of his head; he had a round, chubby face with blood-shot eyes, a round, chubby stomach and short legs that didn't reach the floor of his wagon. His feet were shoeless but covered with so much dirt and mud it looked as if he had on brown slippers. He had a big ball of chewing tobacco in his jaw and every once in a while he would wipe the brown drool off his mouth.

Suddenly the two big horses began snorting, stomping their feet and straining at the reins. Out of the corner of her eye, Olivia caught a movement on the opposite side of the road. Turning her head, she gave it her full attention - for a few seconds she watched as the tall grasses swayed like someone was moving fast towards the trail. Fear clinched her stomach.

Stammering, Olivia managed to squeak out, "Mr. - Mr. Phiney?"

Suddenly she was lifted up and tossed through the air, where she landed with an "Oof!" in the back of Uncle Pud's wagon. A loud thud followed as Mr.

Butler jumped on and immediately rolled onto his stomach, pulled out his pistol and aimed over the back of the wagon.

"Grab your gun, Phin!" Mr. Butler yelled. "We got us one black panther and thur might be more."

Like magic, Mr. Phin was in the wagon bed and with the snap of his whip, Uncle Pud had the two big horses running at full stride and miraculously his hat stayed on his head.

"YEE-HAH!" Uncle Pud screamed out.

The jerk of the wagon threw Olivia tumbling into the tailgate where she eased her head up and peeked over the edge just in time to see a big black panther leap onto the trail and began its chase. Its body was covered with glossy, black fur and its mouth was gaping open, revealing large fangs glistening in the moonlight. Its eyes were the strangest green Olivia had ever seen, and it was moving fast - much faster than the wagon.

The air around the wagon was sizzling with tension as Uncle Pud's whip snapped and cracked through the air with each yell of "Yee-Hah!". The frightened horses were pulling the wagon way too fast through the rutted trail and Olivia was hanging on for dear life.

The panther was quickly gaining on the wagon. Mr. Butler pushed Olivia's head down but she popped it right back up. The huge beast gave out a blood-curdling scream that ripped through the night air like a bolt of lightning.

Mr. Butler and Mr. Phin's first shots were so close to Olivia's ears she was sure the sound would shatter her brain. The wagon was bouncing around so much the shots flew way off their mark.

"Hold up ah bit, Pud!" Mr. Phin bellowed. "We can't get ah bead on 'em!"

"Whoa!" Uncle Pud yelled. He used all his strength to pull back on the reluctant horses as the panther took another leap towards the bed of the wagon. Its paws were about to touch the tailgate and its head was so close Olivia was sure she could have counted its whiskers growing next to its cavernous mouth. The beast's hot breath seemed to blow right onto her face. She was looking straight into the big cat's eyes and he was looking straight into hers, when all of a sudden the big cat winked at her.

As Olivia took a second to wonder if she saw what she thought she did, two quick shots rang out and the panther dropped to the ground, flipping and rolling backwards.

"Got 'em!" Mr. Butler yelled out.

Uncle Pud pulled the dancing horses to a halt and Olivia sat there dazed on the floor of the wagon bed, not moving a muscle.

"You okay, gal?" Mr. Butler asked calmly.

She couldn't manage to get her voice going, so she nodded her head yes and continued sitting there dumbfounded.

"Whoaaa boys, whoaaa!" Uncle Pud yelled as he pulled back tight on the two big horses, fighting to keep them from taking off down the road chaotically. Mr. Phin and Mr. Butler jumped from the back of the wagon, eased up to the big cat's body and gave it a good kick to make sure it was dead.

"It's a goner, Butler. We got 'em."

The two men signed in unison.

"Hey, you two fella's gonna ride in my wagon or are ya gonna stand thar till the moss grows on your feet? These horses are gettin' hard ta hold back."

Mr. Phin and Mr. Butler leaped into the back of the wagon and turned to look at the dead cat as Uncle Pud let the horses, already straining at the bit, take off with another jerk which would have thrown Olivia against the tailgate again if Mr. Phiney hadn't grabbed her.

"Now that was excitin', Livy-gal. Ya ever been chased by a big cat afore? What'cha think?" Mr. Phin asked with a grin. "Ya ride along with me and you'll have some grand adventures. Now, might be ya shouldn't be tellin' Mrs. Turner, cuz she'll be getting' onta me somethin' fierce and prolly won't make me anymore pies," he said with a laugh.

Finding her words, Olivia smiled. "Oh, I won't be telling on you, Mr. Phin. She would fret for days and try to get me back to her house. And, yes," she paused. "It was exciting."

They sat in silence for a moment, bouncing and jerking with the rhythm of the excited horses straining to run.

"That big cat winked at me, Mr. Phin," Olivia whispered softly.

"What?"

"It winked at me. When he was this close to my face," Olivia held her hand out about a foot from her nose. "I was staring right into his eyes and he was staring right into mine, then he winked!"

Mr. Butler's eyes opened wide and his face turned white as a sheet.

"Ya sure 'bout that, Olivia?" he asked.

"Yes, I'm absolutely sure."

"That weren't no real cat, Phin. I've seen it afore. You be watchin' this girl, Phin. That big cat wanted ta get 'er. That cat was a shape-shifter for sure."

Mr. Phiney reached over and pulled Olivia a bit closer to him.

"Me and your Aunt Katy will take care of ya, Livy-lass. Don't you be frettin' none 'bout that nonsense Butler's tellin ya."

Olivia felt Mr. Phiney shake his head at Mr. Butler.

"Well, young lady," Mr. Butler said hurriedly, "I'm jest talkin' through my hat. Ta tell ya the truth I ain't knowin' much 'bout them shape-shifters a'tall."

The three of them turned and looked back at the big cat. Even at their distance, they could still clearly see the big animal lying dead on the trail.

Then, as they looked on, up from the body of that big panther rose a strange, swirling white haze. It rose about a foot above the body and morphed into the shape of a human, hovered there for a minute then with a quick flash swirled right up close to the back of the wagon where it glared at Olivia with its large, green eyes trying to penetrate into her very soul. That was when Olivia realized those green eyes were the same peculiar-looking green as her own eyes. Quickly Olivia gave the apparition an unyielding, forceful stare of defiance. Mr. Phin and Mr. Butler sat staring open-mouthed at the sight, not knowing exactly what to do since you can't shoot a specter. Instinctively Olivia knew exactly how to get rid of it. She squinted her eyes into a glare and made a motion with her hand in front of her face, telling it to leave. With a glistening of light the phantom let out a piercing snarl, flew over Uncle Pud and the two horses then vanished into the black forest, leaving behind a trail of misty vapor.

Again Uncle Pud jerked up on the reins, making the horses rise slightly on their hind legs and causing Olivia to tumble, this time, to the front of the wagon.

"What is tarnation was that?" he blurted out.

"I ain't knowin' Pud! No idee a'tall."

"Let's get on outta here," Mr. Butler said quietly. "Lord have mercy. Move on out, Pud."

Uncle Pud needed no coaxing. Olivia scrambled to the back of the wagon bed and sat a bit closer to Mr. Phiney. Then Mr. Butler leaned over to Mr. Phin and whispered quietly.

"I do hate ta say so, but that was a shapes-shifter. What'd you think, Phin?"

"That's what I'm thinkin', Butler. Yep, I ain't seen a shape-shifter in many a year, but I'm sure 'nuf thinkin' we did tonight."

Mr. Butler looked at Olivia real close-like and whispered softly, "You be careful, young-un, and always keep an eye out for that big cat. That was a strange thing, him winkin' at you and then swooshing up so close-like to ya."

Olivia shivered. She actually did not know what a shape-shifter was, and she really didn't want to see one again.

After traveling down the trail for a few silent minutes, the sound of another wagon could be heard jostling along the rough road at a good pace. Uncle Pud leaned forward to get a good look-see, then yelled for Mr. Phin to come on up beside him and have a look.

"Ain't that your mule and wagon, Phin?"

"I do believe it is," Mr. Phin replied after taking a good look at it. "That old mule knows whur he's goin' and he'll foller the trail right on down ta Memphis.

"How'd he get ahead of us?"

"I ain't knowin' Pud. But he's a sly old dog, fur a mule. Iff'en we hadn't citch'd up with 'em he'd ah made it all the way down ta my cabin in Memphis."

Mr. Phin gave out a shrill whistle and the mule eased over to the side of the trail as he waited for Uncle Pud's wagon to catch up with him.

"Come on, Livy-gal, let's get in our wagon and head on out. What'cha say?"

Olivia let him help her down from the wagon bed and then scrambled up onto the bench of the waiting wagon.

"Ya comin' long, Butler?"

"Naw," Butler said with a smile, "Iff'en ya don't mind I think I'm gonna ride on along with Uncle Pud. He's the only one who knows I didn't do the crime, so if they catch up with us he can be my witness. Is that okay with you, Pud?"

"Don't mind a'tall, I'd welcome the company. After droppin' these two big fellas off, I'm pickin' me up some more ta take on down ta Naw'leens iff'en ya want to ride 'long."

"That's exactly where I'm headed. I'm gonna catch me a ship going to the Islands."

"Sounds good ta me," Mr. Phin said. "I 'spect we might run inta Old Bushy in the mornin'. He's on his way ta Memphis jest like we are. I 'magine they're waitin' up for us somer's."

Olivia smiled to herself because she knew Lily and Ophelia would be with Mr. Bushy and then she would have someone to talk to. The two wagons rode together about another half an hour before the four of them pulled off the road and slept for a few hours until the early morning came.

As usual, the early mornings in Missouri were a delight. The rich warm soil radiated the smell of Mother Nature's fragrance. Sunbeams slipped their fingers over the Mississippi river and edged their way across the lonely trail, chasing away the lingering shadows of night. The night creatures had vanished into burrows or hiding places and the day creatures were waking. The rustle of small critters could be heard as they peeked out from the low-growing grasses to watch the birth of a newborn day. Long-tailed Turtle Doves cooed their laments as they searched for seeds, bringing the peaceful tranquility of promise with the dawn. A chickadee landed on the back of Mr. Phin's mule and sat there staring at the waking Olivia as it chattered its morning message before flitting away to find another perch.

The lonesome whistle of an early morning train announced its arrival to the small villages along the way through the Missouri farmlands. Black smoke from the big, chugging engines left plumes of cinder in the eastern sky that slowly drifted away in the morning breeze. Off in the distance, a rooster's crow seemed to fight with the train's whistle for attention.

Uncle Pud and Mr. Butler were moving on down the trail a bit faster than Mr. Phin and Olivia, but Mr. Phin seemed to pay no mind. Sitting quietly listening to the calming sounds of nature and the plodding of the mule's hooves, Olivia and Mr. Phin watched the sun as it raised its brilliant fingers above the horizon of Tennessee and moved across the mighty river into Missouri. As the last shadows of night slipped to the west, Olivia caught sight of a large dog standing silently in the meadow to her right about twenty feet away and watching them. His fur was a reddish gold and it looked as if someone had given him a haircut, but only on one side. The hair on the other side of his body hung almost to the ground. The big dog lifted his head to the sky and opened his mouth as if letting out a howl to the world, but not a sound came out. Then he began hopping and jumping around as if trying to catch a butterfly. He hopped and jumped a bit while occasionally looking back at Olivia like he was showing off for her.

Olivia smiled. The dog continued. As Olivia gave him another big grin, the sunlight flooded across the land, glistening off his fur like fireflies, and he vanished into the air.

Olivia quickly turned her head toward Mr. Phiney. "Did you see that dog, Mr. Phiney?"

Mr. Phin looked at Olivia curiously then glanced around the surrounding area.

"What dog?"

"He was right over there," Olivia said, pointing to her right, "and he looked kinda strange like maybe someone had given him half a haircut. He was kinda reddish-gold and shimmery."

"Ah," Mr. Phiney said as he smiled widely and gave a soft chuckle. "You're a lucky gal. That's Periwinkle. He's a haint-dog. He went down on a ship crossing the ocean from Europe back in the 1700's or so, I do believe, with his owners. I'm surprised ya din't see that little gal-haint Polly Susannah. I hear she's a pistol of a haint. But, it seems as if they only appear to young'uns like ya'self."

"That reminds me - let me finish tellin' ya what happened when me and Pierre Charron saw the haint ah ol' Napoleon Bonaparte himself."

"After I gave that jar of pickle a toss, hitting that haint square in the chest, he got this here angry look on his face and fell inta a million little pieces then floated away. We all stood there starin' at the fella until not a thing was left of him. The storm passed over and the night critters started soundin' out with their calls again. T'was the strangest thin' I ever did see."

"What happened to Mr. Pierre and his friend Madeline?"

"Oh, them two? Well, they finally married-up, moved to the south of France and had themselves a dozen young'uns with coal-black curly hair like thur ma but blue eyes like thur pappy's. I don't visit 'em much anymore. Those young'uns of theirs's can drive a man insane."

Mr. Phiney laughed heartily.

6

Young Phineas and Aunt Abby

(Told along the road to Memphis by Mr. Phiney himself)

. Olivia and Mr. Phiney sat in silence for a while. Olivia waited for him to tell her about Periwinkle and the little girl-haint, but he didn't.

"Let me be tellin' ya 'bout my younger days, Olivia," Mr. Phin finally said. "It'll pass the time really quick-like and in no time a'tall we'll be near where Mr. Bushy and those other young'uns are prolly waitin' for us.

"You see, Olivia-lass," he began, "I was born on Piel Island which is a pretty little island off the coast of England. It's a lovely place to live as a child or to visit for a jolly-good holiday, if one had a mind to. I was born to a young lass who, at the time ah my birthin', was workin' as a maid at the Ship's Inn and my pappy was working in the shipyards at Rampside. My mum was but fifteen years old when I was born and she died that very day. My pappy never did come to collect me I was told, so I was snatched up by Abigail Eugenie Pennypacker who tol' the authorities she was my mum's aunt. Well, she carted me home to the Ship's Inn and named me Phineas Alexander Georgia, after me mum, Pennypacker. Now, Aunt Abby, as I called her, and me had not a single drop ah the same blood but she was a mighty good woman. She took me in 'cuz she had a heart ah gold and knew if she hadn't told them fellas she was my aunt they would'ah swept me away to Liverpool or London and thrown me inta one ah them orphan houses and by the time I was but five years old, the orphan house would toss me onta the streets ta fend for myself.

"Aunt Abby owned the Ship's Inn on Piel Island. She was a big-boned woman with a loud, happy voice and a ready smile, and she worked as hard as any man I ever did know. Her coal-black hair was always pulled back inta a tight bun at the very top ah her head. She had a face as round as a punkin and 'er eyes was as black as 'er hair. From the very day I can remember, she wore a little flat-topped hat over her bun on the tip-top of her head with a blue ribbon wrapped 'round it. Once, when I asked 'er why she always wore that little hat, she told me it was the onliest thing she had left of her mum's and that she would wear it the rest of her life—which she did! Folks told me she was of East Indian ancestry and that 'er husband James had vanished at sea during a raging battle with a pirate ship. Her own mum had been brought to Piel Island from India by an East Indian pirate and left to fend for herself after he snuck off in the dark ah night, taking a fancy English woman with 'em. I never found out what happened to Aunt Abby's mum, but Aunt Abby grew up in a rough-and-tumble world where you had to fight to survive whether you were a man or woman. And she was no quitter. She was a scrapper, that's for sure."

He stopped talking and chuckled.

"She was nigh on six feet tall and a bit over-sized, iff'en ya know what I mean. She wore men's britches but always had on a lady's frilly shirt and these big black boots that clomped loudly on them cobblestone walkways. She was always in a hurry to get whatever she was doin' done so she could start another chore. She kept herself and me scrubbed clean as a whistle. There were times when I thought she was gonna scrub the skin right off'en my bones till I got old 'nuf ta give myself a good worshin'. And I always made sure it was a good worshin', cuz iff'en she saw dirt behind my ears she would grab holt ah me and plunge my head inta that worsh bucket and give 'em a scrub.

"One time I saw her take on a sailor over a shilling he owed her. Fists were flyin' and they were rollin' round on that dock with ever'body watchin' and grinnin' in openmouthed wonder as she wrestled and twisted 'er legs around that feller ta hold 'em down. Her hat went flyin' off'en her head and I ran over and snatched it up a'fore it got mushed cuz I surely din't want Aunt

Abby ta lose her mum's hat. She held onta that big ole bruiser of a sailor and slapped him good up one side and down the other then reached inta his pocket and snatched out two shillings instead of just one cuz she said he had messed her hat and he had ta pay for it. When that sailor finally got up ta scurry away, she gave him a swift boot in the britches and sent him flyin' off the edge of the dock inta that cold sea as she yelled at 'em that if he started actin' the proper gentleman he wouldn't be gettin' whooped by a woman. He sputtered and spit out water and fumed ah bit but then scrambled back up onto the dock where he quickly darted away from her. Me and my friend Bobby Brookfield stood on the beach with all them other folks watchin' the whole durn—oops, pardon me—thing cheerin' Aunt Abby on. Well, much to our surprise, after she whooped that thievin' sailor, she marched right up ta me and Bobby, grabbed us both by the 'spenders and whooped our backsides fur cheerin' on a fight. She said fightin' was not a proper thing and the only time it was needed was when one body was cheated out of a shillin' or two. Well, Bobby took off for home jest as quick as a jackrabbit and what do ya know but the next day he tol' me after he tol' his mum 'bout Aunt Abby whoopin' us, his mum gave him another whoopin' just in case Aunt Abby hadn't given us a good 'nuf whoopin'. But by the time Aunt Abby drug me home by the ear, she sat me down at the table and poured me a cup ah milk and gave me a gingerbread biscuit 'cuz she said I deserved it for savin' 'er hat from being tramped."

Mr. Phiney was now laughing heartily.

"Well, when that sailor got to the safety of his ship, he turned about and yelled out to the town folks that Abigail Pennypacker was a witch and that he had seen her cast a spell on Daniel Randal's goat right afore that goat jumped off the cliffs of Dover. Well, nobody paid attention ta that there lie, cuz Aunt Abby hadn't ever been off Piel Island - so they all knew he was a big fat liar, but after that thur fight, whenever a sailor came inta the Ship's Inn and Aunt Abby told them they owned her a shilling or two for the food and ale, ever last one of them paid up with a smile and a 'thank ya ma'am'.

"Not too long after that sailor got whooped by Aunt Abby, a man came to Piel Island claimin' ta be Daniel Randal and he wanted Aunt Abby to pay him for a herd of goats, cuz he had been told by a sailor that it was she who had made his goats jump off the cliffs and he truly believed she was a witch. Well, when the constable asked 'em how many goats, the feller mumbled and stumbled 'round with his answer, then he blurted out that it was purt near twenty and right then and there the constable knew he was in cahoots with that sailor, cuz that sailor-fella had said it was but one goat. Well, the constable gave that fella ah stern look and the cheatin' scoundrel took of running like ah scare't rabbit with the constable and ten ah the town-folk chasin' 'em right back onta the ferry he came in on. We never did hear from that particular rascal again."

Mr. Phiney stopped talking as if the story was done.

"Is that it?" Olivia asked as she looked up at Mr. Phin.

"Oh no," he said with a laugh. "That fella left Piel Island but evidently that sailor still wanted ta get back at Aunt Abby fur whoopin' 'em a good one, cuz not too many years later, Aunt Abby had a dream and in that dream she was on her knees plantin' petunias in front of the Ship's Inn when a fella dressed in a long, dark cloak with his hood pulled up blockin' his face floated slowly up the walkway and started in lookin' at the baskets of gooseberries she had for sale. He whispered low so no one else could hear but her, and tells 'er not ta look up at 'em but that she best be leaving the island 'cuz folks be coming ta get 'er and me, cuz that sailor was spreadin' tales of her being one ah them witches and that she was the one who possessed King John's treasure that had gone missin' way back in the twelve-hun'erts. This specter fella told 'er that the town folks wouldn't be able ta defend 'er against the Witch Hunters Commission. Now, back then, they din't mess 'round with witches an such. Iff'en you was accused ah being a witch, they took ya straight-away to the dungeons and left ya ta rot. Well, Aunt Abby thought nothing of the dream till the next day when low-an-behold, a neighbor brought 'er over some petunias ta plant and jest as she was puttin' the last plant inta that ground up walked the very same fella who had been in 'er dream! Without even waitin' ta hear 'em say the words, she stood up, told the fella 'thank ye kindly', invited 'em inta the pub for a free spot ah tea, then right then and thur Aunt Abby walked inta the Ship's Inn livin' quarters, grabbed me up by the 'spenders and that very mornin' we packed up our few belongings. Aunt Abby gave the keys for the Ship's Inn to the Island's King, Camimo Rimini, and told 'em ta sell it fur 'er and keep a portion of the money and she would be sendin' 'em a post when she got settled up. So, the two of us went and took the first ferry to Rampside, and what do ya know, but as we were getting off that ferry in Rampside we spied some ah them Witch Huntin' folks waitin' ta get on the return ferry ta Piel Island. Ya could always spot 'em, cuz they wear them long cloaks with a big angel's halo embroidered onta the back ah them cloaks. Most folks say every last one of 'em ain't witch huntin' a'tall, they're huntin' fur folks ta give 'em gold is what they're doin'. Many a woman went ta the gallows cuz they had no gold ta give them swindler folks.

"Well, Aunt Abby didn't have her usual garb on that day, cuz while we was crossin' the channel she went inta the privy and changed out of 'er clothes. She came outta that privy in a big, brimmed, black bonnet pulled down to cover most ah her face. She was walkin' all hunched-over-like and she was using a cane. That day on the ferry was the only time I ever did see her in a dress. It was a long, black thing and her bonnet had a black veil hangin' down in front ah her face. She looked like them old widder women after thur husbands pass on inta the great beyond. Then, she pulled out a boy's long, black coat and put it on me so's to cover up my clothes and in place ah my usual straw hat, she pulled a stevedore hat down low on my head. When we finally got off that ferry, we skirted the crowd that was waitin' ta get on the return trip and we caught us a hackney and set off for the train depot so's we could catch a ride inta Liverpool where we boarding a ship sailing for the Americas. I didn't know 'bout it a'fore, but on that trip across the ocean, Aunt Abby tol' me 'bout 'er getting' a lot of money from some long-gone relative after her mum passed on, so on that ship to the Americas we had us a fine little room with two portholes and a fine view of the Atlantic Ocean. When we arrived in New York City, we caught us a train and didn't get off till we reached St Louie, Missour'ah. That's where Aunt Abby opened up a boardin' house and raised me 'til she passed on, God rest 'er soul, when I was but thirteen years old.

"What happened was the old boardin' house caught a'far and even though she was sick with some kind of illness, she got up out ah her sick bed and helped get two of the elderly patrons to safety. The very next day she died of unknown reasons, or so Doc Jones told me. He said she had got some smoke in her lungs but that wasn't what took 'er. He wasn't quite sure about the whole thing and that it sure looked suspicious to 'em. But that's the last I ever did hear about my Aunt Abby passin' over. But, afore she passed on, as she was layin' in 'er sickbed, she told me a friend named Elijah Bonheur was gonna raise me up and that he was an upstanding man full of honor. And that he was. He was the best feller I ever did meet.

"I stayed on with Elijah Bonheur for quite a few years 'til one day he told me kindly that it was time for me to leave home and go see the world so's I could figger out what I wanted ta do for the rest of my life. He said I was welcome to come home anytime I needed or wanted to but he din't want to hinder me from seeing the world. So, that's when I took ta sailing the seas."

Mr. Phiney shifted on the wooden bench, reached behind the seat and brought out a jug of water and some biscuits for Olivia and him before he continued.

"So let me tell ya 'bout crossin' that ocean and meeting up with some haints on our way to America. Now, I hadn't ever been off Piel Island a'fore me and Aunt Abby got onta that ferry headin' inta Rampside. I 'member being so excited I din't care what kind ah room we slept in, we were on a ship sailin' for the Americas! I was hoppin' and jumpin' all over that cabin when we got on board the *Queen Sophia*. Aunt Abby calmed me down with a swat on the behind and we went up to the deck and watched as the *Queen Sophia* pulled away from the dock and we were on our way! I rightly remember Aunt Abby whisperin' in my ear and tellin' me to take a look over yonder to the right. There standin' on the dock was ten more of them witch-huntin' folks and they were busy as bees lookin' at the rest of the people on the dock."

Mr. Phin laughed heartily as he remembered the scene.

"Then, the very first night, I was sitting on the winder-sill of our little cabin lookin' out the porthole at a thousand stars twinklin' and shinin' in the clear sky like millions of diamonds and the moon bouncin' its glimmerin' rays off that black, still ocean. I asked Aunt Abby if we could go up ta the deck and have a look-see at the sky for a while since it was mighty hot in the room. She told me to go on up there and she would be follerin' me in a wee bit.

"So, I took on out of that room like a bullet, ran up the steps and there I was on that big, open deck with the whole sky as my covers. I edged closer to the railings, being careful to hold tight to the rails, when up beside me slid another young lad about my age and he smelled like he had been dunked in a keg ah rum.

"He said his name was Baptiste and that he was an orphan from Marsay, France and he was goin' to the Americas hopin' fur someone to adopt 'em so he could have a family. I'll never forget that young boy. He had black, wavy hair and eyes the color of the dark blue sky rimmed in midnight black long eyelashes. He smelled strongly of rum, but he had a quick smile and stood there beside me lookin' up at the sky. Then I introduced myself and we stood silent for a bit.

'Tis' a beautiful night, is it not, mon amie Phineas?" he said with a smile and a strange accent.

'Tis,' I said, still looking out at the ocean.

'Have you sailed before, Phineas?'

'Nah,' I said as I looked over at him. 'Have you?'

'Wee, many times, over six hundred and thirty-one times now.'

"Well, I laughed at him and told him that couldn't be, cuz he wasn't old 'nuf to sail the seas six hundred and thirty-one times."

'Yes, indeed I have, don't ya know? It's so I can go to the Americas and get myself a family, of course. Everybody knows that,' he said back to me with his chest puffed out with pride.

"I stood there looking at my new friend, not understandin' what he meant, then he continued.

'Every time I board a ship and we get as far as Bridgetown, Jamaica and then I can na' remember anything. Next thing I remember is I'm back in Marseilles and I have to go about finding my way to Liverpool and getting on another ship.'

"Well, I looked at him and in my young mind I jest couldn't figure out why he had to sail so many times. Then he continued.

"'But,' he said to me with a frown, 'this time I think I'm going to get off the boat when we make the first stop before Bridgetown and I'll stay there. Maybe I'll find me a family there who will take me in, or maybe I'll just wander about the streets a bit. Barbados is a lovely island, you know. They have bananas and mangos and all sorts of other things growing everywhere a body looks. And the sun is always shining there.'

"Well," I interrupted and asked, 'Why do ya smell like a keg ah rum, Baptiste?'

"He laughed and said, 'I hide in an empty rum keg and that's how I get on board every time I find a new ship.'

"Then Aunt Abby gave me a call and I turned to give 'er a call back. When I turned back to Baptiste, he was gone!"

"What happened to him, Mr. Phin?" Olivia asked curiously.

"Didn't rightly know for a bit. I searched all over that dang ship - oops, pard' me, lass - and I couldn't find hide nor hair of that young fella. Then, one night as I lay in my cot by the open port-hole I hear'd a tappin' on the winder frame and thur he was sitting on the edge of the sill!

"Well, I popped up in my cot and asked 'em how he got inta our room, and he said he could go anywhere he wanted but it was a puzzle to him how he did it. Then I whispered to 'em that he better get out ah the room quick-like or Aunt Abby would be hot under the collar and maybe snatch 'em up by the ear and give 'em a good whoopin'. Then he said thur weren't no harm done a'tall and that he jest wanted ta have a good time being friends with me. And then, jest like that, he was gone.

"I remember layin' back onta my cot and wonderin' what in the world was goin' on, and then I figgered it out. He was a haint! That was the first time I ever did see a haint, and he was a right-nice fella!"

"Did you see him again?" Olivia asked anxiously.

"Oh, yes. Two nights after he sat on my winder sill when Aunt Abby was snorin' like a locomotive, I slipped out of our cabin and scurried up the steps to the big, open deck. Thur was a few of the crew up thur, but not many. Hopin' they wouldn't see me, I slinked along the side of the railing and found me a nice seat on the deck next to the wall ah the capt'n's cabin. There I sat, jest lookin' up at them stars and wonderin' what it was like up in the starry night when pop! thur Baptiste was sittin' beside me again."

'Whatcha doing?' he asked me in a low whisper.

'Wow, ya gave me a scare, Baptiste,' I whispered back. 'I'm jest takin' me a look at all the stars fur a bit.'

'Ya want to play a game of Bones, Phineas?' he asked me.

"Well, I told 'em that'd be a right-fun thin' to do, so he pulled out a small bag ah bones from his pocket and we set about played a few games ah Bones fur a spell. After a bit, we tired ah rollin' bones so we jest sat thur lookin' about the ship when the sea started in swellin' up and down, tryin' ta toss us about the deck.

'Ya want me ta take ya up higher so's you can watch the sea get angry?'

'Nope,' I said, looking back at him sternly. 'I ain't flyin' 'round with no haint. It ain't normal nor right, I do believe,' I told 'em.

'I ain't no haint, I'm a fantôme. What's a haint?' he asked me.

'A haint is what you are, Baptiste. You're dead and ain't got no real body ta hold ya down on earth. I ain't knowin' what no fantômes is,' I said back at him, 'but you are a haint and ya cain't be trusted.'

'What? Why can't I be trusted?' he asked me like he was offended.

'Cuz you're a haint!' I said back at him kindly loud. 'Ya ever think 'bout trustin' a haint? Nope, it can't be done and I'm sure ah that. And I figgered it out on my own thinkin' and I know ya can't be trusted, cuz haints are a tricky lot and a body has ta watch 'em close-like or they'll trick ya up for sure.'"

"Wow," Olivia said. "So what happened next?"

"Well, that lil' haint grabbed holt ah my arm and started in tryin' to pull me up onta my feet, but I was stronger than he was, so I held tight to my spot. Then he yelled at me to let go and he would take me for a jolly ride in the air and show me how the sea looked from above, but I held my spot and gave him a shove with my boot and told him I was gonna yell for my Aunt Abby iff'en he din't let me go. So he let go of my arm and plopped back down beside me.

"'Why would ya do that?' he asked me.

"Well, I looked him straight in the eyes and told him that I knew he was up to a no-good deed and that just like I had told him afore, I din't trust no haint. Then he looked kindly embarrassed and told me I was spot-on right. He said he had planned on takin' me up above the crow's nest of the *Queen Sophia* and then lettin' me drop ta see what happened, but since I was gonna give Aunt Abby a yell he figgered he better not do that cuz he already knew about my Aunt Abby and knew she was sure-shootin' good friends with God.

"Well, I jumped up as best I could with that ship rollin' like a tumbleweed and took off scramblin' fur the cabin and he kept on yellin' fur me to come back and he wouldn't do any such thing now that I knew what he was up to. But I kept right on runnin', and when I got inta our cabin I shut the door good and proper and didn't leave tell the next mornin' when Aunt Abby made me go out for some breakfast porridge!"

"Did you see Baptiste again?"

"Nope, not one time on that whole crossin' did I even get a whiff ah rum, other than that rum them sailors were drinkin'. But, one night at the supper table I asked the Capt'n about Baptiste and he looked at me kindly strange-like and said, 'So, ya seen the lad, aye? Most folks can't see him.' Well, I nodded my head, so he took on the tellin' of Baptiste's story.

"Seemed as if Baptiste De Lafontaine was indeed an orphan from Marsay, France, but he went down with a ship off the coast of Barbados in the 1700's afore he could make it to the Americas and find himself a family. Since then his haint seems to be catchin' a ship ever once in a while, and the *Queen Sophia* seemed to be his favorite. But, the Capt'n said if I told him to go away he probably wouldn't be back to bother me. And, sure 'nuf, Baptiste never did come back onta that ship while we were sailing."

Mr. Phiney scratched his head through his skull cap as if in deep thought.

"Many a time I've wondered what happened to that little fella's haint."

Both Olivia and Mr. Phiney sat quietly in their own thoughts for a bit.

The sun was now slipped completely up from across the Mississippi and the day was going to be the usual hot day in Missouri. Mr. Phiney old mule clomped along the trail in his normal slow movement.

"Let me be telling ya another tale about my adventures after I left Paw Elijah's cabin and struck out on my own."

7

Ghost Ships and Scallywag Scrugs

(As told to Lily by Olivia who heard it from Mr. Phiney

who heard some of it from Scallywag Scrugs; who some

swear is a big fat windbag)

The *Ballyhoo's Plunder* swayed gently with the ebbing tides as she lay anchored a mile from the harbor of Port Royal, Jamaica. Phineas sat propped against the railing, which was attached to the bow, watching the sky darken as millions of twinkling stars quietly appeared. Off in the horizon the enormous orange harvest-moon seemed to be sitting on the top of the water as it cast its shimmering light across the polished, glassy surface of the sea. Not a ripple crossed the dark waters and not a whisper of air hit the sails. The *Ballyhoo's Plunder* rested high in the water, for her holds were empty and waiting to be filled with plunder on her next adventure. Except for the one buccaneer keeping watch in the crow's nest, Phineas was the lone member of Captain Bellows crew still awake.

The *Ballyhoo's Plunder* was a magnificent ship. It was classified as a 'man-o-war' with a total of fifty cannons on each side and seventy-five carvings of mermaids, children and ladies covering the upper hull along the edge of the deck. Its crow's nest sat 70 feet above the deck, and the ship's many sails were kept white as snow. Every morning, Phin and two other members of the crew swabbed the deck until not a spot of tobacco juice could be found. The *Ballyhoo's Plunder* flew under many different flags; it all depended on which country's port they were entering. Along with different flags, Capt'n Bellows would have his men paint an alternative name on her hull so as to gather no grief in the different ports along the way. Then once they were out to sea again, the name would be changed back to *Ballyhoo's Plunder.*

Phin's eyes slowly closed and his head nodded, causing him to jerk awake. Twenty feet from the ship, three dolphins rose majestically out of the bay in glimmering silence. With water glistening off their bodies they arched their dorsal fins and slipped soundlessly back into the deep sea.

Blinking rapidly so as to keep himself awake, Phin scooted around and rested his arms against the railing as he gazed out toward the moon.

Scallywag Scrugs, an old, salty sea-dog who was allowed to stay aboard because he had been a pirate for nigh-on seventy years and had no other place to go, had told Phin the tale of seeing *The Flying Dutchman* one full-mooned night many years ago when he himelf was a young lad dozing on the bow of a pirate's ship just as Phin was now doing. Scally had told Phin that the *Dutchman* appears only when the moon is full, the night is quiet, and misty fog covers the sea like a thick blanket. So that was what Phin was watching for as he sat alone on the deck.

Phin's mind wandered back to the day Scallywag first spoke to him personally. It was the day Phin was ordered by the cook to tote a supper bucket into Scally's cabin, because evidently, Scally was feeling too poor to get up off his sickbed. Phin had hemmed and hawed, not wanting to go inside Scally's sleeping room because the old fella constantly stared at Phin with sharp knowing eyes. But if Cookie ordered him to do something, Phin had no other choice but to do it. So, reluctantly, he tiptoed up to Scally's door and burst inside, sat the vittles bucket down and turned to scurry away before Scally had a chance to say anything. But Scally's arm shot out like a bullet, and with the strength of a much younger man, grabbed ahold of Phin and ordered him to set a spell so they could parlay a bit.

Phin stood still for a bit but finally took a seat on the floor next to the old seadog's bed and turned to look at him. Scally's face was wrinkled; his lips were just a slit in his face and his eyebrows had grown long enough to hang over his eyes. The only thing still normal-looking were his crystal-blue eyes which stood out starkly against his dark, weathered skin. The whites of his eyes were still as clear and bright as a younger man's. His hair was hoary grey and hung in long, unwashed, greasy clumps about his thin boney shoulders. He focused his soul-penetrating eyes at Phin before speaking in his low, raspy voice.

"Ayer ya afear'd ah me boy?"

"Nah," Phin answered sheepishly as he fidgeted nervously.

"Sure ya ayer. Don't be lying ta me, boy." Scally laughed as he kept his stare focused on Phin's face. "Everbody's afear'd ah me."

"Okay, sir, yes I am. You're always staring at me."

"Do ya know why I'm watchin' ya close, an' why you're aboard this here ship, boy?"

Scallywag always called Phineas "boy", even though he was almost eighteen years old and was now taller and more muscular than most the crew on board the *Ballyhoo*.

"'Cuz I asked Capt'n iff'en I could come aboard and learn the ways ah piratin' one day when he was in a pub in the port ah Naw'leens?"

"Nope," the old man chuckled deep in his chest, then gave a harsh, raspy cough.

"Well then, pray tell - why am I on the *Ballyhoo*? Do you know why I'm here?"

"I know ever'thing there is ta knows aboard this vessel, boy. Ever' time a paper drops, I hear it. You remember that and don't forget it," Scallywag shook his finger at Phin and chuckled deeply. "You're here cuz I wanted ya here, boy. I told Capt'n that a bounty hunter was afta ya when me an' him sat in the Ugly Pug drinking ale next to ya. Iff'en ya hadn't come over an' asked, the Capt'n would'ah sent me over ta ask ya myself. He din't know it but I led 'em to the Ugly Pug cuz I'd been trackin' ya fur a good while. And when the Capt'n looked at ya an see'd that ya was a strong, strappin' young'un he jumped at the chance ta get ya on board."

Phin frowned and looked more intently at the grizzled old man.

"Now why might ya be wantin' me ta be on Capt'n Bellow's ship, Scallywag? Ya din't even know me a'fore I came aboard! An' why ya been trackin' me?"

"Cuz, I'm your Gran-pappy!" The old man's spit flew everywhere. "I'm the pappy of that good-for-nothing scoundrel who left your little mum on that bitter, cold winter day on Piel Isle an' didn't go back ta collect ya when your lil' mum passed on, God rest 'er sweet soul." He looked up toward the ceiling and made the sign of the cross. "She was a fine young lass, yes indeed. She was".

Scally sat quietly for a minute as if in reverence for the dead. Then he continued talking with disgust.

"A few years back I watched that no-good scoundrel pappy ah yor'n go down with his bloodthirsty capt'n. The two of 'em standin' thur on the deck of *The Sea Siren's Soul* holding up his cutlass in defiance all the way inta that watery grave. Served the rotter right! The bugger wouldn't ah saved my hide fur love nor money. He and that capt'n ah his was purt-near ready ta make me walk the plank after capturin' our ship, when real sudden-like the *Susannah's Treasure* appeared outta the fog, blasted the *Siren's* hull and but by the grace ah God we prisoners would'ah perished. I swear by me own sweet mum's

94

grave, God rest 'er soul, I saw Davy Jones himself come up outta that sea an in ah flash snatch that good-for-nothing scoundrel off'en that sinkin' deck. So iff'en your ever wonderin' whur your pappy is, he's in Davey Jones locker swimmin' with the fish.

"An," Scally lowered his voice to a raspy whisper, "Capt'n Bellows is your mum's brother. Now, don't ya be tellin' a soul what I just tol' ya, or every pirate aboard this ship will be tryin' ta make ya walk the plank. They don't take ah likin' to ya iff'en they think the capt'n might be givin' ya favors. They'll be lookin' fur ways ta wipe ya off the deck, iff'en ya know what I mean. They don't know 'bout me knowin' the capt'n when he was a lad and they don't know your blood-kin to 'em. I'm only tellin' ya this cuz my days are numbered, boy, my days are numbered. I could count 'em with one hand, iff'en I knew how ta count."

Phin sat stunned for a long while, just staring at Scallywag with a furrowed frown. Then he pulled his head back in disbelief.

"What?"

"Ya hear'd what I said, boy!" Scally croaked, "Capt'n Bellows be your uncle an' I be your grand-pappy."

"Well, I'll be a sawed-off son-of-a-gun," Phin whistled under his breath. "Why din't ya ever come see me?"

"I know'd where ya was all along. Did ya think a pirate could sail right inta Piel Island and stay for a holiday?"

"Well, I guess that wouldn't do. Aunt Abby would'ah twisted your ears good."

"Now," the old seadog said in a muffled whisper, "remember boy, don't ya be sayin' a word ta nary a soul or you'll be swimmin' in Davey Jones' locker with the fish an' your pappy. And, most important of all, don't ya be breathin' a word of it ta the capt'n, cuz he don't know neither an' he don't take lightly ta being tricked."

Phin shook his head in agreement, still staring wide-eyed at old Scally.

"Now," Scally said a bit louder, "I'm wantin' ta talk to ya, boy. Let's pass the time a day for a bit. If I say anything that sounds strange, just take it as a grain ah salt cuz my mind seems ta wander now and again. Let me be tellin' ya 'bout a sight I see'd many years back when I was but a young lad."

Scally gave a deep cough and lay back for a few seconds, closing his eyes as if trying to catch his breath. Phin sat waiting for probably five minutes, then Scally opened his eyes, leaned up and glared at Phin with a deep scowl and yelled.

"Whatcha doin' in here boy? Ya spying on me an takin' me gold? Be off with ya, ye varmint! Get on outta here an' stop nosin' round, so I can eat me some vittles. Come back in a bit an' fetch this bucket a slop that Cookie calls vittles; it ain't fit for the hogs."

Shocked at Scally's words, Phin scrambled up to leave, but once again Scally grabbed his arm. "Wait, wait! Don't go, boy. Don't ya be mindin' me none iff'en I blurt out fur ya to go. Let me gather up my words again and get the cobwebs outta my head. My old brain seems ta jump hither and yon most times."

Phineas sat back down cautiously and waited for the old fella.

"Purt near a life time ago, or so it seems, I was sittin' on the dock in Mobile, Alabamer - it's smack dab right on the very edge ah the gulf. There was times when water lapped up onta the shore and purt-near washed the town inta its belly. Well, I was wishin' an' watchin' for a pirate ship ta come sailin' in and I din't care what pirate ship it was, I jest wanted ta see a pirate ship so ta ease my young mind's wanderlust.

"Well, it was gettin' on to being dark, but I kept right on sittin' there. I din't have a soul ta answer to and I din't have nowhere else ta go cuz my ma an pap had been taken by the cholera some time back an I had no idee where my brothers took off to. Most days I did a bit a stealin' with my friend Jim Tucker and I was always smilin' at them town ladies so they'd feel sorry fur me and give me some vittles. And it worked most times, cuz I was a handsome lad. Or so they told me. So, I'd clean myself up a bit at the watering hole, comb my black, curly hair back and put on my pitiful smile and then knew I was gonna get some good vittles."

Scally laughed deeply.

"But anyways, that night all I wanted ta do was ta see a pirate ship. I'd been listenin' to them fellers in the pubs along the docks talk 'bout pirates and such and I was dreamin' of seein' at least one a'fore I died. I 'member clear as glass thinkin' that I din't care iff'en it was a ghost pirate ship or a reg'lar pirate ship, I wanted ta cast my eyeballs upon one ah them glorious vessels and then my life would be as complete as a twelve-year old's life could be.

"So, there I sat 'til the wee hours' ah the night watchin' through my spyglass for one ah them ships. But after a spell I got a bit tired so I moved from the end ah the dock up onta the soft grassy slope ah the bay where I fell asleep like a newborn'd babe. Well, 'long bout the witchin' hour when I was dreamin' bout sailin' on a pirate's ship an such, I wake up ta this here tap, tap, tap… tap, tap, tap… and real slow-like I opened my eyes and thur she was! The biggest pirate ship I ever did see was sitting high in the water 'bout forty feet from the Mobile dock. It was a pitch-black night, but there she sat, glowing like a heap ah lanterns. She had four sails on 'er main mast and the beams pushed out further than the sides ah the ship and each sail was as if it was filled with air but she was standin' still. Ever last sail, rope and pulley was glowin' like a lit-up Christmas tree. Thur was lanterns hangin' from everthin', an' on the side of that pirate ship was painted *Red's Avenger*, so I know'd right off it was the ghost pirate ship of Jack the Red who had been a merciless scoundrel. 'Tis said old Jack locked his whole crew in his cabin and blew up the ship so his crew couldn't be telling where his treasure was iff'en they was captured or taken by the *Sea Shark* who had jest blown away the main mast on the *Red's Avenger*. I hear tell ol' Jack jumped ship in the nick-ah-time and saved his own hide but din't give a rip 'bout his crew.

"Well, I lay with my mouth wide open starin' for a bit then I crawled on my hands and knees up to ah boulder jettin' out of the shoreline. Peeking 'round that boulder I watched as she sat there, kindly floatin' real slow-like above the water with 'er sails movin' easy-like in the breeze, and stars twinklin' above the tall masts. Being that she was lit up so bright, I could see ever'thing on deck and there weren't nary ah soul moving about, so I belly-crawled a bit closer and got myself hid behind a clump ah reedy bushes. I pulled the spyglass from my britches pocket an' took me a good look-see and that's when I spotted 'em. Little by little I moved my spyglass up to check out the crow's nest, and there he sat lookin' back at me through his own spyglass. Bone legs an' feet was hangin' out the crow's nest, swingin' back an' forth as if he din't have a care in the world. One bone hand was proppin' up his bone head while holdin' that spyglass, an' with the other bone hand he was tap, tap, tapping on the edge of the crow's nest making the sound echo through the night. The hairs on the back ah my neck stood straight up and shivers ran down my backbone like wasper stings, an' I stopped breathin' for a bit cuz there weren't no flesh on them bones a'tall. It was a livin' skeleton and he had a spyglass lookin' right at me. Then, he dropped his spyglass onta the deck far below where it made a loud thud and his bone jaw dropped open with surprise, then he waved at me with one ah his bone hands. Them bone fingers was flappin' up and down and his bone jaw was clampin' open and shut like he was jabberin' like a magpie. I got ta shakin' and tremblin' so bard I couldn't move. Finally, I got my legs goin' and I took off outta there like a jackrabbit. I ran an' ran till I got to the Widder Williams farm, where I slipped inside 'er barn, climbed up inta 'er hay loft and crawled under a big pile ah hay. I lay there gaspin' for air for a bit but when I finally got my air back, I heard the door squeakin' open an' I sure-ah-shootin' thought it had ta be that skeleton. But, when I rolled over to take me a look, it was two men slippin' inta Widder

Williams's barn. They closed the door real quiet-like behind 'em and started in talkin' in whispers.

"They was talkin' about a pile ah money Cactus Curly had been suspected of takin' from the bank, an' one of 'em said Curly let it slip when he was feelin' kindly friendly that it was hidden som'ers on the Widder's farm. Now, right off I thought they was talkin' 'bout Widder Crump, cuz she's a mean'un, but the more they talked the more I realized they was talked 'bout MY Widder Williams.

"I knew ol' Cactus Curly, an' he weren't no man ta be meddlin' with, iff'en ya know what I mean. He was a mean'un. He had a habit ah throwin' them town cats inta the river jest cuz he could. An' I also know'd where his hidey-hole was, so I jest laid there an' studied on their talkin' fur a bit. They said it was hidden somewheres on Widder William's farm, but they weren't sure where, so that meant I could look ever' day iff'en I wanted ta. But first, I was thinkin' I should hunt up ol' Cactus Curly and make a deal with 'em. I'd tell 'em who was huntin' his gold iff'en he'd divvy it up with me.

"Along 'bout that time, the barn door slammed open and them two fellas got quiet as a tomb. At first I was thinkin' it was Cactus Curly and maybe he'd hear'd 'em talkin' bout stealin' his stolen money, but when I, real slow-like, brushed a bit ah hay away from my eyes so's I had me a good view at the whole floor, low-an-behold standin' inside that open barn door was that skeleton from the ghost ship. Them two fellas had the shocked look of ah fox caught in the chicken coop, and was froze with fright. That skeleton started in clinkin' and clankin' and headin' straight for 'em. I was so busy watchin' the three of 'em I din't even know it, but I'd scooted way too close to the edge ah that loft. All of a sudden thur was a big crash, an' it was me fallin' off'en that loft, right smack-dab on top ah that skeletons head with a loud thud! Then the awful'est clinkin' and clankin' started up and bones was bouncin' up in the air flyin' round that room like magic, an' then there I was with skeleton bones fallen all around me!"

"Scallywag," Phin smirked, "I'm thinkin' this story is a big ol' bag ah hot air comin' out of an ol' windbag."

Scallywag ignored Phineas' comment and continued with his story.

"I was lookin' up inta the faces of them two fellas an' what do ya know but it was Skeeter and Stubby Jones! They stood there starin' down at me kindly bug-eyed fur a bit, and then Skeeter, who had tabaccy juice drippin' down his lip, whispered real quiet-like and says, 'Scallywag, ya know'd ya now have the curse on ya, don't ya? Ain't no hope fur ya. Ya done busted up ah skeleton. That's a mighty bad thing ta do, cuz your foolin' round with the dead an' thur ain't no quick fix fur that curse. The onliest cure fur this curse is ta go get ya'self a big ol' toad frog and cut the second toe off'en it's back left hopper-leg and take its blood and rub it on your belly while doing the red-shirt dance. Ya have ta citch the toad frog, whack off hit's toe at the strike ah midnight on a Saturday night when the town clock strikes the first gong ah midnight and hold onta it 'til all them gongs have been struck. Then ya go on home and sleep with that toad-toe layin' on your belly all night long, then get up early in the morning a'fore anybody gets to the church-house. And, ya got ta be wearin' a red shirt an' no spenders on your britches. And ya gotta do the red-shirt dance ever' Sunday, in front ah the church-house, right after the church bells ring out their call for lost souls. Iff'en ya don't do hit fur a month, it'll be mighty bad fur ya.

'Now, the toad frog cain't die or you'll have ta get ya anoth'ern and start it all over again. Iff'en ya don't do it exactly like at, that skeleton is gonna foller ya 'round fur the rest ah your life, hanging onta your shoulder bones clinkin and clankin' and drivin' everbody away from ya and ya won't ever get ya'self a wife.'

"What's the red-shirt dance, Skeeter?" I asked Skeeter.

'Well, I don't rightly know, 'cuz I ain't never busted up no skeleton but I'm thinkin' it's kindly-like doin' the waltz with a lady.'

"Well, Skeeter started in movin' round the barn like he was waltzing with a lady, dippin' and moving slow-like with his hands placed round the lady's waist 'til I got the idee of how ta waltz. Just a'fore he stopped, he bowed deep-like and said thank-ye to his invisible lady."

"You got ya'self ah wife, Skeeter? Cuz ya sure do know how ta dance," I asked after watching him dance the waltz.

'I did, but she run'd off with a circus feller. Said I wasn't e'citin' 'nuf, an' the circus feller knew how ta dance better'n me, an' could even dance to the polka. She din't know it but I can out-Polka anybody 'round and I can waltz better'n anybody she knows!'

"Well, I sat there for a bit a'fore I got up, kicked them bones away an' started out the door. They was still yakkin' when I shut that door and I was purt-near close to the Widder's back porch where I was gonna sleep when I hear'd that skel'ton clinkin' and clankin' again. Out the barn door barreled Skeeter and Stubby, running fur thur lives down the road. I din't even look at the barn door ta see iff'en that skel'ton was comin' out, I jest jumped up onta that porch and shimmied inside the Widder's empty rain barrel an' hoped that skeleton wouldn't see me.

"I could hear 'em comin', but the clinkin' and clankin' sounded kindly strange, iff'en ya know what I mean, so I peeped out the top ah the barrel, an' sure 'nuf, thur was that skel'ton walkin' right at me. But, he had put himself back together all wrong. He was limpin' bad cuz both his thigh bones was on one leg and the other'n had both his shin bones. The short leg had a hand whur its foot goes and his left arm had a foot danglin' at the end. The leg bone that did have a foot on it was turned back'ards and his ribs was twisted round whur his backbone was ta be. Ever'time he took a step he'd walk back'ards a step then he'd have ta shuffle along an' try ta figger out how ta get goin'. Well, I felt kindly sorry for the pitiful feller an figgered he couldn't be too smart or he'd ah figgered out how ta put his-self back together, so I eased outta the barrel a bit an' called out an ask'd 'em iff'en he needed some help. Well, he

101

turned his crooked head, as best he could, towards me and I was thinkin' he nodded yes so I crawled out and walked over ta help 'em, real careful-like. He was a tangled-up mess, that was fur sure; I started in taking all his bones apart and each time I pulled one off to put it whur it belonged, he made a groanin' sound like it was hurtin' 'em, so I did it real careful-like.

"Well, I finally finished puttin' 'em back together and he looked purty good, iff'en I have ta say so myself. Hit was like a puzzle. I had 'bout a dozen or so small bones left over, so he picked 'em up and stuck 'em onta his jawbone like danglin' whiskers, then he jumped up and down and the bone whiskers clanked together like a wind chime. Then he looked at me with them holler eyes and I do believe he was smilin' cuz his jaw bones was going up and down real quick-like and he put his hands on his knees, threw his head back and then a loud cackle came out from his empty rib cage like he was laughing. Then he started in jumpin' and runnin' 'round the Widder's yard like he was doin' ah dance!

"Well, I take off down the road cuz it was Saturday night and it was coming on ta being midnight so I know'd I had ta get me a big, fat toad frog so's I can cut its toe off and do the dance ta get rid ah the curse cuz I sure din't want that skel'ton follerin' me round. I cut 'cross the field to the Widder's waterin' hole and started in lookin' fur ah big ol' bull frog, and I had my eyeball on a big'un when I heard that skel'ton comin' jest a'clinkin' and a'clankin' and scar'd that big ol' toad frog away! I turn 'round ta look at 'em and there he stood with Stubby's straw hat sittin' on his head jest as purty as ya please and he was doin' a dance again. He was clappin' his bone hands above his head, spinning round doin' some kinda square dance and his jaw was flappin' up an' down like he was singin'. It was ah dang funny sight ta see, but I had ta get me a toad frog so I was kindly mad at the bone fella.

"Well, I gave 'em a yell and told 'em he had ta get on outta there cuz he was scarin' the toad frogs away so then he flopped down b'side me, reached inta the waterin' hole and snatches up the biggest old toad frog I ever did see, throws it at me like he's kindly mad, gets up an' stomps away. Well, I grab up that toad frog, takes out my pocket knife and when I heard that first gong from the church bell I whacks off its left hopper toe and held onta it 'til all them gongs rang-out. Then I sat it back down by the pond waitin' fur it to hop away, and it did.

"Well, I go on back ta the Widder's house an' crawled back inta the hayloft with my toad toe on my belly an' take me a sleep. The next morning right a'fore the sun came up, I got up, took my spender's off and figgered I'd go huntin' fur me a red shirt. But lo'-an'-behold, hangin' on the barn door latch is a red shirt and when I put it on, one ah them skel'ton finger bones fell outta the pocket, so I know'd right off that skel'ton got that red shirt fur me. It was way too big fur me, but it was a red shirt so's I put it on and walked towards town. Right after the church bells rang I open that shirt up and mark my belly with a big gob a toad frog blood, all the while doin' the red-shirt dance. So I did that ever' Sunday morning fur a month, an' I never did see that skel'ton again, 'til one night, many years later, after I'd joined up with a cutthroat pirate crew anchored in Port Royal, Jamaica.

***

"I was sittin' in The Tail of the Pup Inn, when all of a sudden that building started shakin' and shimmerin' like it had the palsy. In through the door runs a feller hollerin' bout the killer waves comin' in from far out on the sea and demons from the bowels of the ocean was riding 'em in like they was horses, with Davy Jones himself ridin' on the biggest one. So, we all take off running for the door and down the street, up onta the highest cliff we could find where we turned and watched the waves comin' in. Sure 'nuf, there was Davy Jones his self ridin' the biggest'un. And lo'-an'-behold, sittin' on one ah them waves was that very same skel'ton I'd put back together when I was but ah young'un. After all them years he was still hangin' 'round. He was ridin' that wave like a fast horse, with Stubby's hat still on his bony head and all them little extra bones hangin' from his jawbone like whiskers, but now with seaweed danglin' from 'em. He rode that wave right up to the cliff, swept off'en his hat, gave me a 'howdy' sign, and rode right on past us."

Olivia looked at Mr. Phin and laughed. "Do you believe Mr. Scallywag really met up with a skeleton and had to do the red-shirt dance and then saw the skeleton riding a wave?"

Mr. Phin looked at Olivia as if surprised to find himself back on the road to Memphis, then nodded his head.

"I swear on my Granny's petticoat that's what he said," Mr. Phin chuckled deep in his chest. "Sounded a bit strange don't it. That's what I thought 'til a few weeks later."

"What happened a few weeks later?"

"Well, I'll go back to the part where I was sitting on the deck of the *Ballyhoo* watching for *The Flying Dutchman*. Earlier that day, Scally had grabbed ahold of me as I passed him in the galley and told me that tonight would be the night for me to see *The Flying Dutchman* iff'en I wasn't a sissy-girl and could stay awake that long. Scally whispered to me that it was the very date when the *Dutchman* had gone down to a watery grave during a furious storm around the Cape of Good Hope and I was to wait 'til the stars came out and the moon looked to be sitting on top of the sea. Then the fog would tumble in, covering most of the moonlight, and the stars would hide their faces in terror; the only thing making the ghost ship visible would be the greyish glow from the half-hidden moon. He said it was gonna come for a special reason an' I wasn't ta tell a soul 'bout it cuz they wouldn't believe me anyway. So there I sat with my chin on the deck rail when a warm breeze started blowin' in real soft-like, an out in the bay I see a huge wall ah fog rollin' in like tumbleweeds blowing across the prairie. It was movin' real slow-like and tumblin' 'til sure 'nuf, it covered the whole ship. I could hardly see my hand in front ah my face, and that was when I thought I heard the clangin' of the *Ballyhoo's* bells - but it wasn't the *Ballyhoo* clangin' 'er bells. Right there before my nose sailed *The Flying Dutchman*. She was so close I could'ah reached out an' touched 'er. Then, as if being blown away by a gust of wind, the fog lifted and the air turned clear. She was 'bout ten feet above the water with barnacles hangin' all over 'er hull an 'er sails were filled with wind, an' she was clippin' along pretty durn quick.

"Well, I stood straight up on the deck and with awe watched as she sailed past us. And there hangin' over 'er deck was that skeleton ol' Scallywag had told me 'bout. It still had them bone whiskers and that raggedy old hat ah Stubby's on its head. Its jaws were chompin' up and down jest like Scally said they were a'fore, an' it was wavin' to me like a long-lost kinfolk. Then suddenly, right beside the skeleton stood ol' Scallywags himself! I was never so surprised in my life. I din't know what to yell out at 'em, but Scally yelled out at me in a loud boomin' voice an' says, 'They came ta pick me up boy! Close your mouth an' don't look so surprised! Look in me trunk, boy. Look in me trunk'.

"Then poof! *The Dutchman* was gone and the air felt as if nothing strange had been there a'tall!"

"What did you do, Mr. Phin?" Olivia asked.

"What any fella would do, I guess. I ran down to Scallywag's room so I could tell 'em I saw 'em leanin' over the rail aboard *The Flyin' Dutchman*. I reached up to bang on his door and the door floated right open on its own, so I walked right in and discovered Scallywag Scrugs was gone. So, real nervous-like, I backed outta that cabin and ran up to the capt'n's cabin and woke 'em up. Then me and the capt'n searched that ship from stem to stern but we din't find hide-nor-hair of Scallywags. By that time, the whole crew was up and about searchin' for Scally. Finally, when I was alone with the capt'n, I told 'em 'bout me seein' *The Dutchman*, and real quiet-like he turned and looked at me and said, 'He's gone for good, boy'.

"And that was the last we saw of Scallywag Scrugs. The capt'n grabbed me by the front of my shirt and made me swear I'd never tell another crew member what I'd just told 'em, cuz it was whispered that if any pirate actually saw *The Flying Dutchman* their own ship was doomed unless they made the pirate who first saw that wicked ship walk the plank into the sea on a stormy night. So without the slightest hesitation I agreed. Then we looked high an' low for maybe a sign he had left us but found nothin' a'tall. Then the capt'n told me ta go on inta Scally's cabin and take whatever I wanted and that I could sleep in his cabin 'til we got to the next port where I should get off'en his ship. He was kind about it, but I could tell he meant what he said. He said Scally had already tol' 'em that I was ta get his belongin's iff'en anythin' ever happened to 'em, so I went to his cabin, opened up his trunk and went through the few thin's he had, an low-an-behold ol' Scally had purt-near a hun'ert dollars in gold coin. So I told the capt'n and he said they were mine. When we sailed inta Na'leens port, Capt'n Bellows himself escorted me off'en his ship, then he shook my hand and wished me a good life then turned and walked back to the *Ballyhoo's Plunder* and immediately set sail as if not wantin' to take the chance that I'd sneak aboard."

Mr. Phin laughed deep in his chest and said, "Ol' Scallywag Scrugs was a special person that was for sure. Elijah Bonheur was my hero but Scallywag Scrugs was the most interestin' soul I ever did meet. He tol' me many a tale I reckon I don't believe, but they sure are fun ta hear. I'll tell ya some more of his tales one ah these days."

After a pause, Mr. Phin looked at Olivia with a smile on his face. "Now, Olivia, you can believe me or not believe me, but as the good Lord is my witness, 'tis the honest truth."

With slight hesitation Olivia cocked her head and looked at Mr. Phiney with doubt in her eyes. As kindly as she could, she said, "If you say it's the truth, then I believe you, but it sure sounds unbelievable to me, ya know."

"Yep, it surely does, it surely does," Mr. Phiney laughed. "Iff'en I hadn't seen it with my own two eyes, I wouldn't believe it either. Mostly 'cuz Scallywag Scrugs was a mighty big windbag."

"Mr. Phiney," Olivia said softly, looking up at the older man, "Me, Lily and Ophelia were talking at Mama's burying and Lily said she heard you and Uncle Pud talking about a missing treasure. Is that true?"

Mr. Phin looked at Olivia curiously.

"Yep," he said slowly as he focused his eyes back onto the trail. "I ain't ever found it and I ain't ever found out who took it. Somebody must of took it while I was buryin' Elijah out back of his cabin next ta Esther. He tol' me it was under his front stoop, but when I lifted the boards the next morning, it was gone. I don't know iff'en somebody was listenin' while he was talking to me or how it happened, but it was gone. His cabin ain't close to another cabin so's nobody could overhear him jest talking regular-like, they had to be right there listening on purpose. I thought and I thought on it for a good long while, then one day while I was laying on my bedroll with my eyes closed 'bout two months after Elijah passed on, I remembered something. While I was tendin' ta Elijah that day, warmin' up his blanket and all, I kindly had a feelin' I was being watched, but then when I saw the spirit of Elijah's grandson sitting beside his bed I plumb forgot about havin' that feelin' until that very minute when I was layin' on my bedroll dwelling on it. Funniest thing is when I was layin' on that bedroll that night I saw, in the memory of my mind, the top of a strange looking hat stickin' above Elijah's bedroom winder. Jest for a fleetin' second. I've thought on that ever once'st in a while and wondered iff'en that wasn't the person sneakin' outside Elijah's cabin listenin' and then diggin' up the box. Guess I'll never know 'bout it though. Ain't so sense in worryin' bout it none. Also, there was many a time Elijah, when he got older, would start-in talkin' nonsense that I couldn't make heads nor tails of so I'm thinkin' maybe it was some of that jabber that wasn't even true."

8

The Gypsy Cabin

Early the next morning, after spending a second night sleeping in the bed of the wagon, the sun warmed Olivia's face and she opened her eyes to a new day, one which carried with it the promise of another hot, humid afternoon. Silently Olivia and Mr. Phin readied their wagon and moved down the road towards Memphis. The sweet smell of wild honeysuckle floated in the gentle breeze as the droning of the honeybees buzzed around them. The coos of the Turtle Doves mingled with the Thrush and the Mockingbird songs as they flitted from tree to tree, filling the air with echoes of chirps and chatters. Searching for a tasty breakfast, a rabbit scurried across the trail in front of the wagon and chipmunks rustled in the low-growing brush alongside the roadway.

Propping her bare feet up on the wagon rail, Olivia sat quietly enjoying the welcoming morning of the new day. Within an hour, they approached the main road leading south towards Memphis and a voice called out to them.

"Hey y'all, over here! Come on and have a bite to eat with us!

"We're having some biscuits and buttermilk. There's enough for y'all too. Ott and Paul's ma made plenty, and when she found out all y'all were coming along with us she sent even more."

Olivia recognized Lily Quinn's voice. Parked at the side of the road was a large wagon hitched to an extra-large mule; a big, red-headed man stood waiting for them - a man whom Olivia figured to be Mr. Bushy, along with Lily Quinn and two of the Pruiett boys.

"How-do, y'all?" Mr. Phin called jovially.

"How-do ya'self," Mr. Bushy called back in a booming voice. "We been a'waitin' fur ya."

"Did ya see Pud and Butler pass on by?" Mr. Phin inquired.

"Yeah," Mr. Bushy laughed heartily as Mr. Phin pulled his buckboard up close to theirs. "But they din't want to stop. They was rip-roarin' ta go. Actin' like a couple race horses themselves, Pud said he was anxious to get them horses down to Memphis and Butler was getting kindly antsy 'bout the sheriff maybe catchin' up with 'em, so they moved on right quick-like.

"Hop on down here, young'un," Mr. Bushy said as he reached up to help Olivia down from the wagon. "I'm Mr. Bushy, as ya might already know, and you must be Olivia. Lily's been yakkin' bout ya the whole way. Cain't get 'er ta shut up. I think she's caught the diarrhea of the mouth and just cain't help it." He let out a big, booming laugh. "Come on Phin, and have a biscuit or two; then we can mosey on down the road 'til we get to a camp site. Whatcha think?"

After eating biscuits and butter with honey, the two wagons moved on towards Memphis. They would have to spend a night or two in the dense forest, but there were enough of them that Olivia didn't feel frightened. Lily hopped in the wagon with her and Mr. Phin and told them Ophelia couldn't make it because one of her uncles passed on, and Tom Pruiett couldn't make it because he fell out of the wagon just as they were starting out and broke his arm. But Ott and Paul think it might have happened because he was kindly wary of meeting up with the two fellas with the snake. But his grand pappy said he might bring him down within the next week or two and that even though Ophelia couldn't come along, Lily said she herself wanted to visit Granny Cora so she could be with Olivia.

About dusk, after a day of laughing and talking, Mr. Bushy pulled his wagon off the road and motioned for Mr. Phin to do the same. They both pulled off the road a bit further and stopped in the middle of a clearing.

Dusk was coming on quickly, so they all set about getting their campsite prepared for the night. After building up a fire pit and getting their things arranged, Lily spotted an old, abandoned cabin almost hidden by the forest, built into the side of a hill off in the distance. She then asked Mr. Bushy why they didn't just go spend the night in the abandoned cabin. Mr. Bushy looked where she was pointing, bent and squinted his eyes to get a better look at the old place then muttered something under his breath. Then he looked at Mr. Phin, and Mr. Phin looked at him, but nothing was said between the two.

Finally, Mr. Phin very quietly asked, "Whatcha think, Bushy? Ya think we should move on out?"

"Well, it's gettin' on ta being too dark ta get much further down the road, Phin. By the time we hitch up the wagons again and reload 'em it'll be full-on dark. I'm thinkin' we'll have ta chance it. I surely din't realize we were this far down.

"Chance what, Mr. Bushy?" Lily asked.

"Ain't nothing ta worry 'bout, Lily-Beth, ain't nothing ta worry 'bout."

"Well," Lily said with her hands on her hips, "sounds to me like you and Mr. Phin are worried about something."

"Lily-Beth," Mr. Bushy said sternly as he stood up straight from unpacking his bedroll, "now you listen to me, gal. I'm gonna tell ya not to worry 'bout it and I'm gonna tell ya that iff'en yor thinkin' 'bout goin' over there and snoopin' round, you best not. Iff'en I catch ya tryin' ta sneak over there, I'll turn this wagon round first thing in the mornin' and take you right back to Caitlin and tell 'er you can't go cuz ya don't know how to obey me. That's that."

Lily sighed deeply and agreed.

Paul and Ott stood there staring at Mr. Bushy. This was the first time they had ever heard Mr. Bushy speak sternly to Lily Quinn, and they were stunned. Mr. Bushy had known Lily since the day she was born. In fact, next to Lily's little sister Tessa, Lily was probably Mr. Bushy's favorite young'un around, so their eyes and ears were watching and listening wholeheartedly.

"And that goes for the rest of all y'all!" Mr. Bushy said as he turned and glared at Paul, Ott and Olivia. All three of them shook their heads up and down vigorously.

The forest was dark and the moon was full, but by a strange trick of the moonlight the cabin could be seen as clear as if there were no trees at all in the thick forest. It was as if all the leaves on the trees and bushes had rolled themselves up, intentionally giving them a clear view of the ramshackle cabin. Its every feature and detail presented itself before them. It was a time-weathered log cabin with most of its roof falling in; the single door and windows looked as if they were closing sadly, making the little cabin look forlorn and dismal, as if at any moment, it would just give up and crumble into the dirt overcome with sorrow. Its two windows were partially shuttered, giving it the look of half-closed eyes; the top half of the door gaped wide open, revealing a blackness inside which sent goosebumps up their spines. Vines covered the roof, dangling and swaying gently in the early night breeze as they hung over the edge of the eaves like hair hanging over human eyes. The longer the four of them stared at the little cabin, the more sinister it became - until all four of them gave a shiver and pulled their eyes away.

Lily and Olivia shuddered and Olivia drew her blanket close about her shoulders.

"You don't have to worry about any of us going over there, Mr. Bushy," Ott whispered, as if not wanting an unknown creature to hear him as he spoke. "I sure wish we could move on. Just the look of that place gives me the willies."

Mr. Bushy and Mr. Phin looked at each other again.

"I think it's best if we stay here for the night." Mr. Phin spoke softly as he gazed towards the cabin. "Can't take the chance of getting' lost, can we Bushy?"

"Nope, best if we stay put," Mr. Bushy replied.

Mr. Bushy and Mr. Phiney walked away from the four kids and did some whispering. Lily knew neither one of them would get lost along the road in the dark, but she didn't say a word. For some reason the two men thought it best to stay put, and that was probably the right thing to do. One thing for sure, Lily knew she wasn't going to go snooping around *that* cabin in the dark.

Ott and Paul built a nice, big fire in the fire hole they dug, and the four of them sat in silence waiting for the two men to join them. As soon as Mr. Bushy and Mr. Phin sat down, all of them reached for the baskets of food and dug in. Mr. Bushy asked if anyone would like to hear a mountain-man story and all of them mumbled yes between bites of food. And so Mr. Bushy began his telling.

"Not too many years back I was up in the Ozarks visitin' with the hill-folk and havin' a grand old time at one of their shin-digs. It was for the marryin-up of a couple old folks who had never been married-up before. The brides name was Flossie Mae Frederiksen and the grooms name was Clovis Beauregard Filigreed. Flossie Mae was all gussied-up in her nice green dress and Clovis had on one of them tuxedos he'd borrowed from Conner Johnson. Well, Ms. Flossie's ancestors came down from a well-known family of vicious Vikings, and Mr. Clovis' family came here from Ireland right a'fore the 'tater famine and neither one of them wanted to take-on the other'n last name. So just as the reverend started speaking the marryin'-up words, they got ta whisperin' bout who's name they was gonna carry 'round, causin' the reverend to stop talkin' and wait for the two of 'em to decide.

First off Clovis whispered that he wouldn't take on a woman's name iff'en it killed 'em, and then Flossie whispered back, a little louder than was necessary, that there jest might be a killin' cuz she had a good mind to do the deed herself right there on the spot. Well, Clovis arched his eyebrows, gave out a deep chuckle and mumbled somethin' bout her being a woman and prolly couldn't knock a bug off'en a rag rug. Then Flossie took a good hard swing at him with her cane and smacked him upside the head. He teetered on his feet a bit but a young fella jumped up and caught him and steadied him some. Then Clovis said indignantly that iff'en he wasn't such a gentleman he would smack 'er back fur smackin' 'em, then Flossie tol' 'em ta go right on ahead and "go for it" since he wasn't no gentleman anyway, iff'en he thought he was man 'nuf ta do it.

Then, lo-an-behold, Clovis grabbed 'er cane an' took a hefty swing at Flossie, but he missed her and swung all the way 'round and smacked the reverend right upside the head. Well, the reverend went down with a loud thud onta the wood floor, but both Clovis and Flossie ignored the poor fella, as did the whole church congregation cuz they were leanin' forward watchin' and waitin' to see who was gonna make the next move. Well, Clovis yelled out he never told 'er afore but he never was plannin' on takin' on the name of Flossie's no-good, stinkin', Norwegian pirate-granddad, Erik the Evil.

Then Flossie shrieked out that she wasn't gonna take on the name of a tater-bug picker and that now that she had a good look at 'em in the light of the church-house, Clovis looked pretty much like a tater-bug himself. Then Clovis bellowed out that she looked like a 'mater bug in her green and black dress. Then she let go with 'er cane again and caught him by surprise with a sharp poke in the belly. Well, by that time, the reverend was comin' round and just as he pushed himself up onta his hands and knees, Clovis fell down right on top of 'em, and there he went again onta the hard floor with a big "Umpf"! Then Flossie's sister, Dorcas, who by the way was older than Flossie and just as deaf as a door, gets up and starts in smackin' poor ol' Clovis over the head with her cane an' yelling at him to stop pickin' on 'er baby sister. Then Flossie gets upset at Dorcas for "interferin' with her romance" - that's what she yelled out - and told 'er to leave 'er man alone so she could take on some more smackin'. Well, Dorcas thought Flossie said for *her* to take on more smackin' so she starts in hittin' poor ol' Clovis harder."

Mr. Bushy gave out a big belly-shaking laugh.

"Then Flossie leaned down and grabbed Dorcas by the ear and shouted real loud for her to leave 'er man alone, and after 'bout three tries Dorcas got the idea. She stepped back, smoothed down 'er hair and looked at Flossie kindly strange-like and said all Flossie had to do was to say so.

"Well, by that time the dazed reverend was once again up on his feet tryin' ta help Clovis stand up, when in through the church door stormed Maudie Belle MON-roe, who was also as old as dirt. Along behind Maudie came purt-near half her kinfolk from the next holler over, an all them men was carryin' shotguns. Maudie stomped right up to that reverend and demanded to know what in the world was goin' on. But before the poor fella could answer, Flossie jumped right up onta Maudie Belle's back and started in chompin' on Maudie's shoulder-bone and screamin' for her to get away from her weddin' and her man. Well that maddened Maudie's kin-folk, and her younger brother lifted Flossie off'en Maudie's back and stood there holdin' 'er in the air, with her kickin' and screamin' to beat the band, and Maudie whipped 'round and shook 'er finger in Flossie's face and told 'er that Clovis was her man, an' that Flossie best stay away from 'em with 'er chicken and dumplings!

"Then Flossie yelled out that it wasn't 'er cookin' that took Clovis away from Maudie, it was Maudie's stinkin' body odor, and that it was so bad it could chase a pole-cat away from a pile ah manure. She screeched out that Clovis said he couldn't take any more of it cuz she smelled like horse manure!"

Everyone around the campfire was laughing at this point, even Mr. Phin. Mr. Bushy kept telling the story, not waiting for anyone to stop laughing.

"That angered Maudie even more and she yelled back that Flossie Mae smelled like steamin' pig poop on a hot summer day. Then Flossie bit down on the arm of Maudie's brother and he dropped 'er like a sack ah 'taters. Flossie jumped back onta Maudie's back and down they went onta the floor, cuz Maudie was a skinny little woman. They were rollin' round and wrestlin' like two young'uns."

Mr. Bushy couldn't keep the smile off his face.

"Bonnets came flying off and sailin' cross the room. Their fancy skirts was hiked up and their long, Sunday-go-ta-meeting bloomers was there for the entire world to see. Them two ladies was fightin' like tigers. They jumped to their feet and stood there starin' at each other for a couple seconds, breathin' heavy with red, sweaty faces and gaspin' for air. Then with a big shriek, Maudie Belle jumped onta Flossie. Then they started in with the hair pullin' and the arm twistin'. Flossie Mae, who was no little woman, finagled 'round and got skinny ol' Maudie Belle down on the floor, straddled her and started in lettin' drool drip down onta Maudie Belle's face.

"Maudie's older brother Elmer, who was nigh-on to being 104 and had shrunk up ta be short'ern five foot was having a hard time holdin' onta his shotgun, fired off a shot inta the church ceiling, causin' dirt an' wood to shower down on ever'body around 'em. Both the women stopped their screamin' fits and jumped to their feet. But when Elmer tried yellin' at the two of them to stop thur caterwauling, his voice came out jest a bit above a whisper - cuz he was so old an' all then his face turned red as a beet and all of a sudden, he fell over dead, right smack-dab into the reverend! And down went the poor reverend one more time!"

Mr. Bushy started laughing hard; Olivia thought she saw tears coming down his cheeks into his big beard as he bent over laughing.

"That poor fella couldn't get a break!" He said between heaves of laughter.

"I know it ain't proper ta be laughin' at the dead," Mr. Bushy gasped, "but it was the durn'st thing I ever did see! When Elmer fell on top ah the Reverend, Maudie Belle started in wailin' an bawlin' an sayin' she couldn't live without 'er big brother. She turned ta Clovis an' told 'em she needed 'em ta be with her instead of that stinkin' pirate-spawn Flossie Mae Frederiksen, and that she would take a worsh ever' day iff'en Clovis wanted 'er to. All the while the reverend was strugglin' ta roll out from under dead ol' Elmer; finally, Flossie's brother Randolph, came to the rescue and pulled Elmer off'en the fella. Then the preacher-man staggered up with his hair standin' on end and his broken spectacles sittin' cock-eyed on his face. He sighed deeply and wiped his face off with his torn shirttail, then announced in a very loud voice that it was time for ever'body to go on home cuz it looks like thur wouldn't be a marryin' up after all.

"Then Clovis told 'em ta hold on a second and not to be so all-fired anxious to stop the weddin', cuz Clovis needed ta do some ponderin' on the whole thing. So, the reverend backed off from all of them. Flossie Mae and Maudie turned and stared at Clovis, and ever'body else in the church-house got quiet as church mice again and watched in wonder as Clovis did his ponderin'.

"Finally, after a bit of ponderin', Clovis took in a deep sigh and kindly backed away from the two women like maybe he thought he was gonna get smacked with a cane or two again. With a stutter he said, 'Rev - rev - revend, I - I - I'm d - d - d - done pondering'. Then he started tellin' the reverend he reckoned he wanted ta marry-up with Maudie Belle MON-roe, cuz even though she din't smell fresh as a daisy, 'er fried chicken and huckleberry pie was the best in the whole durn country.

"Well, Flossie slammed 'er cane down onta the floor, marched right up to Maudie's twin brother, grabbed ahold of his arm and declared that she came to the church-house to get married-up, an' that's what she was gonna do! She

116

turned around to all the folks an' announced that even though Ernest Hank MON-roe looked like a squirrel who could open her canning jars with his teeth and he din't have a lick ah sense, she was gonna marry-up with him anyways. Well, old Ernest lets out with a big hallelujah, grabs up Flossie an' gives 'er a big ol' kiss right on the lips in front of ever'body includin' the Reverend and the good Lord. Then he gets a great big smile on his face, does a little dance around the pulpit and said he'd been waitin' for Flossie to marry-up with 'em almost seventy years and he din't give a rip iff'en she was a stinkin' pole-cat pirate herself, he loved 'er for years and he was ready to marry-up with 'er.

"Then Maudie Belle calls out to one of 'er younger brothers and ordered 'em to haul Elmer's dead body outta the church-house so she could get on with her marrying-up business without a dead body hangin' 'round causin' bad luck for marryin'-up. She announced that iff'en a woman married-up with 'er true love and a dead body was sittin' in the room it would put a curse on 'em and they'd never be able to have young'uns. Well, I thought to myself that she ain't gonna have no young'uns anyways cuz she's old as Methuselah himself, but that's what she said and ever'body said 'amen' as iff'en they agreed, so's I din't say nary a word.

"So Maudie's brother did as he was told and pulled poor ol' dead Elmer outta the church-house by his heels, sits 'em up real nice-like beside the outside steps, straightens up his shirt and puts his hat back on his head, then props his shotgun up in his arms and puts his trigger finger on the trigger as if he could shoot it off. Then he runs back in so he wouldn't miss anything.

"Now the reverend din't act too surprised by it all. He calmly announced that iff'en it was all settled he would precede with the marryin' up. Clovis, Maudie, Flossie and Ernest all shook their heads yes, so he started in again. He had to keep rubbin' the back of his head with his shirttail, cuz blood kept drippin' down his collar from one of the bumps on his head, but he opened his Bible and married-up the four of 'em real quick-like, prolly hopin' nobody else would come in tryin' to put a stop to it."

"What happened next, Mr. Bushy" Olivia asked softly

"Weeell, all the women folk gathered 'round Flossie and Maudie an started in giving them congrats an commenced to cluckin' like a bunch of hens and all the men folk were standin' round jawin' with Ernest Hank and Clovis talkin' bout farmin' when all of a sudden a shotgun goes off outside the door causin' all of us ta rush to the door to see what was goin on. And there comes Wilbur Cummins runnin' and hoppin' across a pea patch over to the church-house jest cussin' and hoppin' like a one-legged chicken.

Then Wilbur yelled out at the poor dead Elmer sayin', 'What'd ya do that fur, Elmer?' 'Ya shot my dang toe off! I was jest messin' round with ya when I throwed that rock at your gun. I ain't never done nothin' a'tall to ya less'en it was in funnin'. What's the matter with ya?'

"Then Sheriff Booker spoke up and says... 'He's dead, Wilbur, cain't ya see that? Ya aught not be throwin' rocks at nobody 'specially iff'en they're holdin' a shotgun. It ain't respectable and it's your fault the rock hit his trigger finger.'

"Then Wilbur hunkered down real close-like ta Elmer face, looked 'em straight in the dead eyeballs, waved his hand in front ah Elmer's face and gave 'em a little poke in the nose and says; 'Well I'll be ah bug-eyed bull frog, would ya look at that, he's dead, Sheriff. Elmer's is dead! Who kilt'd 'em?'

'Yep', the Sheriff said, 'I done told yaou he was dead. Ain't nobody killed 'em. He just fell over dead. I cain't arrest a dead man so I guess you'll have to buy a new boot ya'self.'

"Then Wilbur yelled at the Sheriff sayin', 'Well, that ain't right a'tall!'

"But the sheriff told 'em there weren't nothin' he could do 'bout it and that he better get on over to Doc Wilson's cuz his toe was bleedin' like a stuck pig."

Mr. Bushy stopped and laughed again before continuing with his story.

"After that, some ah them fellas hauled Elmer's body over to the undertaker and one of Maudie's other brothers picked up Elmer's gun and gave it ta Clovis as a weddin' present then we all start in havin' the weddin' party. By the end of the night Flossie and Maudie were best of friends again but Clovis an Ernest had too much moonshine so we all helped Bubba Crawford carry 'em off across the holler an deposited 'em inta Bubba's house while Maudie and Flossie stayed at the party gossipin' with the women-folk."

Mr. Bushy and Mr. Phiney had a good laugh since both of them knew all the Ozark mountain folks. The laughter died down after a while and the group enjoyed the rest of their food. After eating their fill, Mr. Bushy started up again.

"Let me tell all y'all bout another tale ah the mountains. Lily, I know you already hear'd this'un, but the rest of y'all need to hear it.

"Ya see, young'uns, what I'm gonna tell ya sounds loco, but it is the honest-to-goodness truth! It all started a while back when I was down at my mountain, sittin' outside my cabin gettin' ready to bed down for the night and all. Now, I usually sleep outside my cabin unless it's too cold for a body to last through the night. The fresh air coming through the mountain night is a right fine thing for the body and soul.

Well, it was a fine night to be sleepin' outside 'cuz the breeze was blowin' just 'nuf to keep the skeeters away. So after my horse, Digger, was all set for the night, I et' my supper and got my night fire burnin low, then I lit up my pipe and leaned back against my big oak tree and started listenin' to them crickets and bullfrogs singin' sad love songs to each other. The breeze was blowin' real soft-like, so I just sat thur watchin' as the sweet smellin' smoke from my ol' pipe drifted up and disappeared amongst the trees. Ever so often I'd join in and whistle a tune or two along with them forest critters for a bit. Well, it was gettin' on to be close to the witchin' hour or so."

Mr. Bushy paused a bit. "Now, you young'uns know how those mountains have a soul of their own and all, and many a time I can almost feel it breathin' right beneath me feet. Well, that night, my mountain seemed to be whisperin' in my ears like a bumble bee buzzin' around a daisy. It was as if it was tryin' to wrap me up in a blanket and start in tellin' me secrets. So, I got real quiet like, thinkin' maybe I could hear what she was whisperin', but I couldn't hear nary a thing. Now, I love my mountain and when she talks to me that way I listen and I feel all warm and safe from anything that might be lurkin' round about. So after I listened for a while, I go on ahead and clean up my grub dish and pulled out a blanket, in case the night chill got heavy.

"I rolled up in my blanket and lay down by the warm embers; I weren't really sound asleep, just startin' off being kindly fuzzy in the brain if ya know what I mean, when all of a sudden I feel somethin' tappin' on my shoulder real steady. Tap, tap, tap. Well, I slapped at what I thought was my old horse," Mr. Bushy stopped and demonstrated how he slapped at his horse, "but my hand hit nothing but jest plain 'ole air. I thought to myself that Digger must've just dodged my slap. I didn't even bother opening my eyes none since I was getting' tuckered out and all and din't want to open up my eyeballs. I din't think a thing 'bout it, so I tucked my hand back up under my blanket and went on back to sleep.

"Well, about five minutes later, I reckon it was, the tappin' started in again. Only this time it pert-near pushed me over onto my belly. And that time it was some pretty dad-blame hard thumpin' on my shoulder. Then I got kindly angry with Digger and all, so I whirled around as fast as I could,"

Mr. Bushy whirled around on the ground, demonstrating how he had reacted, "and I yells out, 'Digger, get on out of here, ya bag o' fleas, and leave me be!' Well, it wasn't Digger a'tall," Mr. Bushy whispered as he leaned in about a foot from their faces.

"Right there real close-like to me was none other than a soldier boy looking straight inta my eyeballs. He was lookin' right at me and he had on the

120

whole kit and caboodle of a soldiering uniform. His hair was kindly long and his face was real thin-like, but I knowed right off who he was."

With his hands on his knees, Mr. Bushy leaned back a bit, and said haltingly, "It was Michael Thorne! Yes sir'ree, it sure 'nuf was Michael Thorne himself, as God is my witness.

"Well I jumped right to my feet and put out my hand, wantin' to shake his hand, and I start in talkin'. I said 'Michael my boy, what a fine sight for sore eyes you are. I am right happy to see ya, where ya been boy? Come on over here son, let's have us a sit-down. But first let me give ya ah belly-button-poppin' hug.'

"Well, I reached out to give the boy a belly-button-popper hug, but he steps back and shakes his head, with a smile. Then I knowed right off, this weren't no actual meeting with a long-lost soldier-boy. Something weren't right and I knowed just what was happenin'. I stopped and squinted my eyes a bit to peer at him real close-like, and lo'-an'-behold I could almost see right through him. Not really, but, kindly like. He was all shadowy, kindly like a thick cloud, but it sure 'nuf was Michael. He smiled and spoke to me in that slow, raspy Tennessee drawl of his and says, 'How-do Bushy? How are ya? Sorry, no more belly button poppin' for me. I'm just here to ask ya a favor and then I'll be on my way. I need ya to help find my Caitlin, iff'en ya would.'

"Well, I just stood there with my mouth hangin' down to my own belly button and then Michael said, 'They need your help in finding her, Bushy. I know I can depend on ya. When ya find her and she's safe, tell her that she's in my heart for all eternity.'

"Then he reached up, pulled his soldierin' hat a little further down onta his head, gave me one of them there soldier hat say-lutes, a smile and a nod, and says, 'had a mighty-fine time knowing ya, Bushy. You're a good man.'

"Then, he up and walks away, kindly like meltin' in with the trees and bushes. So there we stood, just me and ole' Digger lookin' like scare't jackrabbits. My heart had jumped right up inta my throat and was dancin' a jig on my tonsils tryin' ta get on outta my mouth. It was poundin' on my eardrums like an Indian war drum, and I was sweatin' like a buffalo in a stampede! Digger had backed up and was just lookin' off into the forest where Michael had melted away."

As Mr. Bushy told his story, he had been acting out each and every action for the five of them.

"It was one of the strangest durn things I ever did see in all my born days. Now, those hill folks say they see spirits and spooks and such all the time and they ain't one bit scare't of' em.

Mr. Bushy leaned close again and whispered, "They say the dead can talk to the livin' and tell 'em things. Now, I always was thinkin' it was just the jibber-jabber of them women-folk, talkin' and squawkin' about everthin'. But now I'm thinkin' there might be some grit to them tales.

"Well after that happened, I rustled up my blanket, kicked some dirt onta them hot coals and hustled myself up onta my porch where I leaned back against the wall and sat watchin' til the early morning hours came on. And long 'bout dawn I saddled up my horse and started down over that mountain to the Quinn's house and that's when I found out Caitlin Quinn had been kidnapped. But, as y'all know by now, she escaped from them folks who took 'er and married-up with Sheriff Beaumont."

Mr. Bushy sat back and sighed a sigh of relief.

"Ya got another tale?" Paul asked anxiously. The Pruiett boys had been sitting completely still, transfixed by Mr. Bushy's stories. Sitting across the fire from them, Lily could see their eyes open wide, tainted red by the flames while Mr. Bushy spoke.

"Okay," Mr. Bushy said. "One last tale an' then we should all get some shut-eye." He waited for a moment to think of the right story to tell. As he sat in silence for a moment, Olivia watched the fire start to die down a little. She felt comforted by the presence of Mr. Bushy and Mr. Phiney, and also by the sound of the crackling fire.

"Alright. A good while back, I was over yonder visitin' them Ozark hill-folk again as I do quite often, and they was havin' a big 'ol shin-dig cuz some more of their kin was marryin'-up. I just happened to be there and they all insisted I stay around. They said it was gonna be the best shin-dig they ever had put on, cuz it was a marrying-up between two old people who had been in love for years and years but lived in different states and had finally got together after all those years apart.

"Well, I obliged and started in havin' me a jolly time; I was dancin' and talkin' and feastin' on some mighty-fine food, cuz them hill folk can make some fine vittles. Well after a bit, lo'-an'-behold I realized I was as drunk as ol' Cooter Brown. So, I decided maybe I should stumble on out into the woods and sleep it off a while. Well, I went and found me a big tree ta lean up against and I no more than had my first dream goin' when purdy soon I felt someone just ah smoochin' away on my face. 'Well this ain't so bad', I'm thinkin' to myself, cuz I'd been dreamin' of pretty little Maggie Mae Tillman who lives over in England. In my sleepy stupor, I'm thinkin', 'what do ya know, here she is just smoochin' on me to beat the band'! So still being half asleep, I start in smilin' and puckerin' up my lips."

Mt. Bushy puckered up his lips like he was giving an exaggerated kiss which made all of them laugh.

"Then I leaned over and wrapped my arms around her neck, jest tryin' to give her the biggest ol' hug and kiss right on her sweet lips. I had a lip-lock on those beautiful lips of hers and I was thinkin' it was pure heaven. Well all of a sudden-like, I hear a loud squealin' straight inta my ear and it purt-near broke my eardrum! It was so loud, my eyeballs started bouncin' around inside my head and it took me a second or two to settle 'em back into my eyeball holes. Well, when I finally managed to get my eyeballs popped open, all I see is a hog

— a big ol' black mama hog just starin' and squealin' at me real close-like with them beady, little eyes and the biggest old snoot I ever did see, pushed right up against my lips. And that there ol' sow's snoot was completely covered with molasses.

"Well I jumped up from that there tree, reached up to wipe my mouth off, and there was molasses all over my face. Then I hear'd some loud snickerin' and looked up to see four of them skinny little mountain fellers, couldn't be more than twelve years old, taking off into the woods, just whoopin' and laughin' their dang heads off, luggin' a big ol' jug of molasses with them. I start in yellin' at them fellers when that dang mama sow runs right into me and knocks me onto the ground as she tried getting away. I'm halfway to gettin' up when that there big ol' hog gets her foot hooked in my 'spenders, and there I go again, but this time I fell right down on top of her. She takes off runnin' like lightnin', and there I am, hangin' on for dear life. She's still gruntin' and squealin' and I start in yellin'. She took off lickety-split for home with me hangin' onta her back like a tick on a dog. My 'spenders won't come off her leg, so all I can do is latch on tight an' hope for the best. That there hog was pert near as long as I am tall, so it was a wild ride. I got my arms hooked around her neck and my legs around her middle and she kept on runnin' straight out. Well after a minute or two, I started in laughin' and couldn't stop cause she was swayin' back and forth and gruntin' with each step she took and I was slippin' an' sliddin' from the left to the right, back to the left and back to the right again. It was the most fun I've had in my whole dang life!"

At this point Mr. Bushy was standing up and acting out his hog ride.

"After about five minutes, that ol' sow just stopped and dropped to the ground. She was dead! Just as dead as old Abe himself. I thank the good Lord on high that I was on her left side when she went down onta her right side. There she lay, just as if I'd bonked her on the noggin' with a hammer. Well, I managed to get my 'spenders off'en her front leg and stood there just lookin' at her and wonderin' what in the world was I gonna do with this big ol' dead hog. I got down on my knees and put my ear to her heart area, and sure 'nuf, no heart beat! I knew right off that whoever owned that hog was gonna be purty dad-blame hoppin' mad-as-a-hornet when they found out thur breedin' sow was a goner. And I also knew some ah them folks would shoot a feller for killin' a big ol' mama hog like that and not bother ta ask nary a question. So I just scurried right on back to the house where the shin-dig was still goin' on full force, grabbed Digger, and high-tailed it right on outta there. I still had molasses all over my face and my 'spenders weren't doin' a very good job of holdin' up my britches, since that hog ride had pulled 'em all apart. But I jumped on 'ol Digger anyways, held my britches up with one hand and the reins with the other and away we went. I don't know iff'en that owner ever did find out what happened to his hog, an' I ain't wantin' to tell 'em."

Mr. Bushy sat laughing so hard his belly was jumping up and down; everyone was laughing so hard their eyes were watering. Ott had fallen over on the ground with tears in his eyes.

As the laughter died down, Mr. Phin spoke up and said he knew who that farmer was. "I happened ta be up in the Ozarks about two weeks afta' that weddin' to do some trading with a couple farmers, and we got ta talking about a farmer named Porter Smith whose hog came up missing. He searched and searched 'til he found her in the forest with her entire head covered with molasses. Porter had no idea how his hog died or how the molasses got all over her head. He had a feeling maybe it was the witch woman who lives down in holler number seven. Porter said she got mad cuz his kids had run all over 'er vegetable garden one summ'ah, an' she said she was gonna put a curse on 'em all.

"But now I know the answer to that puzzle," Mr. Phin laughed. "The same young'uns who destroyed the garden of that witch woman are prolly the same young'uns with the molasses jug."

"Well, don't be tellin' them hill-folk ya know who did it," Mr. Bushy laughed. "They'll be chargin' down that mountain ta get me."

"That's absolutely right, Bushy," Mr. Phin laughed and shook his head. "One time when I was up there I watched some ah them hill fellas take off an' chase a man for three days 'cuz he picked up one ah their young'uns cats. And when they caught up with the fella, they drug 'em back ta thur church-house and made 'em stand up in front of the whole flock ah folks and apologize to the little gal who had been crying for her cat. Then, for the rest of the day they made that thief fella carry that cat 'round in his arms ever'where that little young'un wanted to go. Them hill folk ain't to be messin' round with, I tell ya."

"Ain't that the truth," Mr. Bushy said. "Well young'uns, let's get us some shut-eye so we can get up and leave early in the morning."

Mr. Phin looked at Mr. Bushy asked him if he thought they should take turns keeping watch.

"Well," Mr. Bushy replied as he gazed off towards the dark little cabin, "I'm thinkin' we'll be okay. Whatcha think, Phin?"

"I ain't noticed nary a thing outta place and I been keepin' my eyes open. I'm thinkin' we'll be okay." He looked at the kids. "All you young'uns pile up on top ah my wagonload ah furs and all y'all will be fine. Iff'en ya get chilly during the night, just cover up with one ah them furs, it'll keep ya warm."

"Okay, thanks, Mr. Phin," Ott and Paul called out as the four of them scrambled to the wagon.

After they were settled on top of the pile of furs, Olivia leaned over and whispered into Lily's ear, "Ya think there's something going on over there at that old cabin?"

"I don't know," Lily whispered back, "but I'm not going to go check it out. That cabin gives me the creeps."

126

"Me too," Ott whispered as he shook his head. "Ain't that right, Paul? Something about that cabin just ain't right, is it? I've been looking over yonder at it the whole time we sat around the campfire and something about it just ain't right."

"That's right Ott," Paul said softly. "Gives me the willies just lookin' at it too. Kindly like it's alive or something, huh? Like maybe anytime now it will start in moving up and down as it breathes. Freaky is what it is!"

All four of them lay on top of the furs with their chins resting on the side of the wagon rails staring at the log cabin. Mr. Phin and Mr. Bushy had stopped feeding the fire and were now lying around the smoldering embers waiting for sleep to catch up with them. Gradually all of them drifted off to sleep.

Slowly something drew Olivia out of her dreams. She felt a presence between herself and Lily; when finally she opened her eyes, there, nestled down amongst them was Periwinkle, the haint dog, and he was all snuggled up like he belonged there.

Gently, Olivia put her hand on his paw, and sure enough, she was able to feel him as if he were a living dog. Periwinkle's whole body glowed in a soft hue of green and with the slightest movement of air sparkles floated from his fur like snowflakes lightly falling from the sky.

"Hello, Periwinkle," Olivia whispered softly.

Periwinkle's fluffy tail began flopping up and down, showering green sparkles into the air. Then he stopped, raised his head and began letting out a low, throaty growl. It began very soft, barely loud enough for Olivia to hear it, but then it grew a bit louder and Periwinkle rose up onto his legs. He was looking towards the log cabin. In a flurry of shimmering bits of light, he jumped down from the wagon bed. Olivia watched closely as he stood beside the cold fire pit, and slowly the green outline of his body began to fade away, leaving only a faint outline of the dog. When the faint outline disappeared,

Periwinkle slowly skulked into the forest; the only way Olivia could tell he was headed for the cabin was by the green sparkles shooting up out of the high grass and underbrush growing along the perimeter of the campsite.

Looking up towards the cabin, Olivia's eyes grew wide and fear clinched her heart; both windows were aglow with candles hanging inside, giving off shadowy orbs of light. The open part of the busted door revealed one single candle suspended from nothing at all in the middle of the room. Olivia watched as the candle began floating on its own, moving from one area to another as if searching for something. The candle stick itself could be seen perfectly, but whoever was holding it was invisible.

Olivia gave Lily a nudge to wake her up. Immediately Lily's eyes popped open but she did not move.

"Is it safe to move?" she whispered softly.

"Yes," Olivia mouthed back, "but be quiet about it."

"What's going on?" Lily asked as she slowly and carefully rolled over and placed her chin on the edge of the wagon rail.

"Look over at the log cabin. Something strange is going on. There's a candle floating in each window and there's another one kind of hovering in the room and moving about."

Lily eased her head around and looked at the log cabin. The candles weren't giving off enough light to make out anything else inside the room, but something or someone must have lit them.

Silently the two of them lay watching and listening. Then, without opening the closed bottom half of the door, out floated a line of beings dressed in black, hooded capes with a single lit candle floating above their heads. There looked to be about ten of them and they all looked alike: heads covered by hoods, bodies stooped over as if they were very old men. Olivia could hear the sound of their feet scuffling on the dirt path.

128

Lily's heart began to beat a rhythm on her ear drums and the palms of her hands instantly became sweaty. "Mother of Moses," she mumbled softly.

"Oh, Lord have mercy," Olivia murmured. "Should we wake up Mr. Phin and Mr. Bushy?"

"We're watchin'," came a soft whisper from the edge of the wagon. "Just hold tight, don't breathe a whisper and we'll see what happens. Real slow-like, all of ya hunker down inta them furs."

Shifting her eyes to the side, Lily saw Ott and Paul peeking over the top of the wagon rail as they too lay watching the same as she and Olivia were doing. Then slowly and quietly the four of them squirmed their way deeper into the furs until each of them were watching through the wide crack between the rail boards.

The moon filled the forest with light, so Lily knew the figures could see their camp site quite clearly. They continued shuffling slowly along the path, and then began humming. At first it was a low, droning, murmuring sound, but it intensified in volume until it reached a high-pitched tone which made Olivia's ears ring. Slowly they turned towards the campsite and stopped when the leader reached the edge of the clearing. Lily heard Mr. Bushy and Mr. Phin ratchet their shotguns, and without even looking she knew both of them had their pistols handy.

Not taking her eyes off of the creatures, she saw Mr. Bushy's hand reach through the opening between the rail boards and hand Ott and Paul each a hand gun.

"Don't shoot 'em off, boys', less'en I tell ya to," he muttered.

The quiet of their surroundings seemed deafening. The moon slipped behind the clouds, leaving only a sliver of light shining down upon them. As Lily stared at the cloaked beings, all she could see was the dark outline of their hooded bodies and the single candles which floated above their heads as if dangling from strings in the clouds. It was so quiet for a moment, a pin dropping on the soft grass could have been heard, but the distant, lonely howl of wolves slipped slowly through the air and made its way through the forest trees.

Suddenly Olivia noticed the form of Periwinkle beginning to take shape beside the smoldering embers of the fire pit. His fur was standing on end and a snarl rumbled deep within his chest. The beings slowly inched forward towards Periwinkle, their feet creating little puffs of dust as they shuffled; Mr. Phin and Mr. Bushy inched closer to the wagon until there they were right beside the four young'uns on the mountain of furs.

Watching cautiously, the six of them stared at the scene being played out in front of them. As the hooded figures closed in on him, Periwinkle's snarl became a growl, which turned into an aggressive roar unlike any other sound ever to came out of a dog. Then, with a bounding leap, he sprang upon them and the battle began.

There were green sparks flying everywhere; the sky around the campsite was filled with fireworks. All the candles had vanished, and in their place Lily could see the milky-pale hands of the beings. Periwinkle ripped the hood off one of the creatures, and there was nothing but a mass of snowy, white hair where its head should have been.

Then, like magic, four wolf ghosts jumped into the melee. It became a massive tangled ball of black hooded beings and glittering animal ghosts. Green sparks were shooting out of the writhing ball of thrashing arms, legs and animals as they hovered above the now blazing fire pit. Black hooded cloaks were being ripped apart, revealing nothing but pale, barely visible creatures with white hands and wild, silvery hair. Hands were snatching and grabbing at the animals, and each animal - including Periwinkle - was latched onto one of the hands which had been flailing madly about. Every hand which was not held firmly in a beast's mouth was pulling out shimmering fur by the handfuls. Periwinkle chomped down onto the hand he held between his ghost jaws and bit off two fingers. The partially invisible being threw its silvery-white hair back, revealing a gigantic mouth with three rows of enormous teeth, and screeched like a banshee. As soon as that creature screamed, there appeared Polly Susannah, the little girl-haint Lily had met when she, Ophelia and Gertie P. had been stranded in a cabin deep in the woods of Mississippi after escaping from the slave traders.

Just as before, Polly Susannah had one side of her hair cut off short, just like her dog Periwinkle. She was still glittering with the sparkly, flickering lights of a haint. She put her hands on her hips and shook a stern finger at Periwinkle.

"Periwinkle!" She yelled, stomping her foot against the packed earth and causing the fighting to come to an instant halt with all the creatures staring at her.

"Get over here and make haste doing so. I told you to stop playing with those troublemaking wolves. What are you doing? Leave off bothering those evil haints. We are supposed to be hunting for that gentleman's treasure. Come hither this instant or I shall have to tell Papa and he will not be happy." Then she stomped her foot again. "And you black evil spirits, get out of here this instant."

Immediately Periwinkle slinked away from the brawl so low his belly brushed along the grass. He crept over to where Polly Susannah stood with his head hung low as if he had been caught in an act of disobedience.

"Come on, you silly pup," she said to him. "Let's go do some hunting."

When she turned to leave, Periwinkle looked back at Olivia, and to their surprise the dog grinned with his big tongue hanging out of the side of his mouth. He did a little jumping and scampering around a bit, all the while looking at Olivia like he was showing off again before taking off in a mad-dash after Polly Susannah. The rest of the tangling mass of creatures hovered over the fire pit all bedraggled and in silence for a few seconds then once again began their vicious fight with snarling and pulling of fur and hair as they floated off into the night.

"Don't move yet, young'uns," Mr. Bushy whispered as the blazing fire went out with a quick sizzle.

Silently, without moving their bodies, the four of them cautiously moved their eyes back to the cabin. There, walking out the door, were four big-muscled, flesh-and-bone men carrying a large, long box heading in the opposite direction of their campsite. Lily was quite sure they had not noticed the campsite because they were talking loudly in a foreign language as they seemingly laughed and chided each other. When finally they too vanished down a slope, the little cabin was once again cloaked in dark and all was silent except for the usual night sounds.

"What's going on in that log cabin, Mr. Bushy?" Ott asked quietly.

Sure that they were now safe, Mr. Bushy whispered back, "Well, let me be tellin' ya."

All four of them turned and looked at Mr. Bushy as he sat up on the pile of furs and cleared his throat.

"Many years ago," he said as he hesitated and lit his pipe, "or so it's told, that cabin belonged to an old gypsy woman who went by the name of Anelka Romani. Anelka is the name of an old African gypsy and Romani is the name of the Romani gypsy band that came from Bulgaria many, many years ago. Anelka and her gypsy band crossed the ocean and made their way inta Missour'ah in the seventeen hundred's where they settled here on this land. Gossip says Anelka's husband Plamen dug gold out of the side of the hill in the back of the log cabin and it's said that still today, in the back wall of the cabin is a big hole where thieves and highwaymen dig for gold. But also, it's supposed to be guarded and haunted by the ghost of Plamen and Anelka.

"Tis said that back in 1781, word got out that Plamen and Anelka had found gold in their hills, and so four thieves came 'long and did away with Plamen. But Anelka hid behind the chimney where Plamen had carved out a hidey-hole and she watched the thieves murder her husband. The thieves tried and tried to make Plamen tell them where Anelka was hidin', but he refused to tell the miserable buzzards and so he saved her life. It was three days before the thieves left, but Anelka stayed in that hidey-hole listening and watching. Finally, when they were gone, Anelka crawled out of her hidey-hole and set to work putting a curse on all the thieves. One by one ever' last one ah them thieves died a cruel death. For one month, every Sunday, one more thief would pass on.

"And not too many months back, I met another old, old gypsy woman in these hills and she told me the tale of Anelka and Plamen. She's the one who warned me never to set foot in that cabin iff'en I ever came upon it in my trappin' travels. And, as a matter of fact, many times while I've been trappin' I saw that old cabin but I never did go inside. I've seen lights floatin' round 'bout it and strange happenings going on while sleeping in these very woods, but I ain't never gone inside even iff'en I have ta stay outside in a storm. And I've seen many a group ah men go in and out, haulin' boxes of gold, but ever'time that happens, just like tonight, within a week or two I always get word that those very men end up goners. I guess ya cain't be stealin' and get 'way with it and ever last mountain-man I know knows not ta go inta that cabin."

Mr. Phin nodded his head in agreement.

"How 'bout you, Phin? You heard any tales 'bout that cabin?"

"Yep," Mr. Phin replied in a whisper, "I have me a tale ah my own. Once'st I was over yonder on the hill overlookin' the cabin and I saw some thieves sneakin' in during the dead of night, pulling four pack mules along with 'em. They went inside that cabin and as soon as they stepped across the front stoop the door slammed shut behind them, and boom! the cabin burst inta flames and started in burning like the blue blazes. Them pack mules took off runnin' and never looked back. That fire burned way inta the night but din't catch a tree, grass or a single weed on fire. I sat there beside my bedroll for a long time, watching that fire until I fell sound asleep and started in dreamin'. In my dream I was sittin' at an old kitchen table with a fire blazing in the middle of it, and there across from me was old Anelka herself. I couldn't feel the heat from that fire, and I could see her plain as day through the flames, but the fire was there. She had all the gypsy dress things on, big ol' round earrings and rings on each finger and a babushka wrapped around her head. Her clothes were bright red, green, and blue and she was staring at me with black, beady eyes. Then she started in tellin' me she wasn't ever gonna bother me, cuz she knew I wasn't a thief and would show respect to her cabin. She told me I best be careful when it came ta thieves an' robbers, 'cuz the trail to her cabin was full of 'em lurkin' round ever' tree. But if I stayed away from her cabin, she said she would make sure they stayed away from me. I din't say one single word, I jest watched 'er and listened. Then slowly she faded away and my mind started in dreamin' bout somethin' else.

"So that's what I do. I ain't never gonna go inside that cabin either, and I try my best to take the night somer's else besides this part of the woods."

"Same here, Phin" Mr. Bushy whispered.

"Well anyway," Mr. Phiney continued, "the next mornin' I woke up and the log cabin looked like it hadn't been touched a'tall, much less burned up! Nary a branch nor twig was burned by that fire and the smell ah smoke wasn't even there. So, I packed up my gear and left because I din't want my curiosity to overcome my sense and lead me inta that cabin. When I reached Memphis, the town was abuzz with the news of four mules, in the dark of night, brayin' an hee-hawin' so loud they woke up ever'body within hearing range. They stampeded through town with clouds of smoke followin' 'em down the street like it was chasin' after 'em. The town folk were so shocked to see such a sight they din't even think 'bout catchin' 'em. They jest looked out their winders and watched 'em run straight through town and headed down the road towards Natchez. I guess when they ran past Billy Butcher's farm, all that brayin' and hee-hawin' straight away woke him up and he jumped out of bed, grabbed his hat and took off out the door in his long-johns. Right off he recognized them four mules as his own that he had put up in the barn earlier that night so he took off after 'em yellin' and a'screamin' for 'em ta stop but that cloud of smoke surrounded 'em and he couldn't see a durn thing, so he said he just stopped, threw down his hat in disgust and went back home and crawled inta bed.

"The funny thing is, a month later when I was down in Na'leens sittin' in a say-loon talkin' ta some fellas, they got ta telling me 'bout four mules that came rip-snorting 'long the levee top, being chased by a cloud ah smoke, and ran right inta the Gulf ah Mexico and started in swimming for Mexico. Ain't nobody seen 'em since."

Mr. Bushy and Mr. Phiney did some good laughing.

"Now," Mr. Bushy said as he looked straight at Lily, "Getting' back to this here cabin, I truly din't want ta camp here last night cuz I know full well how nosey you are, Miss Lily-Beth Quinn. I was scared ta death you was gonna take off and go snoopin' round like you usually do. I'm mighty grateful to ya that ya paid heed to my warnin'. Sometimes it's best to take heed to a warnin'."

Mr. Phin and Mr. Bushy continued lying on top of the animal skins with their pistols beside them until all six of them were sleeping soundly. Daylight crept slowly across the mighty Mississippi. Except for the slow spiral of Mr. Phin and Mr. Bushy's pipe smoke curling lazily up through the treetops, the campsite lay in peaceful stillness. The new morning was soothing as fresh, cold buttermilk as the two of them sat in silence listening to the breaking of the new day. Small day-critters scurried and rustled through the short brush as they began their hunt for food. Off in the distance the two men heard the faint, gurgling music of a small stream tumbling through its rocky bed, rushing with joyful babbling down to the mighty Mississippi river.

The sun quietly eased itself up over the horizon.

"Good morning, Missour'ah!" Paul yelled out loudly as he sat up and jumped down from the wagon bed.

"Shut-up Paul," Ott mumbled. "It's too early for that yelling stuff."

Lily and Olivia continued to lay there for a few more minutes before they too jumped down from the wagon.

"Come on, Ott," Paul reached into the wagon bed and gave Ott a flick on his ear.

"Ok," Ott muttered as he grabbed Paul's hand and gave it a tweak in return, "Ya wanna wrestle? I'm getting up. I'm hungry."

"I'll wrestle ya," Paul said cheerfully.

Ott jumped down and the two boys began rolling around on the ground until Mr. Bushy told them to stop and have something to eat.

"Okay," they both said between gasps, "I'm hungry."

Mr. Bushy laughed and motioned for all of them to go ahead and grab something out of the food baskets.

"Let's get on out of here," Ott said quickly as he remembered what had happened the night before. "This place is creepy, ain't that right Paul?"

"Yep, it is," Paul mumbled through a mouth full of biscuit. "And we ain't wanting to go through that again, are we Ott?"

"Nope!"

After cleaning up their campsite, Ott and Paul jumped into Mr. Bushy's wagon as Lily and Olivia hopped up beside Mr. Phin's, and once again they moved on closer to Memphis.

9

Anglesey Island

(As told to Lily and Olivia by Mr. Phiney)

Lily and Olivia sat quietly on the hard, wooden bench-seat of Mr. Phin's buckboard wagon for a good, long time listening to him whistling a merry little tune which neither one of them recognized.

"Would you mind telling us another haint story, Mr. Phin?" Olivia asked timidly.

"Mind?" Mr. Phin looked over and laughed cheerfully, "That's the reason I'm alive. Anytime y'all want a haint story you just ask, an' I'll oblige."

"Ok!" both girls said at the same time.

"Well," Mr. Phin began, "Now this here is a true story. Not too many years back I traveled across the ocean on a big ship to visit a fella I knew who lived in the village of Llanfairpwllgwyngyll on the Anglesey Island that lies along the coast of Wales in cheery ol' England. Now, I know Llanfairpwllgwyngyll is a mouthful, but that's what they call it. And why they call it 'cheery ol' England' is beyond me," Mr. Phin said as he shook his head. "It ain't cheery a'tall, iff'en ya ask me; it can be downright bitter cold there and it rains so much you'd be thinkin' Noah's Ark was gonna come floatin' alongside ya ever' hour of the day. But, I do have to say, in the summertime, them green fields of England are a sight to behold. There's nothing prettier than a field full of wild flowers.

"Anyway, let me get back to my story. I arrived in the little village of Llanfairpwllgwyngyll on a rickety old ferry boat I took from Wales. I was sure this boat was gonna end up in the drink, but we made it. The capt'n of the ferry hustled me off really quick-like, seeing' I was his only passenger, and tells me not ta dilly-dally along the way but ta hustle on inta the place I was staying then he din't even give me time ta say a proper thank you before he turned that ferry around and chugged back across. He din't wait ta see iff'en a passenger was waitin' ta go back across the way, and he din't even lower the gangplank for me to get off. He just had a big, burly fella hop on shore, reach over and jerk me and my travelin' bag across the openin', then he gave me a slight shove afore he jumped back on the ferry. He had to jump over a widening gap too as the captain was already pulling away! It was a bit from being dark and I had a long walk up the hill to my friend John Smith's cottage, but it was a right-nice evenin' so I took my time wanderin' about the village lookin' at several pubs and small cottages.

"When finally I started up the path ta John's place, it was gettin' on towards dark and the only pub left before I entered the woods was the Slippery Eel on the corner of 4th and Chestershire. That was when I started seeing dark shadows darting here and there between the buildings. I kindly shook it off, figgerin' it was some wild young'uns tryin' ta spook folks as they walked along the way. It was kindly strange though, cuz the day was far from being totally over, but folks started puttin' out their lanterns and fires 'til there wasn't a single light in the village and nary a soul walkin' or scurryin' about, and ever' cottage and business was closed up tight and dark as a dungeon. Well, I stepped inta the Slippery Eel 'cuz I seen a faint light inside and I told the grizzled old barkeep I'd take a pint an a biscuit iff'en he had any.

"Well, as I sat there waiting for my pint, I looked around the pub and nay a soul was there 'cept me and the ol' barkeep. When he shuffled back with my pint and biscuits I asked him where all the folks happened ta be, and then he looked at me kindly strange-like as he shook his head, frowned and says they're all home with thur winders closed an' locked, the same way I should be.

"The old fella stood there staring at me with his green, watery eyes and his white hair stickin' up like he'd been struck by lightnin', and then with his shaky, misshapen hands slipped the pint and biscuits down in front ah me.

"What's with ya, chap? Be ye off your trolley?" He said as he leaned across the bar glarin' at me with eyes bugged out, looking at me as iff'en I was plumb loco, "Cain't ye tell they're comin' quick?"

"'Who's comin' quick?' I said to the old fella.

"'The fog, my boy, the *fog*! Be ya daft?' he graveled as he looked at me like I was crazy. 'Tis the devil's fog coming upon us. Did ya not see the wispy fingers of evil slithering round-about in the alleyway, or the dark shadows lurking and darting about out of the corner of ye eyes? Ye can never catch 'em looking straight on at 'em, it's always in the shadows of one's eyes.'

"Well, I shook my head and told 'em I hadn't never heard 'bout the devil's fog, cuz I jest got off the ferry an' was goin' for a visit with my friend further up onta the hill, and then his eyes got wide then turned inta squinted slits and he asked me where I was stayin' for the night. I told 'em I was goin' on out ta John's cottage 'cuz I figgered I could make it in no time a'tall and I was stayin' for a month-long holiday or so. Then the ol' guy said that wouldn't do a'tall and shook his head vigorously and proceeded ta tell me that I best be stayin' right there in the pub for the night cuz he wasn't steppin' a toenail out that pub door. An' since it was now on ta being full dark, he wasn't gonna let me leave, cuz that fog would zip right inside really quick-like when a door or winder was cracked.

"I looked at 'em real close and his eyes tol' me he was downright serious, so I tol' 'em I'd stay the night but I din't have even a ha'penny ta give 'em, cuz I gave 'em all the money I had for the pint an' biscuits an' was plannin' on doin' some odd jobs 'round town ta earn my way while I stayed at

John's. Well, he said he din't care 'bout the money, he cared 'bout losin' his hide and iff'en I opened that door that devils fog would snatch us both up right quick-like an' we'd we goners.

"Well, I asked 'em what-in-tarnation was the devil's fog, and then he told me the tale. It seems as if in Ireland during the time of the *Dark Ages*, a devil's fog would roll in along the coast. Its misty fingers rolled slowly into the small villages as it covered ever'thin within its grasp. It snatched up people, dogs, cats and any animal it came across. After a night of the devil's fog, folks would find other folks wandering the streets aimlessly with seemingly no brains a'tall; their eyes would be blank and lifeless, kindly like they was scared inta stupidity, like their souls had been grabbed right outta their bodies."

"Mr. Phin," Lily whispered as she leaned over Olivia to look at him, "Mr. Bushy told me about that devil's fog a while back. That was pretty scary. Ya think it's true?"

"I tol' ya these were true tales, ever mountain man in the Ozarks knows about 'em. You can ask me, Mr. Bushy or ol' Jeremiah 'Liver-eatin' Johnson himself, and ever' last one of us will tell you the same tale. Even my friend Pierre Charron from France, who I tol' Olivia about yesterday," he looked over at Olivia, "knows them true-tales comin' outta Ireland."

Lily leaned back against the bench rail and shivered even though it was warm as toast and her back was sweating.

"Well," Mr. Phin continued, "Real quiet-like, that barkeep slid the bolts on his door and winder an doused his lanterns, then motioned for me to foller 'em up the stairs to his livin' quarters. It was slow goin' cuz the old fella could barely get up each step, so on the way he started in tellin' me his name was Aled Gruffudd and that Aled means "from the unknown ages". When finally we got to the top of those windin' stairs an' he slid open the door to his sleepin' place, it was like walkin' inta a knights room ah weapons. Ever kind ah weapon a body could imagine was hangin' on his walls, and he had this massive bed in one corner an' a table that I swear was nigh onta being a hun'erd years old sitting in the other corner.

"But anyways, he signaled for me ta be real quiet then took off'en his boots an' tiptoed to a winder overlookin' the street below, all the time gesturin' for me ta foller 'em. So, I go ahead and take off my own boots and follered 'em to the winder real quiet-like and looked out ta have myself a good look-see.

"Sure 'nuf, that fog was movin' slow as a snails-crawl all over them streets and when it reached a buildin' or a cottage, *zap!* it swoller'd it up like a lizard snappin' up a fly. It was mighty strange, I tell ya. Well, we were pretty high above that lil' village and I watched with alarm as that village became nothing but a blanket ah fog. Then that devil's fog started movin' faster, rollin' and tumblin' like a blanket ah snowy-white tumble weeds, and it made its way up the hill like it had eyes of its own an' knew thur was one more buildin' it could devour, and that was the Slippery Eel. Old Aled quickly shut the shutters on the winder then we both felt our way across that lil' room to the two chairs sittin' round the old table. Quick as a wink he lit a candle that looked as old as the table then he looked back at the shuttered winder. His eyes were green as gourds and seemed to be flashin' sparks. I blinked my own eyeballs a few times thinking it was just me, but his eyeballs kept right on sparkin'. They had turned from the old eyes of an ancient barkeep to the eyes of an alert, young fella. Then he ripped off'en his hat and threw it across the room, then lo'-an'-behold, his hair was not hoary white a'tall - it popped out inta a big, red, bushy head ah hair just as red as an Irishman's.

"Then in a whispery, eerie growl he turned his glarin' stare away from that winder and looked me straight in the eyes an' asked me why was I there an' why had I stopped at the Slippery Eel. I looked at him for a bit as I tried ta get over my surprise and wrangle some sense back inta my brain and then I swoller'd hard and repeated my story 'bout visitin' my friend John Smith. Then with a loud crash, he slammed his fist down on the table top with the force of a hammer, pulled a pistol out from under his coat, pointed it at me and told me John Smith had died many months ago and ever'body who knew John was aware of it. Well, I kindly jumped when he slammed the top ah that table, cuz he did it with the power of ah young man. Then I shook my head an tol' 'em John Smith senior had died but I was sure-a-shootin' my friend John Smith Jr. was still livin'. Then I tol' 'em where I was from and pulled out the letter John had sent me nigh on six months back askin' me ta come visit 'em. Well, the fella grabbed the letter and held it up to the candle so he could read it. Then he very slowly lowered it onto the flame and set it a'far, watching it burn 'til it was nothin' but ash.

"After doing that, he looked back at me an' tol' me never to tell a soul I knew John Smith, cuz I would get myself hung iff'en I did, and he also told me that John Smith Jr. was a goner too. Then he said he was pow'ful sorry ta have insulted me but he had ta be sure as ta who I was cuz thur was some strange thin's going on in the village. Well, I was beginning ta think *he* was the strange thin' goin' on in the village.

"Then the buildin' started in shakin' an' shimmyin' as if it was strainin' ta stay upright. My feet was bouncin' up an down like they was doin' a dance and I purt-near fell off'en my chair.

"Then, right there before my eyes, that ol' man laid his hands on either side ah that table, bowed his head and mumble-jumbled some strange-soundin' words, an' started in shakin' like he had the palsy. Then that ol' barkeep turned inta a haint!"

Mr. Phin looked over at Olivia and Lily with his eyes wide as if to say, "Can you believe it?"

"Well, just in a flash, he became the biggest haint of a Viking I ever did see. He wasn't an ol' barkeep's haint. He was a Viking and he was ugly as mud. His head was gigantic with big ol' teeth shinin' brightly in the light ah that little candle, his nose was so big it spread purt-near all the way 'cross his face and his mouth was wide open in a jolly smile like he was happy as a lark in the mornin'. His entire face was covered with hun'erts ah freckles and his ears were so big they stuck out the sides ah his head like the handles stickin' out on a jug. But the merry look in his eyes was what puzzled me up. I couldn't figger out why the haint fella was so dang - oh, pard' my language, gals - happy! There was some peculiar thin's goin' on outside and I sure wasn't feelin' too happy at the moment, but he was! Then that haint snatched up a metal helmet with ram's horns coming out of each of its sides and then he rammed it onta his head. It had a shiny metal piece hanging down covering part of his big fat nose for protection. He was a big, muscled fella with shoulders wide as a barn draped in bear fur, and over all that fur stuff hung one of them Viking mails. That's a wire, shirt-like mesh-thing hangin' from the sides of his helmet down to his knees. His boots were made of leather with fringes hanging on the tops and in his hands he held a kite-shield an' some strange-lookin' weapons. He gave me a pow'ful poke on the shoulder and danced a lil' jig, then in a deep, excited voice announced that he was off to fight the wizard of the devil's fog.

"Now I ain't tellin' ya no made-up tale, that fella started in fadin' away 'til all that was left ah him was a shadowy outline and his massive teeth shinin' like the moonlight. Fear started raisin' up in my belly and it seeped deep inta my bones, causing my blood to turn to ice. Then in a boomin' voice he bellows out, 'Don't be leaving this place'. Then, quick as a far-fly flash he flew out between the cracks in the winder and vanished inta the fog, and all I could hear was him roarin' the roar of a madman an' then the clankin' of swords slammin' against each other."

Lily and Olivia sat there grinning and staring at Mr. Phin for a few minutes before asking him what he did after the phantom left.

"Well," he laughed as he looked at them grinning, "Don't y'all be laughin' at my tale. This here is a true tale. I stayed right where I was, 'cuz I sure wasn't gonna go outside and risk my neck, that was for sure, and I sure din't want ta cross that Viking haint. But, outside that winder, the wind picked up and it whirled and blew like the blue blazes 'round and 'round that place, howlin' like a banshee. When I finally got my head and brain back inta workin' order, I stood up and walked over to the winder and, real careful-like, I took me a peek through a crack and all I could see was dirt and rubbish swirlin' round that building like a cyclone. I stayed there for a few, watchin' that turmoil goin' on and then I saw Aled come flyin' 'round the corner of the building chasing a wizard haint. It was the strangest thin' I ever did see. They were slashin' and strugglin' with each other like two vicious warriors. Then Aled looked in my direction and the evil eye he gave me made it clear that I wasn't ta be lookin'. So with no hesitation I moved away from the winder and walked over to the bed and had me a rest. Within what seemed like just a few minutes, someone smacked me on the head with a rag and yelled at me ta get up and be on my way. When I opened my eyes, there stood Aled and he had turned back inta that ol' barkeep. I sat there looking at 'em for a few, then he says for me to shut my gapin' mouth and foller 'em downstairs so he could give me a spot ah hot tea and a few scrambled eggs with eel. Then he said that was all he was gonna do for me and I should be thankful for his generosity. Then he said it was best if I be on my way back ta wherever I came from.

"Well, that's just what I did. I din't asked 'em nary a question. I got myself up, went down the stairs to the pub, drank some bitter hot tea, gobbled up a big plate of eggs an' eel and took off down the road to the dock, cuz I wasn't gonna even bother goin' up ta John's cabin. I was fearin' for my life. That lil' village was a'buzz with people goin' bout doin' this and that like nothing a'tall strange had happened. I got on the first ferry that came into the port and as I was standing by the rail watchin' the ferry pull away I overheard some folks talkin' bout some fella walkin' through town and goin' inta the old abandoned Slippery Eel Inn the night before, and they was curious as to what happened to the fella during the night. One fella said he was sure he had seen the man wonderin' out inta the forest with a hole in his chest where his heart used to be and then a woman said she had looked out her winder during the fog and seen the poor man being dragged away by those dark shadows. Well, I din't say nary ah thing to any of 'em, I just high-tailed it back to the States. And that was the end ah that adventure."

"Well," Lily asked curiously, "did you ever find out what happened to your friend John Smith?"

"Yep."

There was a minute of silence.

"Well..." Lily leaned across Olivia and looked at Mr. Phiney with a frown, "What happened to him?"

"Well, three months after getting' back ta Missour'ah I got another letter from John askin' me why I hadn't made it to see 'em, since I had written 'em and tol' 'em ta be expectin' me. I was kindly puzzled up by that letter and figgered it musta been written by someone oth'ern John, but when I dug up some letters he had written in the past and had me a good look-see, I could tell it was actually written by John himself. So, I wrote 'em back an tol' 'em what had happened and then another few months went by an' I got his return letter, askin' iff'en I had been a wee bit sick in the head, cuz the Slippery Eel had burned down nigh on a hun'ert years past. Well, I wrote back an assured 'em I was not off-in-the-noggin, so to speak, and that I had actually been there and had, indeed, took the night in the old Slippery Eel Inn where I talked with that ol' barkeep Aled Gruffudd and I told 'em right there on paper that I wasn't ever again gonna step foot on Anglesey Island, nor any other English island for that matter. Well, finally I got another letter from John and he told me ol' Aled had been dead neigh-on two hun'ert years back and that rumor was that he still haunted his old pub and lured folk in so he could tell them the tales of his warring with other bad haints!

"So that settled it, I wrote and told John I wasn't gonna go over there again and to this day I ain't gonna set foot on that island!"

Mr. Phiney shivered and said he never wanted to do that again.

"Tell us about your family treasure that was supposed to be under Elijah Bonheur's front stoop. Do you know what might in in it? Are we gonna hunt for it, Mr. Phin?" Olivia asked quietly.

Phineas saw the excitement in Olivia's face. He laughed and scratched his head, pondering the idea. He told them that he had no idea what might be inside the box and explained to them how he had not found the box when he dug up the front stoop. "But iff'en you want, give it a go," he said. Olivia and Lily looked at each other and smiled. That was exactly what they hoped to hear.

10

Mr. Bushy's Tales

(As told to all of them by Mr. Bushy himself)

By nightfall, the two wagons had reached their next campsite and all of them set about making camp. Ott and Paul found wood for the fire as Lily and Olivia brought out the rest of the edible food, while Mr. Bushy and Mr. Phin tramped into the forest in search of a rabbit or a couple of squirrels.

After gobbling down a roasted rabbit and the rest of the food, they all leaned back and heaved a sigh of contentment. Ott and Paul rubbed their stuffed stomachs, then as if they had planned it, burped loudly at the same time.

"That's disgusting," Olivia and Lily laughed. "Mind your manners!"

Ott and Paul laughed, then forcing more air out of their chest they both burped out a loud "*Oookaaay*", then fell back onto the ground laughing.

"Well," Mr. Phiney said after he stopped laughing, "I guess we'll have to hunt up some pheasant eggs for breakfast in the mornin' since we were all such pigs and gobbled up ever' last bit of food we brought along."

"Okay," Mr. Bushy said. "Let's clean this up and I'll tell ya another tale."

Quick as a wink, the four of them cleaned the campsite then sat on some bear skins around the fire.

"Well, this here story happened a while back. Lily-Beth, I know you hear'd most ah this story a'fore, but you're gonna hear it again." Mr. Bushy laughed loudly.

"I was off on the other side of the Ozarks doing some trappin' and such. It was only me, Digger and an ol' pack-mule I named Cuss, 'cuz all he understood was cuss words! Well, I had to take that old mule along with us 'cuz we just couldn't haul all them hides by ourselves and at that time I din't have a wagon. Well, anyway, we had just come away from that there big Ozark Lake and was headin' down the side of the mountain, when that ol' mule stopped and wouldn't go another step. I tried and tried to get ol' Cuss to move, but ever'thing I did jest didn't work. Finally, I said to Digger, 'Well, Digger my boy, let's just camp here for the night. It's way too early, but iff'en this here ole' mule won't go, he just won't go.'

Mr. Bushy laid back on his bedroll, lit his pipe and relaxed as if he was ready for a long telling.

"So, I set up camp, unloaded that mule, took all my gear off of Digger and turned them both out to find their own food. The day was mighty pretty on that mountain, jest as it usually is, so I took my time fixin-up my grub and cleanin' it up. Well, after I was done with that chore I decided to take me a walk around for a look-see.

"Well, I start in walkin' toward the west and go about a mile or so when I come upon a Injun burial ground. There was still a lot of them poles with some tattered feathers still a'hangin' on 'em, and the big dead-body-burnin' contraption was standin' right in the middle of the buryin' ground. You know, the thing where they burn their dead afore they put 'em in the ground. Well, I guess that's what they do. I ain't never been to one of them buryin' ceremonies, so I don't rightly know for sure just what they do.

"Anyway, I stopped a'fore I got onto the grounds, out of respect for the dead and all, and started in thinkin' about how far around I should walk to stay

148

respectful but not take forever-and-a-day to do it. And I sure hoped none of them warriors was still out there keeping watch. Well, I start in walkin' around the place, trying to be polite and all, and I get to the other side in no time a'tall, and lo'-an'-behold, there sat an' ol' Injun watchin' over all them dead souls! Well, I make the peace sign of the Osage and the Kickapoo, hoping he's one or the other. Sure enough, he signs back, so I know'd right off that he was Kickapoo. They're a friendly folk and all, so I sit down beside him and we just sat there for an hour or so, not saying nary a word or looking at one another. That's the polite thing to do among the Kickapoo. If you don't mind someone sittin' by ya, ya just stay there, but if ya don't like it, ya get right up in a hurry and walk away. Well, I took it that he didn't mind me sittin' there, since he stayed right beside me for so long.

"Then, real sudden-like, he got up, nodded at me to have a good day and walked straight through the burial grounds and disappeared. Well, I just stayed right there. The view was nice and the tree I was leaning against was feeling mighty fine so I leaned my head back and decided to get myself a wee bit of a nap. Well, right off I start in dreamin' about that burial ground. I dreamed all them dead souls came right up outta their graves and walked over to me and had a sit-down all around me and the tree I was leanin' against. There was warriors, squaws, babies, and all other ages of people. They were all Kickapoo except one. Sittin' right in the front, right close to me, was this here little white gal. She had on a right-nice Kickapoo dress with all sorts of beads and feathers on both her dress, an her hair was as white as the clouds on a sunny day and was long 'nuf to almost touch the ground. Her big eyes were as blue as a robin's egg. I remember, to this day, seeing her hair a'blowin kindly soft-like in the breeze and she had a big smile on her little freckled face. She was as cute as a daisy an' she was holdin' onta a wee lil' pup. She looked to be about nine or ten years along. She sat with her legs crossed, like most Injuns do, and I could see the markings on her ankle. The ankle markings said she was of one particular Kickapoo tribe.

"Well she just sat there for a while grinnin' at me, and then she said in a soft little gal whisper, 'Would you tell my mama I can't go home, cuz me and Bluebonnet fell into the river. The Kickapoo found me and pulled me out. Me and Bluebonnet watched 'em from the treetop and they tried and tried to get me to breathe again, but me and Bluebonnet were already someplace else and couldn't get back down into our bodies. Please tell them that they buried me here with my Bluebonnet and that I'm sorry I fell in the water. Bluebonnet fell in first and I just wanted to try and get him out. But it's all okay now. The Kickapoo gave me the name Sooleawa, which means Silver, cuz they didn't know my real name and they said my hair looked like silver. They gave me a pretty new dress and shoes and drew a pretty picture of a little girl like me, and wrote the name Sooleawa on my ankle. Tell Mama, Papa, Granny and the boys that I love them. Would you do that for me, mister?'

"Well, in my dream, I told her that I would surely do that very thin' iff'en I could, but I didn't know who her mama was or where her family lived. Then in her little whispery voice she tol' me her name was Hannah Barnes and her mama and papa's names were Anna and Jonathan Barnes and they live in Eden Bend along with her granny and her brothers. She told how she had gone on over there and tried to talk to them after she drowned, but no one could hear her. She said she thought maybe her Granny saw her standing in the corner of the kitchen 'cuz she looked over and smiled at her and started in singing one of her favorite songs. That lil' gal said she tried hard as she could but she couldn't get her Granny to hear her. She didn't know why she was able to enter my dreams and talk to me.

"I told that little Hannah gal that I sure will do that, as soon as I can get over to Eden Bend. She gives me another big smile and says, 'Thank you kindly, Mister,' and then her and all them other Kickapoo souls fade away inta the air like they'd never been there a'tall.

"Then I woke up with a start, and sweat was just a'pourin' down my back. I look around that-there burial ground and not a thing had changed. It must have just been a dream, I told myself. With a shiver and a shake I took off back around that buryin' ground to my campsite and ol' Digger and that mule were still chompin' on the grass, so I start makin' up my sleeping blankets for the night, all the while peerin' inta them woods real uneasy-like and kept on saying, 'It's just a dream, ol' boy, it's just a dream.'

"So 'long about midnight I finally fall asleep, and I don't dream a single thing! And seeing that I always start in dreamin' as soon as I fall asleep, that's mighty strange. I got up the next morning and I have the vigor of a fifteen-year-old boy!"

"Well," Mr. Bushy continued, "to shorten up this here adventure of mine, I high-tailed it down that there mountain as fast as that mule would go, stashed my furs and started in huntin' for Eden Bend, since I ain't never in my life heard of such a place. I asked ever'body I met up with but nary a one of them had ever heard of such a place. Finally, I give up and start on back to collect my furs and go on into St. Louie to do some tradin'. I sure felt mighty bad about not being able to keep my promise to that little gal."

Mr. Bushy paused as if remembering the feeling of disappointing the little girl.

"Well, I got a day or two closer to St. Louie, and along the way I ran into a feller coming down from St. Louie goin' towards Naw'leens area to do some trappin' and tradin' with the folks in the South. One of his pack mules had lost a shoe, so I stepped in ta help the feller unload the mule and fix it right up with a new shoe. Well, we strike up ah conversation and he seemed like a right-nice fella, so we decided to set up camp together for the night. And what do ya know, he had some homemade 'shine with him and we started in sharin' it and we get to talkin' and laughin' an gettin' down right gabby when we decided to swap our stories about ghosts and haints and the like.

"After he told me a fist-full of his strange happenin's I started in with my tellin'. I start right off by tellin' my tale about that there little white gal in the buryin' grounds. Well, he sits there starin' at me with his mouth and eyeballs wide open, and when I'm done with the tellin' he sort of swallered hard and says in a low whisper, 'we looked for little Hannah for weeks. We never did find hide-nor-hair of what happened to that young'un. We all ended up thinkin' some mountain man snatched her right up or maybe a bear or panther got ahold of her. Her ma and pa grieve for her still. That was nigh on a year ago now. I'm her Uncle Benjamin.'

"Then all of a sudden like, he stops talking, jumps up and whips out his long skinnin' knife and says, 'Bushman, if you took our little Hannah I'm gonna tan your hide on a tree trunk!'

"Well, real nervous-like, I jumped up and shook my head then held out the palms of my hands towards him and tells him, 'No, Benjamin, I didn't take your little Hannah. I lost my own little gal some years back and I'd never do that to any ma and pa's young'un.'

"Well, he just stared at me for a good, long while, then sits right back down and starts in weepin'. I din't rightly know what to say to the feller, seein' that he was a grown man and all, so I just sat there and let him weep for a bit. I didn't want to embarrass 'em none."

By this time all of them were sitting around the campfire watching Mr. Bushy with eyes wide.

"And then," Lily said anxiously as if she had never heard the tale before.

"After a while," Mr. Bushy continued, "the fella stopped weepin' and shakes my hand and tells me he would let Hannah's ma and pa know what happened to her then I told him no I couldn't let him do that cuz I had to do it myself 'cuz I'd made a promise to that little gal.

"So after that, we din't feel like tellin' anymore tales so we just made up our sleepn' blankets and went off ta sleep. The next mornin', before the dawn even broke the eastern sky, we start on out for Eden Bend. Eden Bend is just a few homesteaders out on one of the points in the Mississippi not too far from St. Louie. When we finally got to the Barnes' small farm, Benjamin walks right in and pulls me along with him and there was the whole family sittin' around the table eatin' supper. There was food piled high enough for the whole northern army. The two women got right up and gives Benjamin a hug and he introduced me all around. There was the little gal's ma Anna, her pa Jonathan, her little brothers Seth and Jacob, and her granny, Pansy. Well, her pa invites us to have a sit-down, and so we do and we all start in eatin'. That was good food and plenty of it. I hadn't had good food like that in a coon's age. My belly was grinnin' from my belly button to my backbone."

"Well after we all 'et, Benjamin asked if the two of us could speak to Hannah's pa private-like in the barn so the three of us went on out. Then Benjamin gave me a nod and I started in with my tellin'. At first Jonathan looked angry, as if maybe he wanted ta pick up his gun and shoot me, but Benjamin told him how he had run into me on his way down to Naw'leens and that I had never heard of Eden Bend in my life and that he himself believed me.

"Finally, Jonathan started in askin' me all kinds of questions about that little gal. I answered them the best I could. He wanted to know how she looked and if she looked happy. I told him about her little pup she had in her arms and he shook his head yes, he had just found her a pup and sure enough she had named it Bluebonnet. I don't think he knew what to do, but he knew he had to tell lil' Hannah's ma about it, so we all went on back to the house and he told his boys to go on outside and do the evening chores. We all sat back down at the table and he starts in tellin' Anna and Pansy about the dream I had.

"Well, Anna just stared at me for a while then tears start in pourin' down her face like water coming out of a bucket and Granny Pansy just sat there shakin' her head the whole time like she knew it was the truth. Then Granny Pansy puts her arms around Anna and told her that she herself had seen little Hannah one time standin' in the corner of the kitchen and that she knew all along that little Hannah was okay. She din't know if she was dead or alive, but she knew she was okay. Anna kept right on sobbin' and then she walked into a bedroom off'en the kitchen an' returns with a wee lil' babe, hands that baby to me and said she wanted me to meet Hannah Lee's new baby sister named Leah Bluebonnet Barnes. Well, I looked down at that silvery haired, blue eyed lit' gal and then that baby looked up at me and gave me a toothless big smile and she looked just like her big sister Hannah.

"And that ain't no tall-tale, it's the honest truth!"

"One more tale, Mr. Bushy?" Ott said asked quietly.

"Nope, you young'uns need to crawl on up there on them furs an' get some shut-eye."

***

Tap... tap... tap...

Lily brushed at the irritating tapping on her forehead.

Tap... tap... tap...

"Hey orphan, wake up!"

Slowly Lily opened her eyes and there sitting on top of her belly was none other than the little pest of a ghost Polly Susannah tapping her forehead with a twig and beside her sat Periwinkle flapping his tail vigorously shooting green sparkles up into the air and grinning at her.

"Whatcha doing?" Polly asked.

"I'm sleeping! What do you want, Polly?" Lily asked in a whisper so as to not wake anyone else.

"Where is the other street-orphan? Where's the other two waifs, Gertie P. and Ophelia? I like Gertie P. because she is nice to me. Did you do-away with them or did the coppers nab them and put them in the dungeons of London Tower?"

"They aren't here and no, they are not in a dungeon. As I told you before, I am not an orphan street-waif, and neither are Gertie P. or Ophelia."

"Well, is your mum and papa alive?"

"No."

"Then I guess you are an orphan!" Polly Susannah lifted her shoulders as if that settled the question, "And you still look like a street-waif with your strange-looking boy's britches and bare feet. If the coppers catch you they will throw you straight-away into the dungeon and hang you by the thumbs until they pop right off for lying! You best be careful, street-waif!"

"Go away Polly Susannah, I'm sleeping. What do you want?"

"I cannot find me mum and granny."

Lily sat up and looked at the little ghost. Polly Susannah was a ghost Lily, Ophelia and Gertie P. had met while escaping from underground slave traders down in Mississippi. Polly looked a bit sad, so Lily thought she would help her if she could Periwinkle was acting like he was licking Olivia's arm then he would look at her as if he couldn't figure out why she was not responding to him and giving him some attention.

"Think about the last place you saw your ma and that's probably where she is now just waiting for you to return."

"Okay orphan, we'll give that a try. Come on Periwinkle, let's go find Mum and Granny at the water mill in Memphis."

Into the night sky both apparitions vanished, but just as Lily closed her eyes, Polly swooped back and quietly murmured in her ear, 'Hey, orphan, go to the old cotton gin in Memphis.'

Then she vanished.

11

The old Memphis Cotton Gin

Horses' hooves resonated sharply off the cobblestone street as a horse feverishly pulled a carriage quickly along the misty, abandoned lane; desperately attempting to leave the seedy river-port district of Memphis. Few people were out and about this late in the evening, and those who were scurried to their destination knowing that muggers and thieves may be lurking in the shadowy corners of each dark, abandoned building waiting to pounce upon an innocent victim. The river fog was sweeping in onto the streets creating the illusion of the streetlights slowly withdrawing in on themselves, becoming faint orbs of light in the dense fog. A sense of foreboding was spreading through the dirty riverfront lane. From a distance came the echo of tinny-sounding pianos from saloons further down by the docks inviting thirsty customers into their establishments.

But the street in front of the Cotton Gin building was quiet. Swirling fog twisted light beams into unknown, strange creatures, sending chills up the spines of the four kids. Sweat rolled down their backs as they stood silently in the dark, shadowy door front of an abandoned building and waited quietly. They knew the men would show up sooner or later, because while sitting on a horse railing in front of the small store down the road from their Uncle George Thomas's farm, Ott and Paul had heard the plots being made by two men who had no idea the boys were listening to every word they said about a stolen treasure. The men had paid no mind to the two innocent-looking boys rough-housing and wrestling with each other. The men discussed meeting two other men at the old, abandoned Palmer Cotton Gin building on Union Street, which stood no more than three blocks from the docks along the river. After listening enough to get all the plans straight, Ott and Paul had taken off to find Lily and

Olivia. Now the four of them were at the Palmer Cotton Gin building waiting for the men to arrive.

Slowly, Ott pushed the old, decaying door open and the four of them quickly slipped inside. Immediately they scurried behind stacked crates and brambles of broken wood boxes pushed against the far wall. When they were well hidden, they stood soundlessly peeking through the cracks between the boxes, waiting for their unknowing informants to arrive.

After what seemed like a lifetime of waiting, two men slipped into the building and quickly pushed boxes and boards in front of the broken window to keep snoopers away. Then they pulled up four empty boxes into a circle and sat down and one of the men pulled some twigs out of his pocket and built a small fire on the dirt floor.

Something was very familiar to the four friends about these two fellas. When they built up the small fire on the earthen floor and turned their faces to the side, immediately the four knew who they were! It was none other than Tater James and Hawg-Jaws Jackman from Malden, the same two greasy-haired hobos who had threatened them with a poisonous snake several days ago.

"Did ya see that thing runnin' long the road jest afore we darted inside here, Hawg? I'm thinkin' it was a haint and I'm thinkin' it was after us," Tater whispered quietly.

"I see'd it and I *know* for sure it was a haint, and it *was* after us. It looked like a big ol' creature from the swamp, din't it? This place gives me the creeps and makes me 'member things I ain't wantin' ta 'member."

"Like what thins', Hawg?"

"Like the one time me and Paw was down in the Loozi'ann bayou fishin' and up comes a pow'ful storm and we had ta find us ah hidey-hole. Paw found this here itty-bitty shack built on stilts way out in that swamp wedged 'tween four of them big banyan trees where we was citchin' some big ol' catfish. Really quick-like we scrambled inside and tied our pirogue to the tree and sat there hangin' onto the boards of that shack while peerin' out that winder openin' when we see another pirogue floatin' our way. It wasn't tossin' or turnin' a'tall, it was kindly floatin' above the water around them cypress tree stumps jest like ridin' on a smooth-as-glass river. When it got right in front of us it stopped dead still, and what do ya know but there was a dead body jest layin' in the bottom ah that pirogue as calm as could be! It was ah sight ta see, I tell ya. That body was a woman and she was dressed in a real clean, nice, white dress with her hands folded in front ah her waist like she was layin' in a coffin! Her hair was so long it was blowin' out the back of that pirogue and floatin' in the wind. But it wasn't whippin' 'round in the wild wind of that storm, it was blowin' real gentle-like, like maybe it was catchin' a cool summer breeze jest a'floatin' down a smooth river. I'll never forget the look on 'er face. She had the whitest skin I ever did see and her ruby red lips was in a soft-like smile. That pirogue looked to be floatin' right on top ah that swirlin', thrashin' swamp water and then it glided up real close ta our shanty and edged its way right smack-dab below that winder we was lookin' out of! Well, Paw grabbed aholt ah my arm, making me jump a foot off'en the floor, and whispered for me ta shush and don't scream, so I din't, and then he pointed off to my right and when I looked over there I saw a big ol' black panther bounding from tree to tree, gettin' closer and closer with each jump! It was the biggest black panther I ever did see! I could see, jest as clear as day, his big, shinin' green eyes, and ever'time he jumped he let out a scream. Paw pulled out his rifle and got ready to shoot iff'en that black devil tried coming inta that shanty ta eat us. But when it got to the tree right smack in front of us, all it did was give out another scream that echoed above the roar ah that storm. Still today I can 'member that scream and how it shook me to the bones. Then it jumped right inta that pirogue with that dead woman and I thought for sure it was gonna eat 'er up. But right away that woman rose up real slow-like and put her arms 'round that black devil's neck and off they went, floatin' cool as a cucumber out inta the middle ah that bayou. That woman wasn't dead a'tall, she was jest takin' a nap

I guess. But it sure was the strangest thing I ever seen, an I ain't wantin' ta see any strange thin's like that again.

"And after we got home and told some folks about what we saw, some ah them old fellers said she was the love of ah evil ol' rich man who was kilt fur robbin' the poor an now she wandered the swamps huntin' fur his black soul. I guess his black soul turned inta a black panther!"

"Well," Tater James leaned close to Hawg Jaws and whispered in a low, eerie voice, "Let me be tellin' ya a tale ya ain't gonna believe."

Hawg Jaws looked back at Tater with wide eyes.

"Oh yeah? Well don't be tellin' me 'bout them haints and fantômes floatin' round in the bayou. I aint wantin' ta hear any more 'bout them, them bayou haints give me the willies."

Tater laughed deep in his chest as he said, "Oh... This will give ya the willies, that's for sure, and I'm gonna *tell* ya anyways."

"A'right. Jest don't be mad iff'en I start in screaming durin' my sleep tonight."

Lily wondered what could be so bad as to give Hawg-Jaws the willies when most times he carried that nasty snake around with him.

"Well," Tater began, making his voice creepy, "one time in the dark of night, 'bout a year or so ago, I was down in Naw'leens with Stick McGregor, and we went inta one ah them ol' boneyards where the dead ain't even buried. They jest put 'em in a coffin-box then put that coffin-box in a cement box and there they are, jest settin' on top ah the ground and all the livin' folks come out and put flare's an doo-dads an such 'round the box and leave notes for the dead ta read, I guess. Stick told me they don't bury 'em cuz iff'en they do and a flood comes 'long, them coffins start in floatin' outta the ground and sometimes they fall over and then there's dead bodies thrown all over the country side. He said it can be a big ol' stinkin' mess and he said he membered

160

a few times when that exact thin' happened and some ah them bodies got right up, brushed themselves off and walked off inta the sunset like they was goin' on some kinda mission or somethin, and ain't nobody can figger out where they walked off to!"

Hawg Jaws was staring at Tater with his mouth open; Tater was leaning in close and every few minutes he would stop and shiver.

"Ya pullin' my leg, Tater. I ain't believin' ah durn thin' you're sayin'."

"No, no. It's the dang truth iff'en I ever did tell the truth," Tater laughed.

"Well," Hawg laughed, "that ain't sayin' much fur ya."

"Well, this'un is a true one. And Stick wasn't the only one who tol' me, some other fellers that was listenin' to the tale nodded their heads and swore on their granny's graves that Stick was tellin' me the truth. One fella said one time durin' a flood, one ah them dead spooks came right up to 'em and snatched his hat right off'en his head and the feller said he was too scare't ta do anythin'. He said that spook croaked out a raspy 'Merci beaucoup' - its French for 'thank you very much'. But the feller said he was so surprised, all he did was nod his head and watch that haint walk away with his hat on his head. And, that feller's friend shook his head agreein' and tol' me it was true cuz he was there and saw the whole thin happen.

"So anyways, me and Stick decide ta try and open one ah them coffin-boxes and see iff'en there was anythin' worth takin'. So we walk on back ta Pappy McGregor's farm and get us two crowbars outta his barn, then we wait 'til it's good and dark a'fore we walk back ta the boneyard. It was the Lafayette's Cemetery #1, and 'til this very day I can still see the old, painted sign in my head. There was moss hangin' from them Cypress trees all the way to the ground and some ah them coffin-boxes was covered in it. Skeeters was buzzin' round our heads and faces like mad and that hot air was sending sheets ah sweat down my back."

161

"I hate Naw'leens," Hawg interjected. "Ain't nothin but skeeters, snakes, gators and sweat."

"Yep, me too," Tater agreed before continuing with his tale.

"Well, real sneaky-like we slip on back inta the far side of the boneyard and found us a big cement coffin-box with purt-near ten names carved on the outside, so we figgered iff'en there was ten people in that box surely one of 'em musta been carryin' some gold or jewels with 'em inta the great beyond, so we start in usin' our crowbars. Well, we get one slab ah that cement off'en one side and are workin' on the top when we heard a strange sound. Kindly like a person walkin' real slow-like and crunchin' the leaves and pebbles with their feet."

Tater shivered. "I get the heebie-jeebies jest 'memberin' it."

"What happened next? Get on with it, Tater!" Hawg demanded as he brushed the greasy hair out of his eyes and glared at Tater.

"Well, Stick hear'd it too, so both of us stopped our crowbars and slipped away from that coffin and got behind one ah them big Cypress trees and peeked through the hangin' moss. Then we seen 'em. It was a long, tall, skinny skel'ton fella, and he was walkin' real slow-like over ta one ah them wooden benches next ta a coffin-box where he had himself a sit-down. When he sat down, his bony body did an awful lot ah clinkin' and clankin', and then his jawbone started flappin' up and down like he was talkin' to somebody. He was a mighty strange-looking skel'ton ghost. He was kindly glowin' in the dark like ah far'fly. He had this big ol' head, and instead of empty eye holes, it had eyeballs! Great-big, blood-shot eyeballs! And they were dartin' back and forth like they were searchin' for someone as his jawbone kept flappin'. Then next thin' we know, along came two more skel'tons, and they had eyeballs too! Well, the first skel'ton fella stands up and they all shake hands, like maybe they hadn't met a'fore. Then one by one they sat down and started in talkin'. Well, we were thinkin' they was talkin'. All their jawbone were flappin' up and down, and ever' once in a while they had to be laughin', cuz they would throw their heads back with their jawbones wide open and slappin' their knees like they was tellin' some funny jokes. Then one of 'em started in jabbin' at the smallest one like he was kindly teasin' 'em, but the little'un acted like he was gettin' mad at the other two. His jawbone was flappin' so hard that one by one his teeth started fallin' out onta the ground 'til finally he had no teeth a'tall! Then he bent over and picked them up, and one by one stuck 'em back inta his jawbone. That made the other two skel'tons start in laughin' again and then that made the little'un madder yet. He jumped up and drew back his skel'ton fist and punched the other two fellers smack in the nose - well, you know, where their nose would have been - making their bony nose holes break inta pieces. Then he turned and stomped away, losin' little bits of bone from his hand as he walked. Well, he walked 'bout four coffin boxes down the path, opened the door on a big fancy coffin box and crawled inside. Jest a'fore he pulled the door, he looked back at those two others skel'tons, ripped off his foot and with a good, hard fling, threw it at them and smacked one of 'em right in the chin. Then he made this 'HAH!' sound and pulled the door to on his coffin box!"

Hawg-Jaws was grinning and gave out a big laugh.

"That ain't no shiverin' story! That there's kindly funny," he said, laughing.

"Well, this here is the shiverin' part. About that time I feel this here *tap, tap, tap* on my shoulder and my heart turned inta a chunk ah ice. I knew what it was a'fore I ever looked over my shoulder. Again - *tap, tap, tap*. Slowly me and Stick turned our heads ta have a look-see and there it was: a real, live haint! He was a big, chunky, haint fella, and he had one ear missing and one arm missin', and hangin' onta his other arm was a big, old badger, like maybe that badger had died with 'em!"

Tater stopped talking and swallowed hard before he continued.

"I ain't never seen anythin' like it a'tall, Hawg. It was like the fella's haint was exactly how he musta died! There was a big ol' hole in its side, like maybe he'd been shot, and there was a hole in the badger's belly. It was kindly like someone had shot both of 'em at the same time! Maybe like his friend was tryin' ta save 'em from the badger an accidentally shot 'em along with the critter.

"Then it lifted its one hand, and with a long, fat finger poked at my nose and said in a low, raspy haint-voice, 'Ya mates be wanting some gold?'

"I din't say a word cuz I couldn't move one single muscle. I was so scare't, drool was drippin' down my chin and my eyes was bugged out like a toad frog's eyes. I jest looked at 'em and then he poked my nose again and says, 'I said! You mates wanting some gold? I know where ye can get gold, but t'will cost ye your soul.'

"Well, I shook my head no, cuz I din't want no gold iff'en it cost me my soul. Then he said in that deep haint voice, 'Where am I mates? I was almost upon the gold me'self when I was blown clean outta the sea by a cannon from the *Emerald Jack*. When finally I reached the shore, this badger got me and me mates fired at the badger. They killed this dang badger but the shot took me along with 'em, so here I am forever hooked up with this stinkin' animal. Then me mates buried me in this wilderness. Where am I?'

"Stick stammered 'round a bit then tol' the haint we din't want no gold iff'en we had ta pay with our souls, but that haint jest laughed real wicked-like and tol' us he know'd we were huntin' gold cuz we was grave robbin'. So we jest stood there starin' back at 'em and then he started turnin' inta one ah them red-haired northern haints! You know, them haints with the big teeth and big ol' tongues flappin' outta their mouths. The ones that come down here from up north and snatch up us southern boys up and drag us up north to them salt mines!"

"I ain't never hear'd ah no salt mines up north."

"Me neither Hawg, but that's what them exper-teeze say"

"Who's them exper-teeze anyways?"

"I ain't know! Jest let me finish doin' my tellin'! That haints head spun 'round with its tongue floppin' out, then that tongue slapped Stick upside the head and the haint laughed like a wild hyena. Then me and Stick took off running outta that boneyard as fast as our legs could carry us with that haint right behind us. We could hear 'em comin' behind us pantin' like he was outta breath and stompin' like a buff'lo. Stick was runnin' so fast his knees almost touched his chin and he was beatin' me by a good foot or two, so I put on some speed and passed 'em up, then I hear'd this yelp like a dog yelpin' and when I looked over my shoulder I came to a skiddin' stop. I saw that haint touch Stick on the shoulder with one ah his fingers, and then Stick's arms and legs was flappin' round like a chicken on a hot stove. Then Stick started in cluckin' and scratchin' the dirt with his feet like he was a chicken huntin' for bugs!"

Tater was standing up, acting out how Stick had been scratching around in the dirt for bugs. Then he bent down to the dirt floor and acted like he had found a bug.

"Then Stick reached down and snatched up a big, fat June bug and gobbled it up like it was tasty! He grabbed a skeeter and gobbled that up too. Then he snatched up another skeeter and gobbled that'un up and he kept right on snatchin' skeeters outta the air and poppin' 'em inta his mouth and smackin' his lips like they was tasty as milk gravy! Well, I din't want that haint ta grab holt of me and make me eat bugs, so I high-tailed it outta there. When I got 'bout a half-mile down the road, here comes Stick with the haint right behind 'em. Stick's legs were churnin' up the air with his knees purt-near bumpin' his chin again, and ever time he took a step his head would bob forward like it was helpin' 'em get up some speed. His arms, legs and head were workin' together like the workin' of a steam locomotive wheels, and he was addin' some space between him and that haint. I knew I was in for it since he was movin' faster than me, so I took off runnin' again but Stick caught up with me and zooms past like a bolt ah lightenin', and then I could hear that haint behind me laughin' like he knew he was gonna catch me. Then off to the right I spied a farm house, so I took me a fast exit and charged up to that farm house door, flung that door wide open and dove in like I was diving inta the river and landed on the floor and yelled at the feller who was standin' there starin' at me ta shut the door quick! Well, he slammed that door shut then turned and stared at me for a minute or two before he tells me I better have a good reason for jumpin' inta his house or I'd be sorry. So, I jump up off the floor where I was pantin' for air, and told 'em there was a haint follerin' me. Well, we both took a peep out the winder, and sure nuf, there was that haint leaned up against a big ol' elm tree with a smirky smile on his face, waitin' for the feller ta give me the boot.

"That farmer feller asked me who the haint was, and I tol' 'em I had no idee, but that I had met 'em in the boneyard and then the farmer got kindly upset at me. He starts in tellin' me how decent folk don't sneak round the boneyard in late of a night, cuz ever'body knew once'st a haint caught ya in the boneyard they would foller ya for the rest of your life.

"Well, I said I know'd it and I was sorry but I had ta get outta there somehow or other. Then the feller's wife came inta the room wearing her nightshirt and said she had the perfect idee of how I could get outta there and be on my way! She opened up an ol' trunk sittin' next ta the back winder and took this here big ol' blue dress out, along with one of them bonnets with the great big rim that hides a woman's face and she handed it to me and tol' me to put 'em on. She said it used ta be 'er mum's dress and bonnet. Well, I wasn't too keen on wearin' a women's dress, much less a dead woman's dress, but I knew I had ta get outta there."

Hawg-Jaws started laughing and had a hard time stopping until Tater kicked him in the shins.

"Stop laughin', ya stinkin' pig!"

"Sorry, I jest can't hep it!"

"Well, so anyways, I put on that dress and that feller said I looked jest like his ol' granny and that nary a soul would recognize me. Well, the farmer and his wife walked out the door holdin' me up like I needed some help, and then the farmer called out ta his young'uns -loud enough for the haint ta hear - that they would be back jest as soon as they took Granny into the doc's house. I was kindly leanin' against the farmer, and his wife was holdin' a wet cloth ta my forehead like I was bad sick-"

Tater's story was interrupted by a slight sound outside the door of the building; Tater stopped talking and took his seat.

The door slid open and two more men slipped inside, shutting the door quietly behind them. One fella was a big, burly guy with copper-red hair and a long, bushy beard. The other fella was dressed in a dandy suit with a top hat, spats and white gloves on his hands. Ott and Paul recognized them as the two men talking outside the store by Uncle George's farm.

As Lily looked at the two men, she noticed the dandy city-fella seemed to fade in and out of focus; as she watched him closely, she knew immediately that he was a haint. The other big fella was unquestionably flesh and bone, though.

The big fella had taken a seat on an empty box, but the dandy fella stayed standing.

"What's the plan?" Hawg-Jaws asked as he glared at Dandy. "We've been waitin' too long and I'm gettin' the willies. Hurry it on up and tell us what ya want us ta do."

"What do you mean? Finding the treasure is the plan, my dear gentlemen, finding the treasure!"

Dandy paused for a second. "I use the term 'gentlemen' lightly," he said with a condescending tone.

"What's the plan on how we gonna find the val-u-ah-bles?" Hawg-Jaws drew out the word with a snarl as he looked up at the citified fella.

"I will advise you not to raise your voice at me, sir," Dandy replied calmly.

"Sir? I ain't no sir, an' I'd advise you that this is Ten'see and we don't cotton ta for'ners from up north tellin' us what ta do, *Sir Randolph!*"

"No need to address me as 'Sir'. I am a gentleman and a scholar, so please, address me as Mr. Randolph."

"I ain't addressin' ya as *Mr. nothin*! Jest tell us how ya want us ta find this so called lost treasure your huntin', and then pay us our fees and we'll be on our way! Fact is, iff'en its true and that treasure *was* stolen a hun'ert years ago, I'd say it's done-gone and we're on a wild goose chase, iff'en ya ask me. Ain't that right, Tater?"

"Sounds purt-near right ta me," Tater joined in. "I'm thinkin' we might should be goin' on out ta Granny Josie's house, Hawg, and see what she has cooked up on the stovetop - an' checkin' out 'er 'mater patch."

"Good idee, Tater. I'm hungry. Let's go."

Dandy's face got beet-red and his hair seemed to go a bit transparent. The copper-haired brute reached out towards Tater and Hawg.

"Sit down," the brute growled in a low, threatening voice. "Ain't nobody going nowhere."

"We ain't your servants, Irish. Get outta the way."

Irish pulled out a pistol and gave Tater a shove, forcing him to sit back down. "If we were onboard, you'd be walkin' the plank."

Both Tater and Hawg-Jaws immediately sat back down.

"Well," Dandy said with a smirk, 'that's better. Now it's said the treasure is in the possession of a Phineas Pennypacker and his Auntie. We have no idea how this Auntie of his got the royal treasure, but the Royal Guard has declared she is the culprit. And since she is no longer alive due to the roughing-up and poisoning from our spies who failed to get any information out of her many years ago, it is now in the possession of this Phineas chap. The Royal Guard is once again on the hunt. Not one bit of evidence has been found to show that a single ounce has been spent. If so, an English agent would have caught word of it. So, they are now quite sure the chap is still concealing it in his dwelling. I would imagine he does not carry it about with him since it would be way too heavy. So find out where this Phineas dwells and go through his house with a fine-toothed comb. Word is that he is out of town and won't be back for a fortnight or so. Find the treasure, then burn the dwelling down. And if you can't find the treasure, burn the dwelling down anyway. If we cannot find it, make sure no one else does. Spare no one."

Olivia grabbed ahold of Lily's arm and squeezed it tightly. She leaned over and whispered that they needed to leave as soon as possible to warn Mr. Phiney. Shaking her head in agreement, Lily nudged Ott's arm and made signals for them to try and get out. Olivia nudged Lily again and pointed toward one of the darkened corners of the room where tiny sparks of light flickered and flashed quietly, moving slowly in several different directions. Gradually the flickering sparkles became more numerous; it seemed an apparition was trying to merge into an unknown shape.

Entranced by the swirling aura of air, the four kids stood frozen to the floor watching the mesmerizing, dancing swirls. It was quite subtle at first, but then the small fire in the middle of the room began to slowly die and the four men stopped talking and looked down at their fire realizing something was amiss, because there was plenty of kindling feeding the flames. Tater and Hawg were the first to notice the spot of glittering flashes. Slowly they rose to their feet, not saying a word, and stared open-mouth at the swirling in the dark corner which was now twisting like a silent cyclone as it evolved into a ghostly silhouette. Then Irish and Dandy turned and spotted the subtle shape in the corner; they watched with horror in their eyes as it became more defined.

The form shivered and shook as it seemed to struggle in its attempt to attain a desired shape, like a butterfly struggling to emerge from its cocoon. Then, with a flash of brightness, there is was - a dark, shadowy form of an old woman. She was dressed in black widow-weeds with her head covered in the dark cloak draped around her shoulders. Her face was dark and angry as she glared at the four frightened men. Slowly she stretched out her black-draped arm and pointed towards the smoldering small fire. Instantly the embers burst into a tower of flames reaching up and through the top of the open ceiling, where droplets of flames danced along the rafters as if they had feet and caught the large, cottonseed oil-soaked beams ablaze wherever the sparks touched. In seconds, the rafters above their heads were blazing.

The city Dandy gasped as he pointed to the apparition.

"You!" he screamed as he spectral body glowed white.

Immediately the four men broke free of their frozen state of mind and rushed through the door; they could be heard running down the cobblestone street with their echoing steps dwindling out of earshot.

Then the apparition turned towards the four kids and motioned for them to come out from behind the boxes. With fear clinching their hearts, the four of them slowly emerged - first Ott and Lily, followed by Paul, who was pulling Olivia along with him. She floated to the open door, pushed the hood of her cloak back and there stood a smiling grandmother's ghost. Her hair was in a little bun on the top of her head and she had a little blue hat sitting askew beside the twisted bun.

Olivia's heart skipped a beat. She knew who the woman was - it was Mr. Phiney's Aunt Abby! Aunt Abby reached out gently and motioned for them to leave. Then with a sizzle and a small burst of sparks she vanished.

Out the door and across the street the four of them ran to watch the flames through the broken windows. Someone must have alerted the firehouse, because within minutes they could hear the echo of hooves and wagons coming closer as the clang of the fire bell rang out sharply through the deserted streets. Quietly the four of them stepped back into another darkened doorway and watched as the flames grew smaller and smaller before the fire wagon removed its hose. By the time the firemen were at the door, the flames were completely gone and the only evidence left was the smoldering embers of the small fire Tater and Hawg had built. Scratching their heads in bewilderment, the firemen reloaded the wagon and slowly went back to the firehouse.

Without saying a word, the four of them emerged from the doorway and ran south towards Olivia's Aunt's house, where they sat in silence on the front porch thinking about what they had just witnessed.

Finally, Olivia spoke up. "I know who that haint was," she said.

"Who?" Lily asked as they all turned and looked at her with curiosity.

"It was Mr. Phiney's Aunt Abby. He told me all about her yesterday. He described her to me and that was undoubtedly her."

"What's she doing spookin' folks? And why didn't she spook us like she did those four men?" Ott asked.

"Those men are after the family valuables she left for Mr. Phiney. She's the person who raised him after his mama died giving birth to him."

"They're not after family valuables, they're after the royal treasure Mr. Phiney has, remember?"

"No," Olivia stated firmly, "They may think it's royal treasure, but actually it's family valuables his Auntie left for him. But I don't think Mr. Phiney knows she was poisoned and hurt by a spy. Mr. Elijah Bonheur told Mr. Phiney he suspected something other than dropsy killed his Aunt Abby, but he wasn't sure."

171

The four of them sat silently in deep thought until Paul stood up and said maybe they ought to go over to Mr. Phiney's cabin and tell him what they had heard at the old cotton gin.

"Good idea," Lily and Olivia said together.

"I need to let Aunt Katy know where we're going," Olivia said as she walked to the door. "I'll be right back out in a second."

12

The Ferry Station

Barn owl's forlorn hoots echoed through the distant forest, floating across the open cotton fields, competing with the loud, deep croaks of the bullfrogs resonating from the swampy lands along the edges of the mighty Mississippi. Other than the owls and the bullfrogs, all was quiet in the stretch of land between Olivia's Aunt Katy's house and the river's edge.

Mr. Phiney's cabin sat close enough to the river that some years, flood waters rose and covered the wooden planked floor inside the little cabin as it flowed inland covering miles of cotton fields.

But tonight, the cotton fields were bone-dry and the ripe cotton bolls lay heavy like a thick, white blanket atop the dark brown, drying plants. The cotton was ready to be plucked from the razor-sharp spiny bolls, which at times could reach a height of five feet or more.

The road cutting through the field was well-worn from travelers going down to the river edge and catching the only ferry within miles which would take them across the swift moving river into Arkansas. The ferry docked on the Tennessee side of the Mississippi at night, but at the first crack of dawn it would begin moving travelers. The weather-worn small building, where the ferry owner Mr. Mobley lived, was built on stilts with steps leading down to connect with the dock at the edge of the river. All the boards were now grey and slightly warped from the hot Tennessee sun.

The four of them walked, silently at first, through the cotton field. But after a while, they felt a bit safer and began chattering like magpies.

"Whatcha think, Ott?" Paul asked as he picked up a clod of dirt and threw it as far as he could. "Ya think there's a real royal treasure at Mr. Phiney's cabin?"

"Naw, I think those men are *hoping* there's a treasure," Ott replied slowly. "They're probably not even from the Royal Guard of England. They're probably thieves trying to steal Mr. Phiney's family gewgaws cuz they heard some loco, slow-witted boozer making up some hair-brained tale about Mr. Phiney and his Aunt." Then he too picked up a dirt clod and gave it a throw.

"If Mr. Phiney didn't have something valuable," Lily said seriously, 'thieves wouldn't bother going through so much trouble to get it. Also, did any of you notice that city dandy? He kept fading in and out kindly strange-like."

"I thought so," Paul said right away, "but I thought maybe it was just me trying to see through the smoke from the fire. Ya think he was a haint?"

"That's what I'm thinking," Lily replied.

"Me too," Olivia chimed in. "He was a strange little fella. And I'm also thinking if there really isn't a valuable treasure, then why would those haints from so long ago be hunting for it."

Ott stopped and scratched his head as if thinking a bit.

"Well," he said slowly, "That's true enough. Gewgaws and trinkets sometimes turn out to be silver and gold, I'm thinking."

Paul picked up another clod of dirt and threw it towards the dull old ferry shack they could see in the distance, but the dirt clod didn't come even close to hitting the shanty.

For a quick second, Lily thought she heard a muffled '*ouch*', but no one else mentioned hearing anything, so she put it out of her mind.

"I bet I can throw farther than you can, Ott. In fact, I'm thinking I can throw it and hit the side of the ferry station," Paul said boastfully.

"So can I," Ott said just as boastfully. "I don't think you can, but we'll give 'er a go. The moon's bright enough. I'll give you a boost onto my shoulders, Lily, and you tell us who throws the farthest."

"Okay," Lily and Olivia laughed.

All four of them stopped while Paul picked up a solid chunk of dirt, reared back his arm and gave it a good, hard heave as Lily watched from Ott's shoulders.

"It went about ten rows over. Now you try, Ott."

Paul lifted Olivia onto his shoulders as Ott picked up a chunk of dirt about the same size as Paul's had been and gave it a good, hard chuck.

"Well," Olivia said, "it went about ten rows over too."

"Let's do it again!"

"Okay," Ott smiled at the challenge. "I'll go first this time."

"Okay, let 'er rip!" Paul laughed.

Ott picked up another chunk of dirt and threw it as hard as he could.

"That one went further than the last one!" Olivia laughed. "Now you go again, Paul."

Paul reached down, picked up another dirt clod, lifted his leg for more leverage, let out a loud grunt and gave the chunk of dirt a heave.

CLUNK.

"That sounded like it hit something!"

Lily quickly slid off Ott's shoulders, held her finger up to her mouth making a motion for them to be quiet, then in a very low whisper said, "There's something over by the ferry station. Paul's dirt clod went purt-near fifteen rows over and when it hit I saw a strange movement in the tops of the cotton bolls. Sparks puffed up like a dust wave!"

"Like a what?" Olivia whispered tensely.

"Like a wave of dust. Like a wave on the water, but its dust. And then the dust rippled out across the top of the cotton plants like an ocean wave."

"Let's go see," Ott whispered excitedly. "It's on the way to Mr. Phiney's house anyways."

"Yeah, let's go!" Paul added with a smile on his face.

Feeling the thrill of an adventure coming on, Lily agreed with the two boys.

"Aunt Katy told me to go straight to Mr. Phiney's house but to turn around and come right back if we see anything amiss, because Eunice Fletcher told her something was amiss down by the river. She said Eunice is a big windbag most times, but she wanted me to be on the watch," Olivia said hesitantly.

"Nothing's amiss, but if you think we should go back, we can," Lily said dismally.

"No, I guess not, I want to find out what that was too. But if it's those men again I'm outta here."

"Okay, sounds good to us," the other three said as they all took off jogging quietly through the cotton plants.

Slowing their pace down and easing carefully though the cotton plants so as to avoid being pricked by the thorny bolls, the four of them edged closer to the spot where Lily had seen movement. Then Ott and Paul came to a dead stop and motioned for them to get down on their hands and knees. The four of them creeped soundlessly through the plants. Slinking along slowly and watching for movement, Lily had to restrain herself so as to not stand up and run for the ferry station. She wanted to have a look inside and see if the fella who lived there was still alive. Her inner bones told her something was not good about the sparks she had seen flying up from the cotton plants.

Ott held his hands up, signaling for them to stop. He turned and pointed towards the small clearing at the back of the ferry shanty. Easing up next to him, Paul, Lily and Olivia saw what had stopped him. There, circling each other, were the ghosts of Mr. Phiney's Aunt Abby and another ghost who looked to be an eloquently dressed man of English royalty.

The Englishman called out in a high squeaky voice. "Put up your dukes, ye wench. I'm about to-"

"Oof!"

Before the words were completely out of his mouth, Aunt Abby's ghost gave him a sharp jab in the belly with her cane and he went down like a sack of potatoes.

"I am the archbishop of Canterbury! And ye have King John's treasure!" he cried out as he lay rolling around on the ground in agony. "By gad woman! Ye have assaulted an official member of the Royalty of Great Britain! Show some respect for your betters, ye mongrel dog! Ye shall hang for striking me!"

Lily gazed with awe at the so-called archbishop. On his head was a tall pointed mitre which had yellowed over the years. Below the mitre hung a long, yellowed, curly wig. His face was as round as a ball with cheeks red as roses. His lower lip was puffed up three times the size of his upper lip and looked as if he had been hit in the mouth with something powerful and his eyes were bulged out like a bull frogs. Above his bloodshot eyes grew one huge continuous eyebrow, all white and bushy. He had at least four chins, and every time he spoke they wobbled back and forth. He seemed quite angry and his one eyebrow was drawn down towards his bulbous nose which, by the way, had exactly five long hairs growing straight out of its end like spikes. He wore a short cape covering the shoulders of his long, elaborately embroidered robe which was stretched tightly around his rotund body. His stockings were covered with dirt streaks above his black shoes embellished with golden thread.

"Never give a warning afore ye strike, old man. Don't be a fool!" Aunt Abby laughed loudly as she gave him another jab and told him to get up and fight like a man instead of a sniveling royal crybaby.

Her laughter and snide remarks angered the archbishop and he jumped to his feet. Well, he didn't really jump, he lumbered around on the ground until he managed to get himself up groaning and holding his stomach the entire time. That was when Lily realized he was not quite five feet tall, which made him at least a foot shorter than Aunt Abby, but his ornamentally stitched slippers gave him three more inches of height. He was having a difficult time balancing on his three-inch slippers in the soft earth of the cotton field, but he finally managed to square off with Aunt Abby. They began circling each other; dipping and dodging as each jabbed out their canes trying to strike the other. Aunt Abby's cane was made of wood, and the bishop's of ivory. Both haints were bent slightly at the waist with their hands out, ready to attack. Then Aunt Abby threw off her cloak, which vanished into the air, and sneered at the old bishop arrogantly.

"I've beat the best of 'em in my day." She snarled and gave out a deep chuckle.

"I'm better than the best of 'em!"

"You don't sound like the best of 'em. You sound like a sniveling little lass. The treasure belongs to me Phineas. 'Tisn't your'n, his mum gave it ta me ta give ta Phineas and ya ain't takin' it, ye crybaby villain. 'Tis blood money for the ancestors me Phineas lost to ye villains."

"Ye'll hang for this, ye witch!"

"I already be dead, ye buffoon!"

"We'll hang ye again, ye despicable wretched swine!"

"Ha! Give it a try! 'Twasn't me who took the treasure," Aunt Abby laughed haughtily. "'Twas Phin's mum's mum who pilfered it, and she said t'was like taking candy from a wee babe. She left it for me Phin and that's where it shall stay!"

"Ye are a thief and a sorceress! Ye put a curse on the sheep of an English gentleman and word is you cast spells on the fine citizens of Piel Island so they would cater to the likes of ya and ye offspring. Ye Mr. Phineas shall hereby go to the gallows for acts of treason!" he snarled.

"T'was for the rebellion, ye dunderhead!" Aunt Abby yelled, "'Twas freedom they wanted and 'twas freedom they got! How do ya think the people won? Did ye think the chickens pooped out the bullets, ye old mugger? Without knowing it, the royal treasury supplied the victory for them. Ye time was up, they had 'nuf of ye picking the pockets of good people and putting fine folks in the tower of London, condemning 'em to their doom for pinching a loaf of bread here an' there ta feed their starving wee ones. T'was too much for ah body ta bear."

The old bishop became enraged at Aunt Abby's words. Aunt Abby took a flying leap towards the bishop just as he took a flying leap towards her. Their bellies did a sharp slam against each other and both of them flew back onto the ground where they jumped to their feet and rushed at each other again. Sparks began flashing as the two of them rolled into one massive ball of snarling ghosts, pulling at each other's hair. Aunt Abby bit at the Bishops ear. The first thing to fly out of the ball was the bishop's mitre. It flew up into the air about fifteen feet then floated down and landed on Paul's head as if that was where it was supposed to be. Tuffs of hair began flying out of the hostile struggle, then out flew one of the Bishop's slippers, then Aunt Abby's boot flew over Ott's head and he caught it with one hand. In a flash, the Bishop's cane flew out and landed within inches of Olivia's foot, sticking straight up in the ground. Olivia plucked it out of the ground and gave it a good look. Slowly the tangled sphere of the two of them fighting rose above the ground and gradually levitated higher and higher, with clods of dirt dropping off, until they simply vanished into thin air, leaving a diminishing trail of tiny sparks and dust flowing behind them.

The four kids sat in the dirt and looked at each other with surprise.

"Was that peculiar or what?" Ott said.

"It was," Paul replied in a whisper as he sat there with the goofy-looking mitre still resting on the top of his head. "So, Mr. Phiney's granny was a highway robber. Wow. Wonder if we should tell Mr. Phiney or should we keep it under our hats?"

All four of them looked at each other thoughtfully.

"Under our hats," they all said to each other in unison.

The kids grabbed the boot, the cane and the mitre and gave them a fling upward. As they sat and watched the mitre and cane rise up into the night, they saw a small light coming down from the sky. All of a sudden, *plop!* There lay both of the bishop's glistening, black slippers and his filthy stockings. None of them moved to pick them up.

"Well," Lily snickered softly, "looks like Aunt Abby knocked the socks off the archbishop." Then all four of them fell back on the dirt laughing at Lily's statement.

"Come on, let's go on up to the station and see if Mr. Mobley is on his front porch," Paul finally gasped. "Back when we used to come down here with

Pa to help Uncle George with his cotton, Pa would bring us down here in the dark of night and every time we came down Mr. Mobley would be sitting on his porch watching the river like it was broad daylight, and he always had a tale to tell. Afterwards, on the way back, Pa would say most of Mr. Mobley's tales weren't true but they sure were entertaining. Ain't that right, Ott?"

"Yep, that's right," Ott whispered back. "And no matter what time of night we came down he always had some sweet tea sitting on the porch. Ain't that right, Paul?"

"Yep, that's right."

All of them fell silent as they carefully and soundlessly walked closer to Mr. Mobley's station. The moon was still shining, but every so often the clouds seemed to stretch their fingers across its face, making it look sinister and foreboding. The kids heard the occasional splash of a large catfish as they jumped out of the river and the constant croak of the bullfrogs. The air was tense with a peculiar feeling that gripped Lily's stomach, urging her to run the other way. She was too curious to listen to it. When they got to the edge of Mr. Mobley's house, they stopped. Ott stepped around the corner and the rest of them followed close behind.

"Come on up onta the porch, young'uns," a raspy voice drawled from the river-side of the house.

The four of them stood stone-still for a few seconds.

"That you, Mr. Mobley?" Paul asked quietly.

"Yep, son, it is. I see'd ya comin' and I got ya some sweet tea ready an' waitin'."

Quickly the four of them scurried around the corner and jumped up onto the front porch. There sat Mr. Mobley with a pitcher of sweet tea and four tin cups resting on a small, wooden box. Mr. Mobley was rocking in his rocking chair and had two wood crates pulled up on one side of his rocking chair and another two on the other side, all facing the river.

"Have ya'selves a sit-down," he drawled in his slow accent. "I was watchin' y'all for a spell, cuz when y'all jumped inta George Thomas' cotton patch over yonder my ol' hound-dog popped his head out that winder in the back and spotted ya. He gave out a low, rumble deep in his chest. I know'd it weren't no bad folks, cuz iff'en it was, he'd ah let out a howl like the gates of hell itself squeakin' open."

"Can old Zebulun still see that far?" Ott asked with a grin. "He must be nigh on fifty years old by now. That's some mighty-good eyesight for an old dog like Zeb."

"Naw," Mr. Mobley laughed hardily, his eyes lighting up with laughter. "He din't actually see ya, I's jest pullin' ya leg. He's blind as ah bat most times, but he has better ears than a young pup. He hear'd y'all coming way back afore ya jumped inta the cotton patch, so I got up outta my bed and got my spy-glass and had me a look-see. That's why I got out my sweet tea cuz I know'd fur sure you Pruiett boys love my tea. But old Zebulun is comin' onta being close to twenty years old so I'm thinkin' I better be gettin' me a new pup soon so Zeb can train 'em afore he leaves me."

Ott introduced Lily and Olivia to Mr. Mobley and he stuck out his gnarly hand and gave theirs a firm shake.

"Nice meetin' ya, young gals," he said with a wide smile. "Been a long time since I had a chat with some young gals. Mostly my time is spent with Jim-Bob from over Mt. Olive way. He's ah strong young fella but he's as prickly as a corn cob rubbin' against your skin. He got in trouble with the law a time or two. His mama should'ah whooped his behind ever so often when he was a young'un and maybe he'd behave himself. I talk all day long and Jim-Bob don't say nary a word nor give out a laugh. But we get 'long ah'right and he ain't never done me wrong. He comes ever' mornin' ta help me with the ferryin' and stays till the last speck a daylight is gone, then he keeps me company while we eat some supper. Long 'bout nightfall, once'st he gets his belly full and has himself a gallon ah my sweet tea, he can turn inta a real jabber-jaw."

Mr. Mobley laughed cheerfully. Although his body was now stooped over from time, he was a tall, thin, stately-looking black man with curly, silver hair, skin the color of caramel, and a ready smile. He wore a straw hat and his clothes hung loose on his rail-thin body; it looked as if maybe he had grown a wee bit after he purchased his shirt and pants. He held an unlit pipe in his mouth and his eyes were light hazel-green. But the most amazing thing about Mr. Mobley was his is smile. It lit up his whole face, including his eyes. And his laugh was contagious. Every time he laughed at something he himself said, it made the rest of them want to laugh.

As Lily looked at Mr. Mobley, she was quite sure he didn't weigh any more than his old hound dog weighed, even with his height advantage.

"Well, we sure do 'preciate the tea, Mr. Mobley," Paul said over the top of the tin cup he was holding up to his mouth.

"Whatcha all doin' out here in the middle of the night walkin' amongst the haints and the spooks?" Mr. Mobley said slowly with a grin. "Ya know, ever once'st in a while I'll see a spook or two glidin' through my trees along the riverbank. Kindly-like they're out for a nice stroll in the moonlight. Most times they mind their own business and don't bother me none, but once'st in a while one will come 'round and get kindly nosey. They'll come floatin' up onta my porch and have themselves a peek through my winder. One time I caught one of 'em climbing through my back winder," Mr. Mobley laughed deep in his chest. "He din't see me but I was watchin' 'em and jest as he got both his legs through the winder I jumped inta the room, yelled out a great big '*Boo!*' and scare't that poor haint ta death."

183

Mr. Mobley laughed heartily. "Well, he was already dead, but it sure did scare 'em. He jumped back out that winder with his eyes bugged out and quick as a farfly-flash, took off inta the night. It was pretty durn funny, iff'en ya know what I mean. Who'dah thought a person could spook a spook?" Mr. Mobley laughed loudly. "That was a new one for me. But anyways, what y'all doin' wonderin' round the cotton fields?"

"We're hunting for clues as to what happened to Mr. Phiney's treasure. Have you heard anything?" Lily asked.

"Well," Mr. Mobley drawled as he scratched his chin, "jest afore y'all got here, I heard two haints outside my winder wrestlin' and tumblin' 'round yellin' 'bout some kind of royal treasure. I ignored 'em cuz it I figgered it weren't none of my business, but other than that I ain't heard hide-nor-hair of a treasure. I was 'bout ta get up and throw some cold vinegar water out the winder onta both of them haints, but then ol' Zeb heard y'all comin'." Mr. Mobley stopped talking and looked at the four of them.

"Y'all did see them haints fightin', din't ya?"

"Yes sir, we did," Paul replied in a whispery voice. "Olivia said it looked like Mr. Phiney's Aunt Abby and an old English bishop."

"Ya don't say," Mr. Mobley bugged his eyes out at Olivia. "Well I'll be a short-legged donkey. I been seeing Abby Pennypacker's haint a lot lately. I'm guessin' she's hangin' round waitin' on something or other. I saw her floatin' 'round over by Mr. Phiney's cabin jest last week. I was out for a stroll with old Zeb, in broad daylight, and I saw 'er float up onta his front stoop and then she had herself a sit-down on his steps for a spell. I called out ah 'how-do' and she waved back at me, but she din't say nary a word."

Olivia looked at Mr. Mobley with curiosity. Never before had she heard a person speak so calmly about seeing a ghost and trying to carry on a conversation with them.

184

"Ever' so often I see some mighty strange thin's 'round my station. One time, not too far back, I was sitting right here on my rocker watchin' this ol' river roll on down ta Naw'leens; not thinkin' bout anything in par-tic-lar, when the night turned dark as pitch and ever' critter in the swamp grass hushed their singing. Even I stopped rocking in my chair and really careful-like pulled my old black quilt up from the floor and slowly wrapped it 'round my shoulders so's nobody could see my white shirt shining in the dark. I flipped my straw hat off'en my head and started in looking real close-like at the thin's around me. Nothing moved for quite some time, then out the corner of my eyes I caught a glimpse of movement. I darted my eyes over to that spot but nothing was there that I could see. Then again, I saw movement out the other corner of my eyes and I darted my eyes over that'ah way and sure 'nuf, nothing was there. So, I squinted my eyes a bit and kept them moving back and forth, and that was when I saw 'em. It was like dark shaders moving amongst the tall swamp grass growing along the edge of the river makin' that grass sway and move kindly like the wind blowin'. They were all hunched over and scrambled hither and yonder like they was searchin' for something. Then all of a sudden, out of those black clouds came this here light. It was the strangest thin' I ever did see. It shined a big light straight down onta the swamp grass around my dock, and then *whoosh, whoosh, whoosh* - ever' last one of them black shaders was sucked up inta that light. I'm still pondering on whether it wasn't just me noddin' off and dreamin' or iff'en it actually did happen. But, the next morning when I got up and walked down to the ferry, ever single blade of grass around my dock was burned up. Now, it could'ah been a lil' fire or it could'ah been me dreamin'. I don't really know for sure. The Mighty Miss holds some strange secrets, that for sure."

Mr. Mobley sat quietly in his rocking chair for a few minutes silently pondering his own story. Then he blinked his eyes a couple times and quietly asked about what we had seen that brought us out to his station.

Ott and Paul hurriedly told Mr. Mobley about what they had seen and heard at the abandoned cotton gin.

185

"Hmmm, now that's a belly full of a puzzle," Mr. Mobley scratched his head in thought. After a moment, he looked out at the river and held up his hand as he pointed to a spot on the water.

"Look over yonder," he whispered quietly as he leaned forward to get a better look at whatever he was seeing. "I think we have us some company comin'. I been seein' some fellas out on the river off-and-on fur the last few nights. They ain't night-fishin' and they ain't going down ta Naw'leens neither, cuz they always tie up along the shoreline then snoop 'round a bit afore paddlin' back up the river. They're up ta something and I ain't figgered it out yet. Would ya look at that, I'm thinkin' these two are comin' ashore right here at my dock."

Turning to have a look, the four of them saw a large raft with two lanterns, one on either end of the raft. Two men were slowly paddling the raft towards the shoreline.

"They ain't seen us yet, so let's slip on inside the house real quiet-like and watch 'em through the winder. Many a time folk come ashore near my ferry thinkin' there ain't nobody livin' here so they can sleep on my dock and won't nobody bother 'em. Most cause no harm, they're jest wantin' a place ta get some rest a'fore startin' out again in the morning." Mr. Mobley laughed quietly. "Word is my house is haunted, so folks don't take the chance on comin' up to the house snoopin' round. They just stay right on the dock 'cuz they're traverlin' folks and just want some rest a'fore movin' on." Mr. Mobley chuckled again deep in his chest and grinned.

Quietly the four of them picked up their tin cups and walked into the house where all five scrunched around Mr. Mobley's big, open window and watched as the raft eased its way up to the ferry dock.

The two fellas didn't bother pulling up next to the dock, they maneuvered the big raft right up next to the ferry, then threw their raft-rope up and tied it well as they could, scrambled up onto the ferry floor itself, blew out

186

the two lanterns they had carried up with them and seemed to settle-in for the night. They sat quietly looking around the area as if checking to make sure they were alone on the quiet stretch of shoreline and then relaxed against their bedrolls. As soon as they began talking the kids knew who they were.

"Whatcha think, Tater-bug?" Hawg said in a loud voice which carried across the quiet river. "Ya think old man Mobley's station has some haints lurkin' round? Maybe ol' Mobley himself is dead and his haint is spookin' the shanty."

"Stop callin' me Tater-bug, ya pile ah hog vomit. I know'd it's ghostly cuz that's what ever'body, includin' my pappy, said for years," Tater replied solemnly. "And, Mr. Mobley ain't dead or his ferry wouldn't be here - it'd be tied up som'ers else with a new owner. I ain't gonna go snoopin' round, that's for sure."

"Aw, don't be a chicken. We can always take off runnin' iff'en we have ta."

"From a haint?" Tater said seriously as he sat half way up, "There ain't no outrunnin' a haint, Hawg! What's wrong with ya? They fly! Thur ain't no getting away from them critters."

Hawg-Jaws laughed loud as he lit up his pipe and scooted around to get more comfortable on the hard ferry floor.

"Let me tell ya a tale about some haints, Tater."

"I ain't wantin' ta hear no tale 'bout no haints, Hawg. I'm not in the mood. I had 'nuf haints with that one at the cotton gin."

Hawg-Jaws laughed and continued.

"That weren't nothin' a'tall. That was jest a shadow of a haint. It din't bother us none. I'm gonna tell ya a true haint tale."

"Iff'en it wasn't no haint, how come you ran faster than any of us ta get outta there?"

"I was jest makin' sure."

Tater gave a big sigh and laid back on his bedroll. "Well, I know'd your gonna tell me whether I want ta hear it or not, so go on ahead and start the tellin'.'"

"Well," Hawg-Jaws made his voice sound eerie. "One time when I was 'bout ten years old, me and my maw were going from St. Louie to Naw-leens and we was purt-near inta Fort Saint Pierre and Vicksburg, and we were travelin' real slow-like along the Miss-sip trail so our ol' mule could make his way without fallin' inta the swamps. Our ol' mule couldn't go too fast cuz he was an ol' feller and purt-near blind. We had this here rickety old cotton wagon full of our few belongings and we were on our way down to Naw'leens so Maw could find a job cookin' in one ah them slop joints.

"Well," Hawg-Jaws whispered as he drew out his words giving his voice an eerie pitch, "long 'bout midnight, or what folks call the witchin' hour, that ol' mule stopped right in the middle of the trail and wouldn't budge an inch. Maw pleaded and smacked that mule and even got out and tried givin' 'em a carrot but he still wouldn't budge. So, she said we might as well camp for the night, so we did. Maw said she wasn't gonna unhitch that ornery cuss 'cuz he din't deserve it. So we got our bedrolls all set up in the wagon-bed, laid down and I went off to sleep in a hurry. 'Bout an hour or so later I woke up for no good reason, or so I thought, and I was wide awake. I din't get up or move, I jest laid there gazing up at the star-filled night when all of a sudden, I hear'd a *whoosh*, and over the wagon flew a blacker-than-midnight haint. I couldn't see nothing but a flash of its green eyes and its body was like a flowin' black bed-sheet all raggedy at the ends and ripplin' out behind it for near-on seven feet. Then *whoosh, whoosh, whoosh,* hun'erts of black haints swooped over our wagon."

"Prolly not hun'erts," Tater spoke up and said nervously. "That's a mighty big number of haints swoopin' 'round."

"Yep, it was," Hawg-Jaws lifted his head up off his bedroll and nodded heartily. "It was hun'erts! I ain't tellin' no lie. They kept right on swoopin' past us tell pretty soon they was so thick it was like a blanket of black haints with their green eyes jest a'glowin'. It puts chills up my back jest memberin' it."

"Well," Tater said as Hawg paused, "Wha'jah do?"

"What'cha think I did?" Hawg replied indignantly as he too sat up. "I just laid there on that wagon-bed scare't stiff."

"What I meant is, did ya keep lookin' at 'em or did ya close your eyes tight?"

"Well," Hawg-Jaws stretched out his words again, "I kept right on lookin' at 'em. Member how a long time ago I tol' ya I lost my maw when I was jest a young'un. Well that was the night I lost 'er."

"It is?"

"Yep. I was layin' there just scare't as a mouse in a room full of cats, when all of a sudden one of them black devils came to a skiddin' stop, reached down inta our wagon and snatched up my maw from where she was sleepin' like she was light as a feather. I felt its cold clammy hand brush against my arm then it took off with a *whoosh* with Maw danglin' from his claws like a caught rabbit!"

"Why'd they go an take your maw?"

"I ain't knowin' for sure, but 'bout a month a'fore that happened my maw took the train down to Naw'leens then went out inta the swampland and had a visit with an ol' witch woman. She was wantin' to know why my paw ran off and left us, and she figgered that ol' woman could tell 'er. Well, lo'-an'-behold, after listenin' to the ol' woman yakkin' on 'bout this and that and whatever, maw figgered out that paw had run off with that woman's own daughter! So, I figger that ol' voodoo woman was 'bout ta die and she sent out them black phantoms ta collect Maw up. What'cha think 'bout that?"

"Prolly so," Tater answered quietly, as he nervously darted his eyes around the water's edge. "How'd your Maw figger out your Paw ran off with the daughter?"

"Now, that's the interestin' part. Maw was sittin' on that ol' witch woman's parlor chair tellin' 'er all 'bout 'er worries and the ol' woman was shakin' 'er head and agreeing with Maw 'bout Paw being a varmint and a no-good scoundrel. Then Maw said the woman got up and started in mixin' up a potion for Maw to throw on Paw the next time she saw 'em and it would turn 'em inta an old, old man for all his born days. Well, just when she handed Maw the potion there was a racket at the back door and in walks none other than my paw all hugged up with the daughter! She said they were laughin' and smoochin' and carryin' on something awful. Well, Maw got so mad she jumped up from that parlor chair and threw that freshly brewed curse-potion all over Paw and in the farfly-flash Paw turned inta an old, old man with white whiskers hangin' down to his belt, all stooped over, and his head looked like the outside of ah coconut 'cept it was white instead of brown, all scabby and rough with white, thick hair pokin' out in spots. Maw said she started in laughin' and that was when she looked over at the ol' woman and saw that the witch was tryin' ta fling some of that leftover potion at 'er. That was when Maw took off out the door, jumped up on somebody's horse that was hitched up to the hitchin' post and high-tailed it outta there. But a'fore she got out ah ways, she heard that ol' woman yellin' out a curse at 'er sayin' she would get even with Maw iff'en it took the rest of 'er born days. So, I'm thinkin' it was time for that ol' woman to pass on and she sent out some haints ta get Maw."

"What happened to your Paw? Ya ever see him again?"

"Nope. Never did see hide-nor-hair of 'em. Some folks said they saw 'em wanderin' 'round the mountains, but me and Maw never did see 'em."

"That's a sure-nuf strange tale, Hawg."

"Now, I ain't knowin' the itty-bitty details ah what all went on, but Maw tol' me never ever go to a witch-woman's house! Never! Ever! Ever! And I ain't gonna ever do it!

"Ya really thinkin' that's why them black haints took your maw?"

"Ain't nobody else who'd want ta harm Maw, that I know of. It was kindly-like they was out looking for 'er."

"Well," Tater said slowly, "I ain't knowin' nothin' bout that-there kinda stuff. So, what'd ya do after them fantômes snatched 'er up and flew off with 'er?"

"I just laid there 'til daybreak came on shiverin' and shakin'. But at the first crack of dawn, I scrambled up onta that bench, picked up the reins to the ol' mule and gave 'em a yell ta get going. I think he was so surprised ta hear me instead of Maw he perked right up and took off down the road to Natchez. I tried findin' some kinfolk but din't have no luck in that, so I just lived on the streets and took what I needed. I got by fair-ta-meddlin' iff'en I have ta say so myself. That was when I started in thievin' and takin' from folks so I could eat. After I growed up, I just kept right on takin' cuz it's easier than breakin' my back in a cotton field, that's for sure."

Tater laid back on his bedroll with a sigh.

"Yeah," he said slowly, "I don't take kindly to workin' hard either. It's ain't good for a body ta overwork itself. And them cotton fields is hard on a body. Did ya ever see your maw again?"

"Yep," Hawg said emphatically. "She showed up one day at the hidey-hole I was sleepin' in and motioned for me ta follow 'er. She took me on down ta Naw-leens on the back of the old mule to a lil' tiny shack down by the docks and that's where we stayed 'til she passed on. Not one single word ever came outta her mouth for the rest of her life, and she never did try telling me what

191

happened after she was snatched from our wagon. She worked 'er fingers to the bone cookin' in one of the honky-tonks and bringin' home some mighty good food - cuz she was a mighty good cook - till the day she was run down by a carriage and died. Some folks said they witnessed it and swore it was that ol' woman's daughter who ran 'er down. They swore the driver was dressed all in black and had glowin' eyes like coals of fire."

All the time Hawg was telling his tale, he had been building a small fire in a large tin can sitting on the ferry floor. Lily saw him push some rocks up against the hot sides of the tin can, then when he finished the story, he bent down, picked up the glowing-hot rocks with his shirttail and put them up to his eyes and gave Tater a nudge with his elbow.

He turned to face Tater and said in a low, eerie voice, *"Like theeeese."*

"AHH! AAHH!"

Quick as a flash, Tater sprang up with his mouth wide-open and began running down the trail leading out of the cotton field. His hands were waving and his legs were churning up the dirt like a fleeing jack rabbit, picking up speed as he kept yelling.

Dropping the glowing rocks away from his eyes, Hawg-Jaws stood up and stared open-mouthed at the bolting Tater, then cupped his hands around his mouth and yelled out to him, "I's jest foolin' with ya Tater! I ain't no haint! TATER! Come on back, Tater! I ain't no spirit a'tall!" Then he plopped back down onto the ferry floor, sighed and called out, "You're a moron, Tater-bug!"

All five of them stood silently at the window staring first at Hawg, then they scurried over to the side window and watched Tater vanish into the cotton field still waving his hands above the white cotton bolls hollering at the top of his lungs. Then they shuffled back to the front window and watched as Hawg-Jaws laid down on his bedroll and flicked a pebble into the water.

"What a ig-nor-a-mouse. Good grief," Hawg muttered loudly before yelling again, "Your as dumb as a stump, ya ol' ugly Tater-bug!"

Mr. Mobley motioned for the kids to move into his back room, and Ott and Paul jumped right in and told him what all they had seen and heard regarding Hawg and Tater since Olivia's mama's funeral.

"So sorry for your loss, young lady," Mr. Mobley slipped off his hat and bobbed his head at Olivia in a humble gesture. "'Tis mighty hard losing your ma at your age. My hat's off ta ya and may God bless ya."

Olivia thanked him for his condolences.

"Now," Mr. Mobley whispered, "We'll have to slip out the back door and get over to Phin's cabin and let him know 'bout these two fellas. Come on with me and we'll try to make it to Phin's cabin. Jeb will stay here and keep an ear open. Iff'en he hears anything amiss he'll give out a howl."

"*Try* to make it?" Olivia asked with wide eyes as she hesitated. "What happens if we *don't* make it?"

"We'll just sleep in the cotton field. I've done it many a time when the fog gets too thick to see where I'm goin'," Mr. Mobley answered calmly as he realized he had made a mistake by voicing his slight doubt.

Quietly they slipped out the back door and ran quickly across the road to the cotton field at the other side of his station, the kids in front and Mr. Mobley bringing up the tail-end. They walked single-file towards Mr. Phiney's cabin, but when they got approximately fifty feet away from the station they came to a skidding stop and turned their heads back towards the station.

Zeb was howling at the top of his voice. It wasn't a normal howl, it was more like a barking howl. The four kids stared at Mr. Mobley.

"What does that mean?" Ott asked nervously.

"It means somethin' ain't right," Mr. Mobley whispered. "Don't move a muscle. Something ain't right in the air." He looked up at the sky.

Before anyone else could utter a word, they heard the sound of heavy panting and watched as the old dog himself ran towards them, moving faster than any of them could believe.

BOOM!

A huge ball of fire shot up into the sky and exploded. All of them, Zeb included, rushed out to the trail and looked back towards the ferry station. It was totally engulfed in flames; the old dry wood was burning like kindling sticks. Then Hawg-Jaws Jackman came tearing down the trail yelling at them as he ran by.

"I saw 'em, I saw 'em, I saw 'em! It had a far-torch and it threw that far' right through the open winder an' it burst inta flames! I saw 'em, I saw 'em! Ya best be runnin' off, folks, 'cuz it might be comin' this'ah way!"

Hawg-Jaws didn't miss a stride as he flew by, still muttering to himself in a panic. They all turned their heads and watched him running towards Memphis.

Quietly the five of them turned back to look at Mr. Mobley's ferry station.

"Let's go take us a look-see, young'uns," Mr. Mobley mumbled.

Surprisingly, within the few minutes it took them to return to the station the entire structure was in ashen shambles and the flames had vanished, leaving behind hot embers pushing tendrils of smoke into the sky. Tiny flickers of red flames flashed within the residue but there was nothing for it to feed on. The blackened chimney rose eerily out of the ashy remains, the only thing still standing upright, and seemingly proud within the scattered ruins. It was framed against the night sky by a subtle glow of reds and purples.

From the corner of her eyes Olivia was sure she caught a fleeting glimpse of the rotund archbishop's ghost slipping off into the dark forest. Thinking it was only her imagination, she said nothing, but immediately Lily grasped her arm and made a motion for her not to say anything, so Olivia knew it was not her imagination.

"That was a dang fast far'," Mr. Mobley murmured as he stared at the pile of ashes that had been his home. "I ain't never seen anythin' like it a'tall. It took 'bout two minutes and the whole place was gone!"

"Not even two minutes, Mr. Mobley," Ott said.

"Whatcha gonna do now, Mr. Mobley?" Olivia asked softly. "Where ya gonna live? I'm thinking Aunt Katy would let ya live at her place if need be."

"Well, darlin'," he sighed and said, "Thank'ye kindly. But I'll go see if ol' Phin will have me for a bit 'til I can build me another station."

"We'll help ya!" Ott and Paul said in unison.

"Us too!" Lily and Olivia joined in.

"Thank'ye kindly young'uns. But for now, let's get on over ta Mr. Phiney's and see what he has ta say."

13

Mr. Phiney's Cabin

The air in the cotton field closed in on the five of them as they walked through the sea of white cotton bolls with the smell of dark, rich earth filling their nostrils. The night fog was rolling in and would soon be followed by even heavier fog settling quickly onto the Memphis lowlands. The damp fog made it hard to see the rows of cotton plants ahead of them, much less Mr. Phiney's cabin. Since he knew the way to the cabin without looking for its shadowy outline, Mr. Mobley quickly switched places with Ott and began jogging so they could beat the thick fog easing up from the river. Except for the random calls of the screech owls, all was silent in the murky haze. Then off in the distance echoed the howls of wolves, but Mr. Mobley kept the group in a steady pace. Only when the scream of a black panther reverberated up from the riverbank did Mr. Mobley's pace quicken. When the panther's scream came closer, their jog turned into a concerned, all-out run.

"Come on, young'uns," he whispered. "Let's beat that panther to Phin's cabin. Ott, Paul, don't let them gals lag behind ya."

"Yes, sir," Ott said in a tense, nervous voice.

Every one of them knew a black panther could hear their prey from miles away and their sense of smell was highly sensitive, especially if they smelled fear, which was definitely flowing out of each of them like a fountain.

Again the panther screamed and be its sound they knew it was coming for them.

Mr. Mobley picked up his speed again; panic fueled their legs to go faster than any one of them believed they could go. Lily picked up Zeb and ran as fast as her legs could carry her.

"Iff'en y'all can make it past me, go right on ahead!" Mr. Mobley wheezed between steps, "Go on, move on ahead of me!" He slowed and pushed the girls in front of him.

Ott and Paul refused to pass him. Instead, they each grabbed ahold of Mr. Mobley's exhausted arms and ran, pretty much dragging him as fast as they could for the clearing. Lily and Olivia were the first to reach the cabin where they pushed the door open with a loud *bang!* Then turned and waited for Ott and Paul to drag Mr. Mobley up the two steps and into the cabin. Once they were all inside, Olivia glanced out the door and saw the big, black cat spring from the cotton field with its white fangs glistening in the night and its eyes glowing green. Immediately an unknown anger surged up into her very being. Raising her hand towards the panther she stared straight into its green, glowing eyes and the panther stopped in mid-air and sank onto the ground, landing on its belly.

It then began letting out a loud rumble from deep within its chest and lifted its mouth to show its teeth. Then the fire faded in its glowing, green eyes. It lay there on its belly as if waiting for another command. Olivia's anger seemed to boil within her mind as she signaled for the panther to leave. Quickly, and without a sound, the big cat slipped into the field of cotton and disappeared. Then Olivia's fear came rushing back and her heart began beating on her eardrums. The entire encounter between her and the panther took only a few seconds and she hoped no one else noticed what had just transpired. Quickly she slammed the door shut and slid the bolt lock. Then, for only a fleeting second, she caught Mr. Phiney and Mr. Bushy's look of surprise as they stared at her before quickly darting their eyes away.

"That was a close one, Phin," Mr. Mobley gasped. "I din't think we were gonna make it. I been seeing a big cat 'round my station, but not a black panther. Normally they stay far away from folks. And, wouldn't ya know it, but this was the first time in my life that I left my pistol at the station of a night when I go out. I won't be forgettin' it again, that's for sure.

"That fire ate up everthin' at my station in a flicker of ah flash."

"What fire?" Mr. Bushy asked quickly as he darted his eyes to Mr. Mobley.

"My station burned into cinders tonight. It happened in the flash of a far-bug. T'was the strangest thing I ever did see. We hadn't left the station but a few minutes when all of a sudden Zebulon came rushin' towards us and then *BOOM*, the station was nothin' but rubble and ash." Mr. Mobley shook his head for a bit before continuing. "What was we comin' over here for, young'uns? My mind's all befuddled. By the way, anybody see ol' Zeb?"

"He's right here by me," Lily spoke up from where she sat, scratching the old dog's head. "And we came to tell Mr. Phin about his family treasure."

"Oh yeah, that's right. Let me get aholt of my breath and get my brains unscrambled then we can do our tellin'. You know, I ain't seen no black panthers 'round here in a coon's age. Wonder what's bringin' 'em back?" Mr. Mobley scratched his head again as if it was a big puzzle to him; he darted his eyes, just for a fleeting second, at Olivia.

"Well, Phin," Mr. Mobley continued after a few seconds, "these young'uns stopped by my station tonight on their way to your cabin and they saw a couple haints wrestlin' 'round out behind my place."

Mr. Bushy and Mr. Phin turned to look at the four of them with interest.

"And...?" Mr. Phin said.

So the five of them took turns telling Mr. Phiney what they had heard and saw until they were all talked out and eventually sat in silence.

"Well, I'll be. Let's give it a night's rest and we'll see how it goes tomorrow," Mr. Phin said. "Mr. Mobley, you can stay here as long as need be."

"Thanks for the invite, Phin," Mr. Mobley said. "It won't take long to rebuild the station, I'm thinkin'."

"Don't even worry 'bout it, Mobley," Mr. Phiney replied. "Ever'body find a spot anywhere ya like and we'll get us some shut-eye."

Ott, Paul, Lily and Olivia settled in a far corner, and as soon as the three men were snoring they silently stood up and tiptoed to the door.

Then ol' Zeb let out a whine like he wanted to go along with them. Before they could shush him, Mr. Bushy's eyes popped open.

"Don't touch that door knob," Mr. Bushy's commanding whisper came from the opposite corner of the room. "Iff'en ya do I'm gonna whoop ever' last one ah ya."

With deep sighs the four of them returned to their corner and lay back down. Within a few minutes, Mr. Bushy's snores were so loud they knew he was sound asleep, so once again they pushed quietly to their feet and tiptoed out the door, taking Zeb along with them.

Once outside they all breathed a big sigh of relief and quietly walked to the middle of the grassy clearing.

"Hey!" Paul whispered softly. "I just thought about something. Look yonder," he said as he pointed towards the forest. "Maybe old Elijah Bonheur wasn't talking about Mr. Phiney's front-door stoop, maybe he was talking 'bout the stoop going into the outside privy. Whatcha think?"

The rest of them turned and stared to where Paul was pointing. There, hidden away in the trees, was an old, outside privy weathered grey from time. Except for the quarter moon opening in the top front and a few visible spots of weathered wood, it was veiled with wild vines and branches. All of them stood staring at it for a few minutes then cautiously began walking closer to the old abandoned privy, all the while peering into the dark forest for signs of the big cat or unknown spooks who may be lingering around watching the cabin.

Lily and Olivia let Ott and Paul pull away the vines from the front of the old door and there it was, the front stoop all covered in moss and dead twigs. It looked as if nothing had touched it for many years.

Ott pushed away the twigs and scraped the moss off the stoop with his shoes.

"It's a solid block of wood," Ott said as he tried unsuccessfully to remove it from the black dirt.

"Let me give it a try," Paul replied as he pushed Ott aside and bent down to give the chunk a tug. It didn't budge.

"Stay right here and I'll be back with something to move it," Lily whispered quietly.

Within minutes Lily was back with a large pig's foot.

"Okay," Ott said a bit nervously. "Keep a look-out for the big cat. Hopefully Zeb will let us know if it comes back around."

"I don't know about that," Lily said as she looked at the old dog laying with his head between his paws. "He looks as if he might fall asleep any minute now." Zeb looked up at them with one cloudy eye and gave out a whine as if to say he would keep watch.

With Paul pushing the pig's foot into the ground and under one end of the solid block, the other three pried on the other end with their hands; finally they were able to roll it out of the hole and onto the ground, leaving a dark, gaping hole in the ground.

The four of them scrunched their heads together as they peered into the black hole.

"Hold on a minute, let me go get a lantern out of Mr. Phiney's shed," Ott said quietly.

Within a few minutes, he was back with a lantern and matches and sat the lantern down next to the hole and lit the wick. Lifting the lantern a bit so as to get good look into the dark hole, all four of them stared at what was inside.

There sitting in the hole was a small, engraved box, about the size of a square hat box.

Paul used the pig's foot and pried the box loose so he and Ott could pull it up onto the ground next to them. Using the hem of her pant leg, Lily wiped the dirt off the lid, and there before them was an elaborately engraved wooden box studded with pearl and what looked like silver. Stunned, the four of them sat there on the hands and knees staring at the box for a few minutes.

Then, Zeb began emitting a low rumble in his chest, which caused the four of them to spin around and look at him. There Zeb stood with his hair straight up all over his body; floating before him in the clearing was more ghosts than the four of them ever wanted to see in one spot.

On one side of the grassy clearing stood the ghosts of Aunt Abby, Elijah Bonheur, Isaac Bonheur, the young French boy Baptiste and the pirate Scallywag Scruggs and on the other side of the clearing stood the ghost of the pirate with the badger hanging onto his side, two of the ghostly horsemen from Roscoff-by-the-Sea, Napoleon Bonaparte and the large grotesque ghost of an old, grey-backed grizzly bear. Which Olivia immediately recognized as the Banshee. Alongside the grizzly stood the city Dandy from the cotton gin, and standing in the very middle of the clearing was the archbishop. The archbishop's ghost was swaying quite a bit as if maybe he had received a knock on his noggin. He was holding a long, thin pole and doing his best to bang it onto the ground.

"Hear ye, hear ye!" the Bishop announced loudly in his high-pitched, squeaky voice as he unrolled a parchment paper he held in his other hand and held it up in front of his face when he realized he had finally gotten their attention.

"Here ye, Hear ye. By decree from King John this treasure box is hereby declared to be property of the Royal Treasury of Great Britain. Henceforth no man shall lay claim to it or its contents being he dead or alive. As ordered by the parliament of Great Britain, the archbishop of Canterbury shall henceforth take into his possession the Royal Treasure and shall delivered it straightaway to the Royal Treasury. Any man or woman who tries to resist this duty of the archbishop shall be hung by the neck until dead outside the Tower of London immediately with no pre-hanging trial."

Then the archbishop rolled the parchment decree up, stuck it under his arm, and glared at the group of ghosts as he puffed out his chest and sniffed loudly as if he had resolved the entire affair. There was an odd moment of silence; Olivia, Lily, Ott, Paul, Zeb, and the plethora of haints of varied colors and sizes looked at each other, wondering what was going to happen.

Then, unsurprisingly to Olivia, Aunt Abby's haint yelled out a loud *'CHARGE!!!'*

The two lines of haints stormed across the clearing with the force of a mighty tornado and battle commenced. The grizzly focused on Scallywags and charged with a massive roar, but just as the grizzly knocked Scallywags to the ground, Elijah, Isaac and Baptiste jumped on its back and began wrestling with it. Aunt Abby give the bishop a solid shove with one of her boots, causing him to roll almost to the very spot where the four of them stood watching with amazement. Kicking his tiny feet, he managed to stand up and then demanded to be given the box, but instantly, another ghost - who must've to be nigh-on seven feet tall with muscles bulging through his shirt sleeves - whom none of them had noticed before, swooped in behind the bishop, lifted him up and rolled him onto his shoulder like a rolled-up rug.

"Percival!" the bishop stammered, his arms waving frantically, "What are ye doing, man? Ye *must* protect me from these heathens!"

"Na' any longer, sir," Percival the giant ghost answered. "Na' any longer. I am hereby announcing to ye that I no longer work for the royals. I am but a commoner in me death and I shall defend my fellow commoners."

The bishop began blabbering on about Percival being thrown in the London Tower and how much he disliked such common heathens; Percival wrapped his free hand across the bishop's mouth, turned and gave the four of them a bow, and vanished into the night.

Turning their attention back to the battle of ghosts in the clearing, the four of them could not believe that Mr. Phiney, Mr. Bushy and Mr. Mobley had not been awakened by such a racket. Elijah Bonheur and Scallywag Scruggs had the grizzly's ghost by the front legs, and Baptiste was sitting on top of him pulling his ears back so far it looked as if his white cloudy eyes might very well fall out onto the ground. Then Baptiste gave the bear's ears one more yank, making the big bear gave out a mighty roar and shake his large, ghostly body so hard that the three of them flew off his body. The beast took off into the dark night just as Percival the giant had done.

The badger-arm pirate was battling Aunt Abby, but Aunt Abby was getting the best of him. Napoleon Bonaparte's ghost was standing off to one side of the clearing with his hand still slid into the front of his jacket as if he were too cool to do battle; he was fading in and out. The city Dandy's ghost was trying to fight with Isaac Bonheur, but Isaac had a white, glowing rope and was winding it around him, wrapping him into a mummy.

Suddenly Paul picked up the box and took off for the cabin, yelling for the rest of them to follow. Within seconds they all made it to the door, with Paul carrying the box and Lily once again carrying old Zeb, and they burst inside with a loud *BANG,* where they found all three men gawking out the window. Before any of them could yell out an audible word over the ruckus going on outside the window, Mr. Mobley pointed at the mayhem and yelled out a warning.

"Look yonder in the corner of the clearing! There's a wrinkled-up, old, green ghost with a far' torch; I reckon he's the one who burned down my station! We best be gettin' outta here 'cuz he's comin' this'ah way!"

"Run!" Mr. Phiney yelled as the three men began shoving everyone towards the back door.

Sure enough, running towards them was a short, bony haint all grizzled-up with baggy skin hanging off his shriveled body. His skin had a deep green hue and his arms and face were spotted with clumps of hoary grey hair. He had a ginormous nose and huge ears which were flapping against his checks as he ran. His feet were bare and his only piece of clothing was his baggy britches which were held up with sagging suspenders. His skin was *so* loose that with every running step he took, his extra rear-end skin would bounce up out of his baggy britches and he had to keep pushing it back down into his britches. On his face his had a huge grin which spread from one gigantic ear to the other and his teeth were dingy yellow. He was zipping and zagging through the brawling bedlam as he made his way closer and closer to the cabin.

Out the back door all seven of them fled with Paul still carrying the treasure box and Lily still carrying old Zeb. Once they were hidden in the overgrown trees, they heard a loud *POP* and turned around just in time to see the fire torch explode as the little creature threw it at Mr. Phiney's cabin. The cabin burst into flames and within seconds became a pile of ash just as the ferry station had done.

With open-mouthed unbelief, they watched as the shriveled little ghost sat down and began laughing and rolling around in the fire as if it were a swimming hole. After a couple minutes he rolled onto the grassy clearing, sat up and looked around to see if anyone was watching, then stretched and laid down as if he was going to take a nap.

But with a crackle like popcorn, his toes popped out into giant toes, then his legs and arms began stretching longer and longer. His neck grew about two feet, and then he stood up. His skin was no longer baggy, but his torso was still small and shriveled. He now stood about eight feet tall and his arms were so long they scraped the ground. His head had not grown at all, but his nose and ears were bigger than ever and his eyes looked like big, black saucers.

The creature took a step in their direction. Then *whoosh!* There stood Percival, the archbishop's old bodyguard, with his hands on his hips. In a flash, Percival snatched up the gangly ghost and twisted its arms around and around its body; then he grabbed its legs and tied them up into a knot and threw him over his shoulder just as he had the bishop.

"Ye ain't goin' anywhere, Bellybone. Don't even think about it. You're going back where ye belong!"

Another *whoosh,* and they too were gone.

Easing out of the trees, the seven of them stood watching the disorderly chaos continuing beyond the ashes and cinders of the destroyed cabin. Aunt Abby had the badger-pirate tied up in knots with what looked like her cloak, and Isaac Bonheur had Dandy's ghost tied up with that glowing rope wrapped around Dandy's body. Scallywags was poking at Napoleon with what looked like a red-hot poker, but Napoleon was totally ignoring him.

Then just as suddenly as they had appeared, all of them vanished - a breeze blew up from the river, sweeping across the clearing and taking with it every ghost and all the ash from the burnt cabin, leaving behind the chimney, a few pieces of wood, and the lone badger who had evidently fallen off the pirate and was now standing in the middle of the clearing wide-eyed with a piece of the pirate's arm hanging out of its mouth. Looking around as if in a panic, the badger dropped the piece of arm and zipped away into the treetops.

"Well now," Mr. Phiney gave a slight laugh and just as calm as a cucumber, as if nothing out of the ordinary had just happened, said, "That lil' fella looked a might scared, din't he?"

"Well, I reckon he was. Cuz this whole thing purt-near scared the hide off'en my bones," Mr. Mobley drawled in his slow soft accent, "I reckon we best be goin' on over ta Katy's house and see iff'en she'll put us up for a spell."

***

Sitting anxiously at the big, round table in Aunt Katy's kitchen, the seven of them leaned close and eagerly with baited breath as Mr. Phiney opened the box and dumped its contents out onto the tabletop.

Papers, buttons and various babbles rolled onto the surface. There were buttons from what looked to be a soldier's uniform, a lock of blond, curly hair wrapped carefully in a soft deerskin hide, a small family Bible, and a few trinkets which Mr. Phin picked up gently and smiled as he remembered a long time past when each trinket sat on a certain shelf.

The last thing to roll onto the table was a small leather pouch. Picking up the pouch, Mr. Phin dumped the contents onto the tabletop. There sat two shiny gold coins. Mr. Bushy reached over and picked up one of the coins and studied it closely, then shook his head in disbelief.

"Well Phin," he said in amazement, "you have yourself a bit of money here."

"Hmmm," Mr. Phin muttered as he too studied the other coin. "Well, here's to a new ferry shanty, Mr. Mobley, and a new cabin for me. Where in the world did Aunt Abby get these coins? There must be a bit of information in the box."

Immediately he picked up the box and shook it hard and out from the bottom fell a small piece of yellowed paper. Turning it every which way, he laid it on the table.

"Bring that light over here real close-like, Olivia."

Then, he picked up the aged paper and held it up to the light.

"My eyes cain't make out the words. Olivia, would you give it a try? Maybe you can do it better'n me."

Picking up the old, fragile paper, Olivia studied it closely for a bit.

"It says, 'Find the mouse, Phiney,' Olivia said with a slight frown. "Wonder what 'find the mouse' means?"

Immediately Mr. Phiney picked up the box and slammed it onto the table, causing it to break into four separate pieces. He picked up the bottom board and pulled it apart, revealing a letter folded in half which had been slipped beneath the outer board and the board of the box.

Ah-ha! Here 'tis!" he exclaimed, "jest like ya find a mouse, between the out and inner boards! Tis a letter from me own Aunt Abby.

Gently Mr. Phin sat the paper on the table without unfolding it and pushed to towards Oliva.

"Olivia dear, would you read this for me, please?"

Carefully Olivia unfolded the paper so as to not destroy it, sat it down on the table and squinted her eyes as if trying to make out the scribbled words which had faded through the years of sitting in the box in the wet moist earth of the forest, before she began reading it loudly so everyone could hear. Finally, she cleared her throat and slowly began reading the page as if she were the Arch Bishop reading his parchment paper.

207

'Me dearest Phiney-boy, Tis yor treasure ta use as ye see fit. Stay away from the green-skinned giant. He be a crook and a heathen for he be the scoundrel who left yor sweet mum on that cold island so he could sail with those black-hearted demons called pirates. He be cursed by Davey Jones himself and sad I surely am ta have ta tell ya he be yor rightful Pa and I be yor rightful Granny. Yor darling mum, Betsy Georgina Pennypacker, be me only sweet child. May the good Lord forgive me for lying to ya, me sweet Phiney-boy, but I had ta tell ya a lie ta keep ya safe from the greedy devil himself. Love ya dearly, me boy...Granny Abby.'

All of them looked at Mr. Phiney and waited for his reaction.

"Mr. Phin" Olivia muttered quietly

No one paid attention to Olivia because they were still gazing at Mr. Phiney waiting for him to say something.

"Mr. Phin!" Olivia stammered again a bit louder.

Then all of them looked over at Olivia and saw her pointing at the front window with wide-eyed fear.

They turned and looked at the window and there it was. The big black panther had its paws on the windowsill with its head pushed close to the glass and his huge emerald green eyes glaring straight at Olivia. Its mouth was wide open in a snarl with its top lips curled above its white fangs, exactly how a barn cat would do just before it pounced on a mouse.

It let out a scream that shook the glass as if it would splinter into a million pieces.

Then, with wide-eyed fear the seven of them watched Olivia's Aunt Katy walking slowly towards the cabin carrying a bucket full of fresh water whistling a merry tune, but before any of them could jump up and warn her about the big cat she stopped, stared at the cat with a scowl on her face for a few seconds then held out one hand and pointed a finger at the creature. With a loud *zap* a bolt of white lightening shot out the end of her finger, bounced off the cat, slammed him against the wall then threw him into the air where he vanished into the pre-dawn darkness at the same time Aunt Katy flew back and with a thud landed on the ground in a cloud of smoke and dust. As she stood up she swayed a bit, as if dazed, reached down and brushed her blouse and britches off, shook her head as if to get her brain back in place then once again began walking calmly towards the cabin as if nothing unusual had just happened. Her long black hair was singed and standing straight up in the air like a big fan of peacock feathers surrounding her head. Her eyebrows were also singed and her face and hands were covered in black soot making her look like a raccoon. She then stopped once, sat the now empty water bucket down and with both hands gave her head a sharp tweak as if getting it back into place. Then, just as cool as a summer breeze, she walked into the cabin and stood looking at them with a big smile on her sooty raccoon face. She let out an comically booming laugh and yelled loudly…as if she had lost most of her hearing…

"Did ya see that? Dang cat! I lost the water."

Interesting Facts

Interesting Facts

Roscoff-by-the-Sea:

Located on a peninsula jutting out into Morlaix Bay on the north coast of Brittany, Roscoff is a particularly charming seaside town that has earned it a place as one of the region's 'small towns of character.' It boasts a pleasant harbor and beaches, and its town center has maintained its attractive architectural heritage, with sixteenth and seventeenth-century buildings from its prosperous history as a port. Just offshore, a short boat ride away, is the small island of Île de Batz (pronounced 'ba'). Free of cars, it offers an idyllic getaway from the mainland, with quiet beaches and a well-known botanical garden, *The Jardin Exotique Georges Delaselle*, created between 1897 and 1937 by a Parisian businessman.

The Grizzly Bear:

Lewis and Clark named the huge bear a "grisley" or "grizzly", which could have meant "grizzled"; that is, golden and grey tips of the hair or "fear-inspiring". Nonetheless, after careful study, naturalist George Ord formally classified it in 1815 – not for its hair, but for its character – as Ursus Horribilis. Most adult female grizzlies weigh 290–400 lb (130-180 kg) while adult males weigh on average 400–790 lb (180–360 kg) Average total length in this species is 6.50 ft, with an average shoulder height of 3.35 ft.

The largest known grizzly bear was taken down in Alaska with a head measurement of 27 ½ inches and height of 14 feet.

Ha'penny or halfpenny:

Design date. 1937. The British coin simply known as a *halfpenny* (pronounced HAY-pe-nee), was a unit of currency that equaled *half* of a *penny*. Originally the *halfpenny* was minted in copper, but after 1860 it was minted in bronze.

King John's Treasure:

King John's treasure is considered one of the largest treasures in the world. If you want to get rich, finding the treasure is one of the ways how you can go from zero to hero. The estimated value of the treasure is $70,000,000. The treasure contains crown jewels, silver plates, gold goblets, the sword of Tristram, golden wand with a dove and many, many gold coins. The treasure was lost in 1216 somewhere in Great Britain, and it is yet to be found.

Llanfairpwllgwyngyll

This small British village is located on the isle of Anglesey which lies close to the shores of Wales on the main island of Great Britain. To properly say Llanfairpwllgwyngyll, pronounce each section separately   LLAN - FAIR - PWLL - GWYN – GYLL. The internet gives an extensive amount of information on Llanfairpwllgwyngyll. This village has existed since 4000 BC.

Yellow Fever

The disease is caused by the yellow fever virus and is spread by the bite of an infected female mosquito. It infects only humans, other primates, and several species of mosquitoes. In cities, it is spread primarily by Aedes aegypti, a type of mosquito found throughout the tropics and subtropics.

The entire Mississippi River Valley from St. Louis south was affected and tens of thousands fled the stricken cities of New Orleans, Vicksburg, and Memphis. An estimated 120,000 cases of yellow fever resulted in some 20,000 deaths.[24]

Memphis suffered several epidemics during the 1870s, culminating in the 1878 epidemic (called the Saffron Scourge of 1878), with more than 5,000 fatalities in the city alone.

<u>Glossary</u>

Glossary

Southern other slang words used in this book

A pint	"A pint " refers to pint glass of ale
Bloke	A male who is not liked by another person.
Bowler Hat	The Bowler hat is also known as the Bob hat or the Derby hat
Capote coat	A long coat made from a wool blanket
Compagnons	French word meaning companions or partners
Davey Jones	According to the mythical legend of sailors, is the fiend who presides over all the evil spirits of the deep, and is often seen in various shapes; perching among the riggings of a ship in the eve of hurricanes, shipwrecks, and other disasters.
Epaulettes	Rank displayed on epaulettes or shoulder pads of a military uniform
Fantômes noirs	Black ghost
Farthing	An old English coin worth a quarter of a penny.
Haints	Ghosts
London Bobbie	British policemen

Mitre	Head wear worn by Arch Bishops
Off your trolley	Crazy
Pig's Foot	Crow-bar, used to pry open boards.
Poppycock	Nonsense
Salty Sea-dog	Nautical slang for an experienced sailor who has spent most of his life aboard a ship at sea.
se dépêcher	Hurry up
Shape-shifter	Having the ability to change from human to animal form.
Shinny	(shin-knee) - To "shinny" or climb up.
Stoop	A small platform leading to the entrance of a building
Tremolo	Wavering effect in a Loon's call
Widder	(wid-der) A widow woman
Widow's weeds	Old American slang for the customary black clothing worn by widows after the death of their husbands
Winder	A window
Yellow Fever	A disease transferred by mosquitoes.

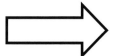

Coming in 2018 – Book #5

"Lily and the Ghost of…"

Your chances of seeing a ghost....

Maybe

Your chances of hearing a ghost...

Maybe

Your chances of talking to a ghost…

Well, probably never

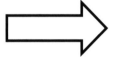

Your chances of becoming a ghost…

Pretty much guaranteed

Your chances of reading about ghosts....

100%

Made in the USA
Columbia, SC
09 November 2017